Secrets
of a
Scandalous
Marriage

VALERIE BOWMAN

St. Martin's Paperbacks

This is a work of fiction. All of the characters, organizations, and events portrayed in this novel are either products of the author's imagination or are used fictitiously.

SECRETS OF A SCANDALOUS MARRIAGE

For information address St. Martin's Press, 175 Fifth Avenue, New York, NY 10010.

ISBN: 978-1-250-00897-8

Printed in the United States of America

St. Martin's Paperbacks edition / October 2013

St. Martin's Paperbacks are published by St. Martin's Press, 175 Fifth Avenue, New York, NY 10010.

10 9 8 7 6 5 4 3 2 1

For Mary Behre and for Holly Blanck Ingraham
who both loved Lord Medford
from the moment he stepped onto the page.

Secrets
of a
Scandalous
Marriage

CHAPTER 1

The Tower of London, December 1816

The large metal door to her cell scraped open and Kate closed her eyes. She stepped forward, summoned from one cold dank cell into another. She had a visitor. Her first since she'd been taken to the gaol.

She opened her eyes. The harsh winter light filtered through the only window in the antechamber. The yeoman warder wore a blank expression on his face. He and the other guards always gave her the benefit of respect due her title. Whether they liked it or not.

The guard stepped aside, revealing the room's other occupant. Interesting. Her visitor was a man. She narrowed her eyes on him. Who was he and what did he want with her? He stood with his straight back to her. He was tall, that much she could discern. Tall and cloaked in shadows.

The smell of mold and decay, rife in the Tower, made her stomach clench. The unforgiving winter wind whipped through the stonework, raising gooseflesh across her arms. She shivered and clutched her shawl more tightly around her shoulders.

"Ye 'ave ten minutes an' not a moment more," the gaoler announced before wrenching open the door and clanging it shut behind him as he left. The loud scrape and subsequent clank sealed Kate and the stranger in the small room together. She took a step back. A small rickety table rested between them. She was glad for that bit of separation at least. Whoever the man was, his clothing marked him a gentleman. He had better behave like one.

The tall man turned to greet her. He doffed his hat, but she still couldn't make out his face. He wore a dark gray wool overcoat of considerable expense. A stray beam of sunlight floated through the dirty air, let in by the one small window nestled in the stone wall across from them.

He executed a perfect bow. "Your grace?"

Kate cringed. Oh, how she detested that title. "Bowing to a prisoner?" she asked in a voice containing a bit of irony. "Aren't you a gentleman?"

He smiled and a set of perfectly white teeth flashed in the darkness. "You're still a duchess, your grace."

She pushed the hood from her head and took a tentative step forward. The stranger's eyes flared for a moment and he sucked in his breath.

Kate's stomach clenched. No doubt she looked a fright. She hadn't bathed in days and could only imagine her own smell. Her hair, normally piled properly atop her head, was a mass of tangled red curls around her shoulders. She might be grimy and in trouble, but she wasn't broken. And she refused to let the stranger see that his reaction affected her. She pushed up her chin and eyed him warily.

He stepped forward then, into the light, and Kate narrowed her eyes on his face, rapidly assessing every detail. She didn't know him. But whoever he was, the man was handsome. Devastatingly so. Perhaps in his early thirties, he had dark brown cropped hair, a perfectly straight nose, a square jaw. But his eyes were what truly captivated. Hazel in color, nearly green, assessing, knowing, intelligent eyes. They stole her breath. Her gaze moved lower to where the faintest hint of a smile rested upon expertly molded male lips.

"Do you know who I am?" His voice splintered the quiet cold like a hammer hitting ice.

She regarded him with a steady stare. "Are you a barrister? Come for my defense?"

The man furrowed his brow. "You haven't yet been given access to a barrister?"

She straightened her shoulders. "I've been . . . waiting."

The stranger's captivating eyes regarded her calmly. "From what I understand, you've been in gaol for weeks. I find it difficult to believe a lady of your station has not yet met with a barrister."

She lifted her chin. "Be that as it may, I have not."

"I'm sorry to disappoint you, your grace, but no, I am no barrister."

"Not a barrister? Then who are you and why have you come to visit me? Please don't tell me it's merely to see the spectacle of a duchess accused of murder."

His gaze remained pinned to her face, his eyes still assessing, wary. "I am here to assist you, your grace."

"Assist me?" she scoffed, stepping forward to get a closer look at the man. "I rather doubt that. Assist yourself perhaps. Tell me, how much did you bribe the gaoler to let you see the infamous duchess who shot her husband?"

The stranger arched a brow. "Did you? Murder your husband?"

She clenched her jaw. "Did you come here to insult

me with your questions? Or do you mean to coax a confession from me?" She squeezed her fists against the fabric of her shawl, twisting it so tightly her fingers ached.

He shook his head. "My apologies, your grace. It was not my intention to offend. I assure you, I'm not a common gossipmonger come to witness your degradation. I intend to assist you. And yes, in return, there is something I want."

Kate raised both brows. She respected the man's honesty, but whether she intended to continue this conversation depended entirely upon what exactly the handsome stranger desired. "So, tell me, then. What is it you want?"

He swept another bow. "I've come to make you an offer. One that can benefit us both."

Pulling her shawl over her shoulders more tightly, Kate crossed her arms over her chest. "Forgive me if I am a bit doubtful, sir. I've seen enough deception in my twenty-eight years to be highly skeptical of the promises of men."

His head quirked to the side and he regarded her with an inquisitive look. Her statement had obviously surprised him. "I understand, your grace. And I fully intend to explain. But first, I must ask for your discretion. If we are to help each other, I cannot reveal my identity unless you promise to keep what I am about to tell you entirely secret."

She pursed her lips and narrowed her eyes on him. "Secret? Are you a spy?"

His brow rose, and tension seemed to radiate through his body. "Would you aid me if I were?"

She pointed toward the door. "Get out," she said through clenched teeth.

"Pardon?"

Her nails dug so hard into her shawl she was certain she would rip the fabric. "I may be accused of a murder I did not commit, but being called a traitor to my homeland is not an insult I will bear. If you are seeking my aid in that manner, you most certainly have come to the wrong person. I am not, and never will be, that desperate." She turned toward the door to call for the gaoler.

The stranger quickly held up a hand. "I assure you, your grace. I am no spy."

Kate snapped her mouth closed and turned back to him, still eyeing him warily. "Then what exactly do you want from me?"

He nodded slowly. "Your promise, first?"

She watched him, assessing him from the top of his handsome head to the tips of his precisely polished—and obviously expensive—top boots. Apparently, this man was willing or desperate enough to trust an accused murderess, too. Interesting. She had absolutely no reason to trust him, however. Every reason not to, actually. But conversing with a good-looking chap about whatever daft idea he had was preferable to counting the cracks in the walls of her cell or writing letters to . . . no one. "Very well, you have my promise. Now tell me, who are you and why are you here?"

The stranger clicked his heels together and bowed again. "James Bancroft, Viscount Medford, at your service."

She couldn't help the tiny gasp that escaped her lips. The man was a peer. Why on earth would a peer pay her a visit? "Why are you here, my lord?"

Brushing back his coat, he pulled papers from an inside pocket and tossed them on the wooden table.

Her eyes still trained on him, Kate stepped forward and picked up the papers. It was a pamphlet. She scanned the first page and shuffled through it quickly, but the pages were blank.

She gestured to the papers with her chin. "What is this?"

His mouth quirked again. Distracting, that. "You might say I have a bit of a hobby on the side. I own a printing press."

Her gaze snapped to his face and she stepped back, clutching the pamphlet, genuinely surprised. And a little bit intrigued. "A viscount in trade?"

He grinned. "That's the secret." His grin faded and he strode forward. Bracing his hands apart, he leaned across the table. "I offer women in scandalous situations a unique opportunity. This, your grace, is a chance to tell your side of the story."

"What do you mean . . . exactly?"

His eyes blazed at her. His jaw tightened. "Write a pamphlet for me. It will be a top seller, I assure you."

She shook her head. "A pamphlet? Telling my story? I don't understand. What do I stand to gain from it?"

His eyes, dark green now, captured hers. "What do you want?"

Kate spun around, pacing across the small room. A chance to tell her story? A frisson of hope skittered down her spine. Yes. An opportunity to inform the entire city what a hideous husband George had been. To tell the truth. It was tempting. She must handle this carefully, however. There was something else she wanted.

She turned back toward the viscount. "Out of curiosity, *if* I agree to do it, what exactly will the pamphlet be named, my lord?"

His jaw relaxed and his eyes lost some of their intensity. He stood up again to his full height and regarded her down the length of his nose. *"Secrets of a Scandalous Marriage."*

CHAPTER 2

"Medford, how can you be so flippant about all of this?" Lily Morgan, the Marchioness of Colton, asked, plunking her hands on her hips and tapping her foot on the wide Aubusson rug that adorned the floor of James's drawing room.

They had just adjourned to the blue salon in James's town house. A fire crackled in the hearth next to them and the smell of burning logs permeated the cozy room. James signaled to his butler, Locke, to pour the tea. Then he settled in for a visit with two of his very closest friends, Marchioness Lily and her sister Annie, the Countess of Ashbourne.

"Who's flippant?" he asked, giving them both a grin.

"You are and you know it," Annie replied, taking a seat and busily setting about plopping an extra lump of sugar into her teacup. She stirred the drink with a tiny silver spoon. "I, for one, think the poor duchess has been sorely mistreated. I've heard no evidence to make me believe she's guilty."

"I agree." Lily nodded. Hands still on her hips, she paced the floor, refusing to take a seat. "Besides, I had the misfortune to meet her husband on more than one occasion and the man was a complete scoundrel. He made overtures to me time and time again. Can you imagine?" She turned back to Medford. "But asking her to write a pamphlet is entirely flippant of you."

"I disagree," James replied. "I think it will be a welcome opportunity for her. Not to mention I've asked her to name her terms."

"And what did she ask for?" Lily wanted to know.

James shrugged. "Nothing yet. I'm returning to the Tower today to get her answer . . . and her terms."

Lily shook her head. "Hmm. Shrouded in mystery Lady Katherine Townsende has been."

Annie set down her cup. "I read that she was the daughter of a landowner in Kent. Apparently, she caught the Duke of Markingham's eye when she was eighteen. They married, and she's been kept tucked away in the countryside all these years." She cleared her throat. "Ahem, until her husband's untimely death, that is."

Lily tapped her cheek with her fingertip. "Yes, well, now she's a complete scandal. The entire *ton* is convinced she's a murderess."

Medford grinned. "Yes, but she's a murderess with a story to tell. And *that* makes all the difference."

"I didn't say she was a murderess, I said everyone *thinks* she's a murderess. I intend to reserve my judgment until I've heard more facts about the case. What did *you* think of her?" Lily asked, with an arched brow.

James's mind retraced to his meeting with the duchess the day before. She'd stepped into the room. So slight. A dark cloak with a hood covered her head. Her face had been in shadow, but James hadn't mistaken her momentary uncertainty, nor her pride. She'd held her shoulders erect, her head high. There had been a bit of anger, too. He sensed it when he'd narrowed his eyes on her delicate form. He didn't blame her for being angry, his was not a social call after all. She was thin, perhaps too thin. Of medium height, she did not seem capable of murdering a grown man, let alone Markingham. The duke had been tall, and strong. A large man, her husband.

When the duchess had stepped into the shaft of winter sunlight and pushed the hood from her head, James had sucked in his breath. The Duchess of Markingham was absolutely stunning. In his thirty-three years he'd never seen her equal. She had alabaster skin, a straight thin nose, and a riotous mass of golden-red hair that tumbled over her shoulders and down her back. She'd glanced up, her cornflower-blue eyes shooting sparks at him from beneath the velvety blackness of her impossibly long eyelashes. The smudge of dirt on one of her high cheekbones only served to highlight the ethereal beauty of her face.

James had glanced away. He'd heard the duchess was a beauty, but he hadn't been prepared. She was more than beautiful. She was a goddess come to life.

He glanced back at Lily. "She seemed . . . like a lady in a great deal of trouble."

"Is she as beautiful as everyone says?" Annie asked with a sigh, a dreamy smile on her face.

Leave it to Annie to ask such a direct question. James tugged at his cravat. "She is . . . beautiful. Yes, I might call her that."

Lily watched him carefully. "But what did you *think* about her? How did she seem?"

"To be honest." He tugged at his cuff. "She surprised me. I'd half expected a termagant the likes of which I'd never encountered before. Instead, I wasn't quite sure what to make of the woman."

Lily stopped pacing. Her gaze scanned his face. "Why?"

James bit the inside of his cheek, considering the question for a moment. "I suppose it was because she didn't seem fearful."

"What do you mean?" Annie asked, leaning closer.

James shrugged and settled back in his seat. "She was poised. Calm. She carried herself like . . . like a duchess."

Lily rubbed one finger across her chin. "Is it possible that she wasn't afraid? She's soon to be on trial for her life."

"I cannot imagine." Annie shuddered. "They say she was there, with her husband's body, when they found him. He was lying on the floor of his bedchamber, shot with his own pistol in the chest."

"It's absolutely ghastly," Lily agreed. "Not a wonder the rumors have been rampant. And if she didn't kill him, it certainly doesn't look good for her defense."

"Yes, and unfortunately, it stands to reason," Annie said.

James cocked his head to the side. "Why's that?"

"Because just days after his murder, Lady Bettina Swinton, a close friend of the duke's, told everyone that the duchess had recently informed him that she intended to seek a divorce," Annie replied.

James arched a brow. "Is that so?"

Annie nodded.

"It does look bad for her," Lily said. "The case has caused riots. I read that crowds had gathered around the coach that brought the duchess from her husband's estate in the countryside to the Tower. The traveling party was nearly overrun with the rioters. The king's guard was called in to bring her to the prison unscathed."

James scooped up the newspaper that rested on the table beside him. "It's not every day a duchess is accused of murder."

Annie lifted her teacup to her lips again and shook her head. "I still refuse to rush to judgment. It's completely unfair that that poor young woman is sitting over there in a freezing gaol while the entire *ton* speculates about whether she shot her husband. I admit I've never met her but it's entirely possible that she is innocent."

Lily turned to face James. "*We* haven't met her, Annie, but Medford has."

The two sisters eyed him carefully.

"So, Lord Medford, what do *you* think?" Annie asked. "Based on your acquaintance with the Duchess of Markingham, is she an evil murderess or an unfortunate innocent?"

James folded the paper in half. "As far as I'm concerned, it doesn't matter either way. The fact is, the *ton* is vying for details of the story and what better details could one possibly gather than those that came directly from the lady herself? Scandal is my trade. Regardless of her guilt or innocence, I want the duchess to write for me. *Secrets of a Scandalous Marriage* will be immensely popular."

Lily sighed. "Once again, you're being flippant."

"On the contrary," James replied, tossing the paper aside and straightening his already straight cravat. "I am merely attempting to provide the public with what it desperately wants, a pamphlet written by the Duchess of Markingham. There has been nothing like this scandal to set the town on its ear since . . . ever. People want to read about the details. Sorry to say, but even *Secrets of a Wedding Night* and *Secrets of a Runaway Bride* weren't as popular as this stands to be," he said, referring to the pamphlets the two sisters had written for him earlier in the year when they'd both been involved in their own adventures.

Lily rolled her eyes at him. "That's not my point and you know it. Those pamphlets were written *anonymously*. This will be entirely different. Everyone will know the duchess wrote it, if she agrees to, that is. She's involved in enough scandal as it is without adding a tell-all pamphlet to the list. Personally, I think she should refuse you."

"That's not very loyal of you, my lady," James pointed out, still grinning.

Annie took another sip of her tea, then bit her lip. "I'm not sure what to think. If the duchess really does have a story to tell, the pamphlet may help her with regard to public opinion. But, if she is guilty . . ." Annie winced. "I cannot imagine she'd agree to write it, however, if that were the case."

James stretched his legs in front of him and crossed his feet at the ankles. "Either way, the decision is up to the duchess. She intends to give me her answer today, and I've every expectation she'll say yes."

"What makes you so certain?" Lily made her way toward the fireplace where she warmed her hands and looked back over her shoulder at James.

He flashed a grin at her. "Why, because I've offered her an indecent amount of money."

Annie leaned forward, her dark eyes sparkling. "How indecent?"

"Sufficiently indecent," he replied with a wink.

Lily tossed a hand in the air. "What good will money do a woman who's sentenced to death?"

"Quite right." Annie nodded, shuddering.

"It shall help pay for her defense for one thing," James replied. "If she's wise she'll hire a Bow Street runner to investigate the case separately from the official investigation. Now, come sit down," he said to Lily. "Speaking of indecent, I've put an indecent amount of cream in your teacup and we all know how much you love cream."

Annie laughed. "That's true. She's like a cat."

Lily turned away from the fire and hurried over to join them. "The fact that the duchess didn't already take the offer makes me think she intends to turn it down."

"Nonsense." James pushed Lily's teacup toward her. "She wanted to consider my offer, that's all. She'd be a fool to refuse it."

"She's a duchess. She's already rich," Annie pointed out, slyly pulling a teacake from the little porcelain plate in the center of the table.

James arched a brow. "Her husband's assets have been seized by the courts until the trial is finished. She has no access to his money, and I sincerely doubt her mother-in-law is in much of a generous mood at present."

"If she's innocent, Medford, we expect you to help her," Lily said.

"Help her? What do I have to do with it?"

Lily gave him a small smile. "Don't forget who you're speaking to, James. We happen to know you have a soft spot for damsels in distress." She gave her sister a conspiratorial grin.

James pursed his lips. "There's no chance of that happening here. I intend to keep my business with her entirely secret . . . and entirely business."

"But if you learn she's not guilty, you'll help her. I know you will," Annie added, leaning over and patting his hand.

James shrugged. "I don't know whether she's guilty, and to be honest, I don't much care. All I know is her story will sell pamphlets."

"And that's all that matters to you?" Annie asked, a frown on her face. "Selling pamphlets?"

"Of course not," James replied with a grin. "I intend to sell a great *many* pamphlets."

Lily rolled her eyes at him again. "But what if the duchess is innocent?"

"I'm giving her a chance to tell her story, aren't I? Besides, it's not as if I pulled the trigger and shot her husband, nor did I accuse her of doing so. This entire situation was already well made before I ever got wind of it."

"But how can you be so nonchalant when an innocent woman may be sentenced to die?" Annie had left half of her teacake on her plate, a sure sign she was thoroughly distracted.

"You don't fool me for one moment, James Bancroft," Lily interjected. "I give you one week of dealing with the duchess before you're assisting with her defense."

James shook his head. "Now *that* is utter nonsense. I draw the line at aiding a murderess."

"But you don't know for certain that she is a murderess," Annie pointed out, brushing crumbs from her skirts.

James stood up and tossed his napkin on the table. "Indeed, I hope the truth will out, for the duchess's sake. Now, if you'll excuse me, ladies. I have a prisoner to visit."

CHAPTER 3

This time when she was led into the small, cold room in the Tower, the duchess greeted James with something of a curious smile on her face.

"Good morning, your grace." He bowed over the delicate hand she presented him. No. He hadn't been imagining it before. She *was* ethereal.

"My lord," she replied in an unhurried tone.

James was once again captivated by her startling beauty. No wonder Markingham had married her. The man must have snapped her up the moment he'd laid eyes on her. James didn't blame him. But, alas, the duke obviously didn't realize what marriage had in store for him.

"I trust you slept well," James said, wondering why his stomach was in a knot around this woman. He was never nervous. Ever. It was a singularly unique experience for him. He watched her closely as if her countenance would give a clue as to why his heart beat a bit faster in her presence.

The edges of the duchess's mouth turned up in the hint of a smile, and James was immediately reminded of how different she was. She was supposed to be all refinement and perfection but instead she had a sort of realness to her that drew him in. Made him want to see what she would do or say next. She was . . . captivating. That was it. That was what he was responding to.

She tugged on her shawl. "I never sleep well in this place." She gestured with her chin to the stone walls surrounding them. "It's freezing and not particularly comfortable, as you might imagine."

James furrowed his brow. His voice deepened. "Are they treating you ill?"

"No, of course not. They're treating me with all the respect due my *illustrious* title." She nearly spat the last two words.

James motioned for her to sit and he waited until she'd done so before he took a seat across the table from her. "You don't enjoy being a duchess?"

Her bright blue eyes pinned him. "Enjoy it? What has being a duchess ever brought me? A loveless marriage, a lonely existence, and now a death sentence." She laughed a humorless laugh.

James ducked his head. For a moment he felt a twinge of regret for her. Regret and a bit of guilt. Here he was, attempting to profit from her situation. *If* she were innocent. But that was a very large if. For if she had indeed killed her husband, James had no reason to feel sorry for her. After all, it was possible that she was just angry that she'd been caught. Regardless, it did little good to discuss the details with her. She'd have the opportunity to put whatever she wanted into the pamphlet. Once she agreed to write it, that was.

It was time to discuss business.

He cleared his throat. "Have you made your decision, your grace? Will you write for me?"

She watched him, crossing her arms over her chest.

"You're very direct, my lord." She raised a perfect golden-red brow.

James nudged at his cravat. Was it hot in the room all of a sudden? "I'm not sure there is much else left to say."

"Locked in the Tower," she murmured, a faraway look in her eyes. "Not something I ever expected when I was growing up on a farm." With one fingertip, she traced a pattern on the rough-hewn tabletop. Her voice was tight. "Life is unexpected sometimes, is it not, my lord?"

He nodded. "Indeed."

Expelling a long breath, she stood and paced to the window, arms folded over her chest. She glanced out. "There." She motioned with her chin. "There is the lawn upon which Anne Boleyn lost her head." She turned to face James who looked at her with narrowed eyes. What was she getting at?

"And what was Queen Anne's crime?" she continued.

"Adultery," he answered. "Treason."

Kate's head snapped around to face him. "Ah yes, treason, or so said her husband, the one with the power, the one who made the laws. She was brought through Traitor's Gate and put to death, the mother of the future queen, and all for failing to make her husband happy."

James stood and cleared his throat again. "Anne Boleyn was not accused of murdering King Henry."

Kate turned on him with flashing eyes. "'Tis true, though not the best way to win my favor, my lord. Tell me again why you think I should agree to your offer. A dead woman needs no money, you know?"

He relaxed his stance a bit. "No, but a woman who is on trial for her life needs the best defense she can afford and the opportunity to tell the public her side of the story, which is priceless. Writing the pamphlet will provide you with that opportunity."

"Do you think I'm innocent, then?" she challenged him, drumming her fingertips along her opposite elbows.

He met her gaze directly. "That I do not know."

"Then why provide me with the opportunity to state my case?"

"Every accused person deserves as much, do they not?"

She tossed a hand in the air. "I'll have my day in court, and the papers will cover every bit of it."

"True, but the papers will only cover what your barrister will *allow* you to say in court. The pamphlet can contain whatever you choose."

She arched another brow at him and scoured him with those arresting eyes. "You've thought of everything, haven't you?"

"You'll do it?" James pulled a set of folded papers from his inside coat pocket. "I've brought the contract."

"A contract?" She smiled ever so slightly. "My word isn't good enough? You don't trust me?"

He tossed the papers on the worn wooden tabletop that stood between them. "I always use a contract."

She tipped up her chin. "That was a jest, my lord."

He turned toward the door. "I'll ask them to bring a quill and—"

"Just a moment," she said, grabbing up the contract with one hand and perusing it. "I haven't agreed . . . yet."

He turned back to face her. "You plan to refuse?"

"I haven't said that either."

He bowed. "I await your decision, your grace. Though you should know that if you agree, you'll be breaking Society's rules again and the reaction may not be—"

Her sharp bark of laughter stopped him. "Society's rules. Bah. What do I care for Society's rules? Did you know that I'd been planning to ask my husband for a divorce? I'd already accepted my future being ruined by scandal. Besides, I've learned a bit about you, my lord. There is a lady here whom I've befriended. She knows you. She tells me you are a rule follower yourself, Lord Medford, despite your illicit printing press."

He kept his face blank. "Ah, so my reputation precedes me."

"I followed the rules my entire life, too," she continued, "and look where it got me. In a loveless marriage with a death sentence hanging over my head."

James glanced away, but for some reason her saying her marriage had been loveless made him feel sad for her although inexplicably pleased for himself. Why was that? It made no sense.

He shook his head. Regardless, he had to ensure she knew what she was getting into. He'd be no sort of gentleman if he did not explain it to her in detail. "Be that as it may, the pamphlet will have a very wide distribution, and there's every reason to expect—"

She regarded the papers again. "As I said, I'm done following rules, my lord."

She spent the next few moments reading before she tossed the papers to the tabletop and met his gaze. "I'll agree, upon two conditions."

He watched her face closely, trying to ignore her stunning beauty. This was business. Only business. "Two? What are they?"

"First, I want you to employ for me the best barrister money can buy."

He nodded. "I was expecting such a request. You'll have the very best. What is your second condition?"

She straightened her shoulders and faced him head-on. "I may not have long to live, my lord. I know that much. I'm not a fool. I have a matter of months at the most. I've spent the last ten years practically a prisoner at my husband's estate in the country, and now I'm sentenced to death." She smoothed her hands down her dark skirts. "I may not have much recourse against the charges that have been brought against me, but I can and will choose how I spend my remaining days."

"I see, and how do you wish to spend them?" he asked, reminding himself he shouldn't care what her answer was.

She moved back over to the window and glanced outside. "I want to do the things that make me happy. Enjoy myself a bit." She turned her head to face him. "I want to live."

James furrowed his brow. Live? "I'm not sure I understand."

She whirled around and made her way back to the table where she planted her palms firmly on the top and leaned toward him. "The law allows for me to reside under house arrest as long as I am under the supervision of a peer."

James's gaze shot to her face.

She squared her shoulders. "I want you to get me out of here."

CHAPTER 4

After Viscount Medford left, Kate collapsed into the wooden chair that sat next to the small table in the room they'd provided as her cell. She let her head drop into her hands and took a deep breath. She was shaking, trembling. Good heavens, how had she ever summoned the nerve to ask Lord Medford to get her out of prison? Yes, he wanted something from her in return, but still, she was taking a gamble. A risky one. If the viscount left and didn't return, she might have just missed her one chance at telling her side of the story to the masses. Had she been a fool to ask for so much?

She'd learned what she could about the viscount in the small amount of time she'd had since he first came to visit. There was another lady imprisoned at the Tower, a woman who was to stand trial at the House of Lords for treason. She was accused of being a spy, a supporter of the French. Lady Mary's trial had been delayed again and again. She'd been in the Tower since before Waterloo. Kate knew only too well how an innocent could be locked away. Lady Mary was the only friend Kate had in the gaol.

The prisoners were allowed to take walks along the grounds in the afternoon, and this afternoon, Kate had asked Lady Mary what she knew about a certain viscount.

"They call him Lord Perfect," Mary had said, a sly grin lighting her ice-blue eyes. "The Lord of All Rule Following. The Viscount of Flawlessness. And quite a handsome chap, too, if you ask me." She ended the last part on a wink.

Kate had hid her smile. A rule follower? She'd keep her promise to Lord Medford. She would not tell Mary about the viscount's printing press. Obviously, the man enjoyed his pristine image and went to great lengths to protect it. But there had to be a bit of a rule breaker in him if he secretly published scandalous pamphlets. And *that* is what intrigued Kate the most. She bit her lip.

But if it were true, if he were a rule follower, she may have pushed him too far with her request for sanctuary. She wrapped her shawl more tightly around her shoulders. But the damage was done now. She'd just have to wait for his answer.

Thankfully, Lord Medford had said he would consider her request and left shortly after, giving Kate a much-needed opportunity to sit. Her legs had turned to water, and her stomach roiled as if she might retch.

Good God. When had her life turned into this? A nightmare. Was it only ten years ago that she was playing with the animals on her parents' farm? And now both her mother and father were dead, and she was a miserable twenty-eight-year-old duchess, about to stand trial for her life.

She rested her head against the wall behind her. Lord Medford had looked surprised when she'd asked him to free her. Even more surprised when she'd indicated the reason why. But Kate had had little else to do in the last several weeks but think, and in that time, she'd come to understand what she truly wanted from the last days of her existence on this earth.

She was going to fight the charges. Fight them with every bit of strength she possessed. But in the meantime, she intended to live. To truly live. Of course, even if Medford harbored her, she wouldn't be allowed out in Society, not that she'd ever relished it, but she wanted to eat good food, and sleep on fine sheets, to pet a puppy, and to . . . dance. Yes. She wanted to dance and dance and dance. She'd gone from her parents' property to her husband's and a life greatly unlike what she'd envisioned for herself. Now that she had very little life left, she refused to allow an unfair legal system to take away her last bit of remaining joy. Her husband had never loved her. And she had never loved him. Not really. Oh, she'd thought she had loved him when she'd been the naïve girl who'd married him. But it was obvious nearly from the beginning of their marriage that they did not suit. They quarreled nearly constantly and George always wanted to be out with friends and enjoying sports. He never chose to be at home with Kate, spending time together as a couple. In fact, she'd discovered barely a week into their marriage that he still had a mistress whom he had no intention of relinquishing.

Kate had lived a life of loneliness and unhappiness, punctuated by infrequent visits from her husband, and very little to do with her time. She'd been useless. Useless and powerless. And she intended to make up for it now. James Bancroft wanted a pamphlet from her? Well, she would use what little power she still possessed—her story—to get exactly what she wanted.

A loud knock sounded at the door to her cell. "Your grace, are you in need of anything?" the guard asked in a muffled voice that carried through the heavy oak.

Kate momentarily lifted her aching head. "No, I'm fine," she called back.

She couldn't help but smile at the question. Lord Medford had asked if they were treating her well. Her answer had been the truth. The guards at the Tower had all treated her with nothing but deference and respect. A wry smile touched her lips. If the people who held her captive believed she was a killer, they didn't indicate it by either word or deed. But they all had to think it. What else were they to believe?

She may not ever have been loved by her husband, but she would never have killed him. And she regretted that he was dead. She was sad even. Sad for all the years they'd made each other unhappy and sad for the memory of the man she'd thought she'd once loved. Yes, it was true that when she'd discovered that George refused to even discuss a divorce, she'd been devastated. Devastated and then furious. She'd written to him, pleading her case, informing him that a divorce was obviously the best decision for both of them. It was true that a divorce was difficult to obtain and they would be forced to invent a suitable reason, but George had to agree that they were not happy together. In fact, if he didn't get a divorce, he'd never have a legitimate heir. They both knew that.

The next thing she knew he'd stormed into the country estate, railing at her for even suggesting it. His mother would be disgraced. The Markingham name would be dirtied. Then he informed her that he intended to have her move to his property near the Scottish border. He was banishing her. She'd thought it was the last of the ignominies he'd heaped upon her throughout their marriage, including parading his string of mistresses to stay under the same roof as Kate. But now she supposed the final act of betrayal was seeing to it that she lost her life along with his. Ah yes, things were truly ironic sometimes.

And somewhere out there a murderer was still at large. At first, she'd briefly worried that whoever had killed George might come for her. But as the days passed and the investigators seemed intent upon blaming her for her husband's death, she realized that whoever had killed George fully intended to allow her to be sentenced to death for it. No. The murderer wouldn't harm her. She was his scapegoat.

She stood up, hugging herself, rubbing her arms briskly for warmth, and walked to the window. The cold seeped through the stone walls. The wind whistled through the ancient windows. She sighed and traced a fingertip along the freezing-cold pane. The lawn where Anne Boleyn had been put to death was brown and withered, a bit of lackluster snow lay in a dirty heap. The sky was gray and dark. Was it this dark and gray the day the former queen had died? And would the sky remain gray on the day she was put to death herself? Kate shivered. Yes, she and Anne were kindred spirits now. The guards had brought her books, and Kate had spent the last several weeks reading everything she could about the Protestant queen. They were alike. Falsely blamed. Betrayed by the men they'd sworn to love forever. And now here Kate was imprisoned in the same gaol where Anne had once been kept.

Kate made her way into the tiny adjoining chamber and retrieved the wool blanket that lay sprawled on the small bed in the corner. She wrapped the fabric tightly around her shoulders. It was so cold. December. Almost Christmastide. Where would she spend the holiday? If Viscount Medford didn't accept her offer, she might spend it here, alone, in this sad place. If the viscount did agree to harbor her, she'd be in the home of a stranger. Either prospect was disheartening, but at least she'd be alive. *This* Christmas. She shuddered. Almost certainly her last such holiday on this earth.

She shook off the unwelcome thoughts and turned her attention to the viscount. She didn't relish having to trust another man with her freedom or her secrets. And the money he'd offered meant little to her. But his other offer, the one to widely publish the pamphlet, to allow her to tell her side of the story, was tempting, even if it would redouble Society's censure. Even if no one believed her, if the pamphlet were printed, her story would be there, published for all eternity, and that would count for something.

She squeezed her eyes shut. Would Lord Medford accept her offer? According to Lady Mary, he was known as a gentleman of honor and integrity, but he also seemed intent upon his trade. Despite his fine clothing, at first she'd had to wonder if he was poor. Why else would a peer engage in trade? But Lady Mary had quickly disabused her of that notion. "They say his fortune rivals the king's," she'd said. And it must be true. Obviously the viscount was rich, or he couldn't have offered Kate a sum of money that had nearly made her choke. Either that or he was extremely confident that her pamphlet would sell very well.

The viscount was an eccentric, she'd decided. For some reason, printing scandals amused him, and he'd set his sights on the most scandalous of them all. Even sequestered in the country, Kate had managed to read his other famous works, *Secrets of a Wedding Night* and *Secrets of a Runaway Bride*. Though she hadn't known they were his at the time. They'd amused her, made her laugh. But the story he was asking her for, there was nothing amusing about it. It seemed the viscount had turned his sights to a much more serious topic. *Secrets of a Scandalous Marriage,* he'd said. She hated that title. But she supposed it would help to sell the thing, and that's why she wouldn't object. The more copies that made it into circulation, the better, regardless of the salacious label.

Lord Medford had explained it all to her in intricate detail. His plan to publish and sell the pamphlet. His strategy to ensure it received the most notice and the widest distribution. He was obviously a skilled tradesman. He'd leaned over the table, smelling like a mixture of leather and soap, and looking like a statue of some Greek god come to life. Eccentric Lord Medford might be, but the man was also ridiculously handsome. Lady Mary was quite right about that. It surprised Kate, to be sure, to find herself attracted to the man. Any man, actually. She'd thought that part of her had died along with her freedom. Her own husband, who hadn't touched her in years, might be dead, but she was still a woman who could recognize and appreciate a handsome man when she saw one. James Bancroft, with his long, lean build, sharp hazel eyes, and short, cropped dark hair was quite handsome indeed.

She curled up into a ball on her mattress, still hugging the shawl around her shoulders. Yes, she would write the pamphlet for Lord Medford, as long as he agreed to her bargain. She wanted to be freed from the Tower of London, as soon as possible. There was a degree of risk involved for the viscount, of course. After the riot that had taken place upon her arrest, the Tower was probably the safest place for her. Anyone found harboring her would certainly be placing himself in danger. But Kate refused to spend her last days in a prison. She wanted to live in a house and pretend to be as normal as possible. The truth was, she'd prefer to spend the days on her father's farm. What she wouldn't give to go back to a simple life for one month, one week, one day. Pretend she'd never met the Duke of Markingham, never agreed to be his wife. Oh, what she wouldn't give for another chance at her past.

Kate closed her eyes. Viscount Medford had told her he'd be back today to give her his answer. What was her story really worth to him? Would he be able to convince the lord chancellor to allow her to stay under his protection? Would Lord Medford take the risk?

CHAPTER 5

"How exactly do you plan to carry this one off, Lord Perfect?"

Devon Morgan's voice snapped James from his thoug..ts. He was sitting in a wide leather chair at his club and the Marquis of Colton had just arrived.

"Yes, I for one cannot wait to hear this." There was also no mistaking the voice of Jordan Holloway, the Earl of Ashbourne.

James glanced up at the pair. The two men were the husbands of Lily and Annie, and as such, James had developed something of an unspoken truce with them for the sake of his friends. In fact, Colton and Ashbourne were two of the only peers who knew for certain that James owned a printing press. Otherwise, he kept that fact a secret. He'd had to tell Kate, of course. He could only hope she didn't disclose it as she'd promised.

He eyed the two other men again. Regardless of their more recent common bonds, the truth remained that the three had been classmates at Eton and Cambridge and they had long been rivals. Prior to their marriages,

Colton and Ashbourne were known for their rakishness and serious drinking bouts while Medford had earned the nickname Lord Perfect for his love of order, his stellar reputation, his history of excellent marks, and his inherent tendency to always do the right thing. Today, James needed their assistance. So he'd summoned the marquis and the earl to Brooks's for an afternoon drink. The perfect invitation with which to lure those two particular chaps from their warm studies on such a blustery day.

"It's simple," James replied, offering them both a seat. "I intend to speak with the lord chancellor."

Colton and Ashbourne took their seats next to him in the large leather chairs near the windows. A fire crackled in the hearth across from them, and the smell of fine cheroots being smoked by a pair of gentlemen on the other side of the room filled the air. The club was nearly deserted this afternoon. It seemed many of London's finest had decided not to brave the elements in search of their usual afternoon amusements.

Colton settled into his chair. "And you expect the chancellor to just turn her over into your care?"

"Yes. I'm a peer, aren't I? That's the law. As long as she's in my personal care, she can be released from the Tower."

Colton replied with a skeptical look. "And you want a murderess living under your roof?"

"There's no proof that she's a murderess," James replied simply. "Yet."

Ashbourne snorted. "And there's no proof she isn't."

James shrugged. "I'm willing to take that chance. All anyone is talking about is this trial. If I have the story straight from the duchess, it will sell thousands of copies."

"No doubt about it," Colton replied. "I might even read it myself."

"I won't," Jordan replied. "But something tells me Annie will and she'll apprise me of every detail."

Colton laughed. "You're absolutely right there."

Somehow Ashbourne had already managed to procure a drink and he tossed it back. "Sure you don't want one?" he asked, holding his brandy glass in the air toward James.

James rolled his eyes. "No, thank you."

"Are you certain, Medford? Not even some *blue ruin*?" Ashbourne replied with a smirk. The two had had an unfortunate incident involving gin at a house party the previous autumn and there was hardly an encounter in which Ashbourne let him forget it.

"What does the duchess's barrister say?" Colton asked, signaling to a passing footman to bring him a drink.

"She hasn't got a barrister," James answered.

Ashbourne nearly spat out his drink. He sat forward in his chair and braced his elbows on both knees. "The devil you say. Hasn't got a barrister?"

James shook his head. "Not yet at least. I will provide the honorarium for one with the money I'm giving her. She's requested the best in town."

"The lady is soon to be on trial for her life." Ashbourne replied. "She'd best get a barrister and quickly, I'd say. Montgomery or Cartwright—"

"Abernathy. Abernathy is the best," James interjected.

Ashbourne arched a brow. "Looked into it already, have you?"

"Really, Ashbourne, you should know better. Am I ever unprepared?" James countered.

Colton took the drink from the returning footman and crossed his booted feet at the ankles, waiting for the servant to leave so he wouldn't overhear their conversation. "Seems to me, the real problem with harboring the duchess will be keeping the public from finding out she's with you. If anyone breathes a word . . ."

Ashbourne whistled. "You'd be a dead man yourself. There is a great deal of public condemnation of her already. She's *persona non grata* to be sure."

James nodded. Once. "True. But regardless of their feelings for her, everyone wants to read her story."

"They might want to read her story, but they won't take kindly to it if they find out you're harboring her in one of your properties." Colton took another sip.

"I understand the dangers," James replied.

Colton narrowed his eyes on James. He lowered his voice. "What is it, Medford, that makes you care so much about your bloody printing press? It can't be money, we all know you're richer than the king."

"Madder than the king too, I'd say, if you intend to take in a murderess," Ashbourne added. "I don't see how you would even get her out of the Tower without a mob following you home."

James steepled his fingers and eyed the other two men coolly. "Leave that to me. I just need the two of you to back me if the lord chancellor requires additional peers to convince him to allow me to keep her in house arrest."

Ashbourne gave him a long-suffering stare. "As if the lord chancellor would tell you no. You're thick as thieves with him and everyone else in Parliament, not to mention more than half of London. You're Lord Perfect, for Christ's sake. Need I remind you that's why we've never liked you?" He laughed.

"Oh, was *that* why?" James replied with a grin. "And here I thought all this time it was because the two of you were total arse—"

"Let's not start with all that," Colton said, downing his drink. "Suffice it to say we have faith in you, old chap." He leaned over and patted James's shoulder.

Ashbourne snapped his fingers. "Yes. Care to make a wager on whether Lord P here has his wish granted?" He gave Colton a devilish grin.

"Ha," Colton replied. "I wouldn't take that bet in a hundred years."

"Smart man," Ashbourne replied.

"Yes, well, I'm honored by your belief in me," James replied, clearing his throat. "And, of course, you must keep all of this silent."

"No one said we weren't willing, Medford." Ashbourne grinned from ear to ear. "Personally, I would love to see you involved in the scandal of the century. And of course you may count upon my discretion." He flourished his hand in the semblance of a bow.

James fought the urge to roll his eyes. Instead, he nodded. "Thank you."

"Absolutely, count me in, Medford," Colton replied. "I want a view from a box seat for this particular escapade."

CHAPTER 6

Bang. Bang. Bang.

Kate's eyes snapped open. It was the middle of the night and someone was knocking loudly upon the wooden door to her cell. She bolted up, her heart pounding. Sweat beaded on her forehead despite the freezing night air. She clutched the blankets to her throat and swallowed hard. "Who is it?"

"Yer grace, please get dressed an' pack yer things." In addition to its usual gruffness, the guard's voice sounded a bit sleepy.

"Yes. Yes. Just a minute." Kate scrambled out of bed. She quickly pulled off her night rail and fumbled around in the cold darkness for her gown. She'd only brought a few items of clothing with her when she'd been arrested. She promptly stuffed them all into her only bag. Smoothing a brush through her hair once, twice, she piled it atop her head as best she could. She stuck a few pins into the coiffure to hold it precariously in place. Then she quickly made her way to the door.

She cleared her throat and pushed up her chin. "I'm ready."

The door swung open, and her guard stood there, a candle in his hand, a sleeping cap on his head, and a robe wrapped around his massive frame. "He's come ta take ye out o' here, yer grace."

Kate shuddered and closed her eyes. "Oh, thank heavens," she murmured. She didn't need to ask who. Viscount Medford had come for her.

She pulled on her pelisse, grabbed up her bag, and hurried after the guard who was already rapidly making his way down the winding dank staircase. The stairs ended abruptly in a small dark antechamber, and Kate skidded to a halt in the middle of the scuffed, wood-planked floor. She hadn't had time to put on her stockings, and the cold wind that blew in from the partially open door wrapped its icy fingers around her ankles. Kate's teeth chattered, but she didn't care. She'd walk out of there naked if she must. She glanced about. Only darkness. Where was he?

Just then, a dark-cloaked figure in the corner spun around, and Kate caught her breath. She hadn't seen him standing there before. He emerged from the shadows.

Lord Medford looked every bit as handsome as he did the first day she met him. His face was made of stone. Handsome stone. He nodded toward her bag. "Is that all you have?"

"Ye—yes," she stuttered, shivering this time for an entirely different reason.

He stalked over to her, leaned down and whispered in her ear. "You said you wanted to live. Are you ready?"

"Yes," she whispered, nodding.

He grabbed her bag with one arm, and hefted it over his shoulder. He stopped and tossed what looked to be a guinea at the guard. "Thank you for arranging this," he said. Without another word, he pulled Kate by the hand out the wooden door and into the freezing dark night.

She did her best to keep up with his long strides. When they reached his mount, she watched in awe as he fastened her bag onto the saddle then hoisted her up onto the large brown gelding, all without saying a word. He swung up behind her moments later, and Kate tried to ignore the feel of his hard body against her backside as they took off at a gallop through the Tower yard. She was riding astride. That was a scandal in itself. But it felt like . . . freedom.

Courage. Courage. Courage. She repeated the words over and over in her mind. The great drawbridge lowered as they drew near, and Kate fought against the urge to close her eyes, sure they would be stopped before they cleared the entrance, as if there had been some sort of mistake.

The freezing wind whipped her hair, and it soon came unlodged from the tenuous bun she'd created moments earlier. The long red tresses wrapped around her face, partially blinding her. She tried to pull them away, tugging at the hair in her eyes, breathing in the icy night air, and watching the bridge draw closer and closer. She widened her eyes. In that moment she was absolutely exhilarated. She dug her fingernails into her palms as they approached the gate. The horse's hooves thundered across the wood, echoing in her chest and giving her an even greater thrill of freedom as they made their way across the bridge. The guard in the watch tower saluted them, and Medford hoisted his hand to return the gesture. Kate bit her lip, wanting to smile. They were going to make it. They were going to get away.

And then they were gone, into the shadowy alleys of London, into the dark cold night. Kate shuddered again, but she didn't look back, afraid she would see a troop of guards behind them. Afraid they hadn't indeed made this escape after all.

"Why did you come for me at night?" she managed to ask over the thunderous beat of her heart and the horse's hooves.

Lord Medford leaned his head down next to her ear, and when she turned her cheek slightly she saw dark stubble along his jaw. He hadn't shaved since morning, and oh my, but it made him look good. She shook her head to clear it of such thoughts, and then she shivered against the biting cold.

"It's safer this way," he replied. "I'm sorry I couldn't bring a coach to make you more comfortable. Are you cold?"

He must have felt her shudder, and she read in his response the truth. He hadn't brought a coach in case there was trouble. They would be more nimble this way.

Was she cold? All she could do was nod. Handling the reins with one deft hand, he somehow managed to whip his cape from his shoulders with the other and pull it around her. "Here, use this," he said in a commanding voice that made Kate's insides tremble.

"Won't you freeze?" she asked hesitantly.

"I'll be fine," he intoned.

She didn't wait for his answer. She was already tugging the cloak closer. It felt so good, warm from his body, and it smelled like him. She pulled the fine fabric against her face and inhaled its scent. It smelled like leather and something spicy and indefinable. Something wonderful. She prayed he wouldn't notice her sniffing his cape.

"Live, live, live," she whispered to herself, the words snatched away by the harsh night wind.

Kate closed her eyes. Who was this man? Lord Medford was obviously no ordinary viscount. Not only did he own a printing press for some unknown reason, but he obviously possessed the power and connections to free her from the Tower of London and to have a special request granted to do so alone in the middle of the night. There were no crowds or rioters because of his intelligent thinking. She was immensely grateful to him. But of course he had his own well-being in mind too. If he were planning to take her to one of his properties—and Lady Mary had assured her he owned a great many properties—and leave her there to write a pamphlet for him, he wouldn't want anyone to know.

She clutched at the cloak at her throat. But what did any of that matter now? She was free. She smiled to herself and closed her eyes, sucking in the wind through her nostrils. She pulled the cloak around her, trying to ignore his scent on it. What *was* the maddening scent? Printing ink? She stifled the small laugh that bubbled to her throat. Good heavens. That had been the first time she'd laughed since George had died. Wait, no, since she'd been married, rather, she quickly amended with a wince. A sobering thought.

Lord Medford's strong arm wrapped even more tightly around her waist, pulling her snug against him. Kate gulped. He was drawing her close, trying to warm her. A small smile popped to her lips. That was nice of him. Very nice indeed.

She held her breath as they raced through the streets. Kate concentrated, trying to remember every landmark, every building. It might be the last time she saw them. While under house arrest, she wouldn't have much opportunity to leave whichever house Lord Medford brought her to, and her next trip might be to the gallows or worse . . . being burned to death. She shuddered.

The spire of St. Paul's rose in the black night sky, and she stared at it in wonder as if seeing it for the first time. Christopher Wren's masterpiece. It made her feel tiny and powerful at the same time. She'd first seen it when she'd traveled to London with her mother eleven years ago to shop for her wedding trousseau. Back then she'd been so full of hope, the city so full of promise. She'd talked her mother into stopping at the famous church, and she'd entered slowly, reverently, gazing at the cavernous ceilings and soaring heights. It had taken her breath away. And it did so again, tonight, even just its outline standing proudly in bold relief against the night sky. She had paused in the great cathedral. Bowed her head and prayed that her marriage would be happy and blessed. That particular prayer hadn't been answered, of course, but tonight she said a new one as Lord Medford's horse thundered past the shadow of the church. A new prayer that she desperately hoped would be answered this time.

She swiveled her head, intent upon taking in the sights and sounds of the town even as it lay quiet, dark, and cold. Minutes later, they passed the Houses of Parliament, racing alongside the Thames. She breathed it all in, savored it. Enjoyed it. *This was living.* Flying along on horseback in the dark of night, the wind whipping her hair, a handsome man's arm wrapped around her waist.

"Are you all right?" Lord Medford asked, brushing her cheek with his stubble again and sending a shiver through her.

"Yes," she nearly shouted. "I'm alive!"

"Ah, so this is what you meant when you said you wanted to live?" he asked. She could feel the hint of his smile against her cheek.

She nodded eagerly. "I want to play with animals, smell roses, and dance the night away."

She heard his laughter this time. "Let's get you home safely, and then we'll see about the rest of it."

Kate nodded. "Where are you taking me?" she asked as they passed St. James.

"Mayfair," he answered. "We're nearly there."

Mayfair, of course. She'd assumed he'd install her in one of his lesser properties, but perhaps all the viscount's properties were grand houses in Mayfair. Or perhaps he wanted her close to keep an eye on her. She could hardly blame him. She had no intention of running off, but he wouldn't know that, and his reputation would be in jeopardy if she did escape.

The horse thundered through a paved alley and around a set of mews, a public house, some grand looking white town houses. Her husband's town house had been here somewhere though she'd only seen it once. Was it nearby?

They turned down a short alley and came to a stop behind an impressive four-story town house. "Here we are," Lord Medford said in her ear, leaning down again. His stubble brushed her cheek once more, and she had to force herself to concentrate on his words.

He dismounted quickly, tossed the reins to a groom who materialized from the shadows, detached her bag from the saddle, and reached up and swung her down. Her body slid against his, and she didn't meet his eyes. He was strong and hard and muscled in all the right places. He'd lifted her as if she weighed no more than a doll.

He let her settle on the ground and then pulled her by the hand through the gravelled alley and up the back steps. He opened the door with the same hand that held her bag. He shoved open the door with his booted foot, swung her inside, followed her in, and pushed it closed with his elbow.

They were standing in what looked to be a breakfast

room, and Kate could tell immediately the town house was quite grand. If this was one of Lord Medford's lesser properties, the man was quite wealthy indeed. She glanced around. No doubt there would be a housekeeper or someone who might help her find her way around, otherwise she'd most likely be quite alone here. Still, better than the Tower.

Clutching Lord Medford's cape around her shoulders, Kate turned to say her good-byes to him. "Thank you very much, my lord. Will you be coming by tomorrow to discuss the pamphlet?"

He arched a brow. "Coming by?"

"I mean from your house. I assume you will want to discuss the details before I get started. Do you live nearby?"

"I do want to discuss the details," Lord Medford replied with a firm nod. "Very much so. And I live extremely nearby." He smiled at her then and her knees melted. "This is my house. You're staying with me."

CHAPTER 7

What happened next was all a very efficient business. Lord Medford issued orders to a variety of servants who soon materialized from the interior of the house. Kate had never seen such smartly dressed servants. Not a wrinkle in their clothing. Not a hair out of place. Not a single frown. Lord Medford pointed, ordered, and issued commands, and his words were met with a flurry of precise activity and a minimum of folderol. Kate watched the proceedings with wide eyes. Whatever else Lord Medford was, the man was entirely in control.

Lord Medford finally turned to Kate where she stood inching toward a corner, watching everything with great interest. "Mrs. Hartsmeade here will see you to your room," he said. "A fire has already been started, and she's laid out some furs and blankets to warm you."

Kate nodded jerkily and glanced around. She looked up to see an older woman who stepped forward and took her bag. She was obviously the housekeeper. "And I've already got a nice, hot bath waiting for you, your grace," the older woman said in a soothing, friendly voice.

Kate nodded again. It was all she could do. It had all happened so quickly. And it all sounded so wonderful. Since coming in the back door, she was already warming up, and she hadn't had a proper bath in over a fortnight. No doubt she smelled like a foot. A very dirty foot. A bath would be absolutely heavenly.

She followed the housekeeper out of the room, with a backward glance and a thankful smile directed at Lord Medford.

Kate didn't entirely realize just how grand a house the viscount lived in until the next morning when she had a chance to explore. She still couldn't quite believe that Lord Medford intended for her to live under his very own roof. And how grand a roof it was. Even her husband's town house hadn't been this grand.

The man must sell a great many pamphlets. She eyed everything with wonder, the delicate French wallpaper, the expensive Aubusson rugs, the ormolu clocks, the priceless works of art and portraits that hung on the walls. She'd never seen such a well-ordered home. Every single item was perfectly in place. The maids scurried about plucking nonexistent bits of dust from tabletops, the footmen stood at attention in perfectly pressed livery, and the butler and housekeeper were so thoroughly organized, Kate got the impression that they had their days scheduled to the second. In the humming precision that was Lord Medford's house, Kate felt like a pigeon in a peacock's nest.

Her breakfast had arrived that morning on a shining silver tray that held a precisely pressed linen napkin embossed with a scrolling letter *B,* a scone and homemade jam, a pot of chocolate, a china tea service. Even a tiny crystal vase filled with roses graced the setting. Kate plucked one of the sweet flowers from the vase and swiped it under her nose. She closed her eyes and breathed in its delicate scent. Where in the world did Lord Medford get roses in winter? She bit her lip. It wasn't possible that he'd arranged for them after she'd mentioned wanting to smell roses last night, was it? No, it had only been a matter of hours since she'd made that comment. No doubt Mrs. Hartsmeade had chosen the flowers.

Kate watched with wide eyes as the efficiency that was Lord Medford's household worked its magic around her. Everything was choreographed to the smallest detail. One maid whisked in and plumped the pillows behind Kate's head, another brought her a decadently soft robe, a third stoked the toasty fire in the hearth across from the bed, and Mrs. Hartsmeade herself had brought the breakfast tray along with a wide smile. Oh yes, Kate had made a good bargain coming here.

"Are you feeling better this morning, your grace?" the housekeeper asked, deftly sliding the tray onto the bed next to Kate and promptly filling her teacup.

Kate couldn't help but return the woman's smile. "I am. Very much so. I must say I wasn't treated this well at my own . . . my husband's home."

Mrs. Hartsmeade's brow furrowed. "Lord Medford indicated that you were to be treated to our best and given whatever you desire. So please do not hesitate to ask for anything."

"Thank you very much, Mrs. Hartsmeade."

"I've taken the liberty of pressing the clothing you brought with you, and Lord Medford has sent one of the footmen to Markingham Abbey to fetch more of your things."

Kate blushed at that. Lord Medford was fetching her clothing? Did no detail escape the man's attention?

"And not to worry, your grace," Mrs. Hartsmeade

said in a lower tone. "You may rest assured that all of Lord Medford's servants are utterly discreet. No one will know you're here, not from the servants." She gave a firm nod.

Kate expelled her breath. She had been a bit worried about that with so many people flitting about, but they all seemed so flawlessly proper. She couldn't imagine any one of them gossiping the way the servants at Markingham Abbey were wont to do. She smiled at the older woman. "Thank you for that, Mrs. Hartsmeade."

"I'll leave you to your breakfast, your grace," the housekeeper replied. "And later, Louisa will be in to help you dress."

Kate nodded. Oh how she wished she could ask Mrs. Hartsmeade not to call her "your grace," but she could just imagine the proper woman having conniptions were Kate to suggest any such thing.

After enjoying the breakfast that was infinitely better than the fare that had been served to her at the Tower, Kate stretched and relaxed back into the pillows on the bed. Ah, treated as a guest of honor in a fine town house in Mayfair. So much better than her cold dank room at the Tower. The hot bath she'd had last night had been so heavenly she'd nearly cried and she'd slept better than she had in weeks. It was all like a dream.

But even as she tried to enjoy herself, apprehension clawed at her insides. She had no idea what would happen next. Her life had been anything but predictable of late and there was no indication that pattern would cease any time soon.

A knock at the door signaled Louisa's arrival and the efficient little lady's maid with bright green eyes and neatly braided blond hair set about helping Kate into one of the few gowns she'd dragged with her from her husband's home. She eyed the light blue morning dress she wore. It was inappropriate. She hadn't even had time to have the gowns dyed black. And she certainly wasn't about to inconvenience Lord Medford's servants by requesting that they do it. But did it even matter? Would a Society that assumed she had murdered her husband truly fault her for failing to properly mourn him? She shook her head. Even when she was trying to break the rules, they crowded into her brain and mocked her. No. No. No. She refused to care anymore. Society and its rules had ruined her.

"I hope you don't mind my saying so, your grace," Louisa murmured, after she'd arranged Kate's hair in a loose chignon. "But you must be the prettiest lady I've ever seen."

Kate's cheeks heated. "Why, what a nice thing to say, Louisa. Thank you."

The maid returned her smile. "Lord Medford asks that you meet him in his study at half past, your grace," Louisa announced, bobbing a curtsy and retreating from the room.

Kate glanced at the delicate clock on the mantel piece. Fifteen minutes yet. She squared her shoulders and smoothed her skirts. She might as well go in search of Lord Medford's study. Louisa had rushed away before she'd had a chance to ask its location.

Taking a deep breath and opening the door to her room, Kate made her way into the hall, through the corridor, and down the grand staircase in the foyer. She glanced about uncertainly. Which way? Might as well begin here. No doubt she would find the study eventually. She poked her nose into the first few salons in the front of the house. All perfectly appointed like the rest of the mansion. Where were all of the helpful servants when she needed them? All probably industriously occupied elsewhere no doubt. She couldn't imagine any one of them being lazy for even a moment. She gingerly made her way toward the back of the house, where she came upon two large wooden doors. Either the study or the library, she decided. She knocked lightly and a deep voice answered, "Come in."

Ah, the study.

She opened the doors with both hands and pushed them wide. She twirled around in a large circle to take in every detail of the vast space. The study was a grand room, and it didn't have so much as one paper out of place. A large mahogany desk sat in the center of the room framed by floor-to-ceiling windows behind it. Two large coffee-brown leather chairs rested in front of the desk. Bookcases lined with an enormous variety of tomes marched along the walls and a warm fire crackled in the hearth across from the desk. A big yellow dog lay on the rug in front of the fireplace. The dog jumped up and wagged its tail eagerly, watching Kate, but the animal remained in its spot, obviously awaiting a command from its master.

I want to pet a puppy. The memory of what she'd said to Lord Medford when he'd made her his offer in the Tower came floating back to her. He hadn't mentioned that he had a dog.

She smiled brightly. "Oh, but she's adorable. I love dogs! I haven't seen a dog since I lived at home with Mother and Father." A wave of homesickness hit her and she pressed her lips together tightly.

Lord Medford had looked up from his papers and was watching her. "Would you like to pet her?" he asked with a smile that made Kate's heart flutter.

She nodded. "Yes, very much."

Lord Medford gave a short whistle and the dog bounded forward. She stopped in front of Kate and sat politely, wiggling and putting up one paw that Kate took and shook. Kate laughed. "Well, well. Someone has extraordinary manners. What's her name?"

"Themis." Lord Medford stood up and walked around the side of the desk. He rested a hip against it and smiled at the scene in front of him. "I've enjoyed training her," he said. "Though sometimes I think I may have gone a bit too far." He laughed.

"Themis." Kate put a finger to her jaw. "Why do I know that name?" She tapped her fingertip to her face. "Ah yes, the goddess of custom and order."

"You know her?" Was that a look of admiration in his green eyes? "Themis isn't one of the more popular goddesses."

"She's the goddess of divine justice," Kate murmured. "Perhaps that's why I know her. I need to call upon her now."

His eyes shifted back toward the dog and he gave a little laugh, perhaps to lighten the mood. "Well, here she is."

Kate bent down and patted the dog's head. "Themis," she said. "You and I shall become fast friends." Themis stamped a paw on the floor and breathed out through her snout.

Kate smiled at Lord Medford. "I've never seen such manners. What else can she do?"

Lord Medford issued commands for the dog to sit, lie, roll over, and bring him the paper, all of which Themis did without hesitation. She obviously loved her master.

Kate clapped her hands. "Amazing, truly. How long have you had her?"

Lord Medford sighed. "She was a stray, actually. My friend Lily, Lady Colton, she and her sister have made it a habit to rescue animals in need. This poor girl was not long for the world, I'm afraid. She had no one to take her in."

Kate watched him carefully. "So you agreed?"

"Yes, and I must admit I never thought myself one for owning a dog until I met Themis."

Kate ducked her head to hide her smile. How wonderful. The man had saved a dog out of the kindness of his heart. And he obviously loved the animal. She could tell just by watching them together.

"I used to have a dog that looked very much like Themis," Kate said, her voice trailing off softly.

Lord Medford braced his palms on the desktop on either side of his hips. "Did you? What happened to him?"

"I couldn't take him with me when I married. My parents kept him. Eventually he . . . he died of old age just before my parents did."

"What happened to your parents?" Lord Medford asked softly.

Kate glanced up at him and it struck her then. Lord Medford had kind eyes. Very kind. "They both had the fever," she murmured, swallowing.

Lord Medford nodded. "I'm sorry."

Kate cleared her throat and straightened her shoulders. She pinched the delicate skin on the inside of her arm. Why had she told him about her dog and her parents? No doubt Lord Medford wasn't interested in such drivel. She had a job to do. A pamphlet to write. "Shall we get started?" she asked, schooling her features into the most professional manner she could muster. "Discussing the pamphlet?"

"By all means." He stood and moved back around to his seat behind the desk, gesturing for Kate to sit in one of the facing chairs. Themis trotted away and curled up on the rug in front of the fire again and closed her eyes.

"Before we discuss the pamphlet," Lord Medford said. "I wanted to speak to you about your defense. I've sent for Mr. Abernathy. He's the most experienced barrister in town."

Bracing her hands on the arms of the chair, Kate sat up straight and blinked. "Mr. Abernathy?"

"Yes. I promised you the best and I'll deliver." He winked at her and Kate's insides felt funny again. "I must admit I was quite surprised to hear you didn't already have someone employed. Abernathy was working on another case, but I . . . persuaded him to put his work on hold."

Kate settled back into the chair and expelled her breath. "Thank you, my lord. I'm going to need the best. But I've seen enough of how the aristocracy works to not trust the House of Lords, to be honest. I doubt even Mr. Abernathy will stand much of a chance against the charges I face."

Lord Medford cleared his throat. "Abernathy will do everything he can. He'll be here at one o'clock."

She took a deep breath. "I look forward to meeting him. In the meantime, perhaps you should tell me what exactly you have in mind for the pamphlet."

He leaned his elbow on the arm of his chair and propped his chin on his fist. "I ask nothing more than that you tell your story, in your own words."

Her gaze snapped to his face. "Truly? You don't want the salacious details? I thought surely—"

"Trust me. The *ton* will be interested in whatever you have to say."

Kate shook her head. Trust me, he had said. That made her stop. She didn't trust him. Didn't even know him. True, he'd been kind to her so far, but he wanted something from her. Though he had surprised her by giving her free rein to write the pamphlet. And seeing to her defense. But there had to be a catch . . . somewhere.

He leaned back in his chair and steepled his fingers in front of his chest. "What is it that you want to tell people?"

"That I'm innocent," she said in a loud, strong voice, quite sure her eyes were flashing with all the passion she felt on the subject. "Though I expect most won't believe it," she finished more softly.

His eyes narrowed on her face. "May I ask you a question?"

She smiled. "I believe I cannot say no to that."

He leaned back in his chair. "You might have an easier time of it if you had friends in the aristocracy. Why is it that you were in the country for so long? Why did you never come to London? Never meet anyone? Make friends?"

She swallowed and glanced away. "What does any of it matter?"

"It matters to your defense."

Kate bit her lip. "Very well." She paused, expelling her breath. "After we were married, my husband and I . . . we soon realized we didn't suit. He wanted to pursue his . . . pleasures in London, and he didn't want me there, reminding him of what an awful choice of wife he'd made."

Lord Medford pursed his lips. "Awful choice?"

She stared at her hands that were folded in her lap. "You must have heard about me, Lord Medford. My past. It's been in all the papers."

He nodded. "If you mean that your father was a gentleman landowner, not a peer, then yes. But how does that make you an awful choice?"

She raised her head and gave him a skeptical look. "You know how vast the divide is. I was never a part of my husband's world. Despite the fairy tales, one does not go from a farm to a ducal estate. Not successfully at least."

"You didn't enjoy your new position?"

She looked up at the ceiling and searched her memory, trying to locate the right words. "I tried. I truly did. I tried everything to fit it, to be a good wife. But I just couldn't, and I wasn't. I was miserable and George was even more so. We'd made a terrible mistake."

Lord Medford's brow remained furrowed. He shrugged. "Many couples find they aren't a love match. It's not uncommon."

She glanced away, her face heating fiercely. She should stop talking. She'd already said too much. "There were other . . . reasons." She cleared her throat and shook her head. "But none of that matters now. None of it changes . . . anything. Including the reason why we're here." Oh God. Why was it seemingly so easy to talk to this man? He was a stranger. Did she have to remind herself of that again? And here she was sharing the intimate details of her life with him.

He nodded. "I understand. And all I ask of you is that you write your story, your grace. And that you write the truth."

CHAPTER 8

When Mr. Abernathy was ushered into the study, Lord Medford invited the man to sit. Lord Medford pulled out the other chair in front of his desk for Kate. She walked toward her seat slowly while Lord Medford nodded to the butler asking him to bring tea.

Kate swallowed convulsively but kept her eyes trained on the barrister. "Thank you very much for agreeing to represent me."

"It shall be my pleasure, your grace," Mr. Abernathy replied with a precise nod and a matter-of-fact smile. The man was older with a trimmed white beard, a lean, able build, and sharp, discerning eyes. He seemed like the type of man who didn't miss a thing, and Kate had the awful feeling that she was being closely scrutinized.

She cleared her throat and straightened her shoulders. "I assume you have . . . experience with this sort of thing."

Mr. Abernathy extracted a pair of silver-rimmed spectacles from his inside coat pocket and placed them on the tip of his nose. He sat up even more straight and regarded her over the rims of the spectacles. Oh excellent, more scrutiny. "I'm experienced, your grace, but the fact is there's never been a case quite like . . . with these exact circumstances, and I—"

"I understand," she replied, putting up a hand. "You'll do your best."

"I'm quite qualified," Abernathy replied. "I assure you. I'm enrolled to practice before the House of Lords, which, of course, is where your trial will be held, should it come to that."

She furrowed her brow. "Should it come to that?"

Abernathy bobbed his head in a brisk nod. "Yes, well, we hope for the best, of course, but we must plan for the worst."

"I see." She swallowed. "What can I expect, then?"

James lifted his brows. Impressive, the way Kate was taking charge of the conversation. She seemed even more interested in her defense than he'd expected. Good. He'd been a bit worried that she'd be meek or even worse, act guilty, but the confidence with which she'd said, "I am innocent," earlier had given him hope. There was definitely a fighter beneath her beautiful surface. One he'd witnessed when she'd demanded that he free her from the Tower. One that he wanted to see more of.

Mr. Abernathy pulled a large stack of papers from his well-polished leather bag and set them on the desk in front of him. He consulted the stack, flipping through it and pulling out a small group. "In this case, Lord Medford's solicitor has employed me directly. I will be in charge of your defense, leading the investigation on your behalf, and drawing up the necessary paperwork."

Kate shook her head and met James's eyes. "I don't understand. Hasn't there already been an investigation?"

Mr. Abernathy gave a curt nod. "The magistrate

near your husband's country house has performed his investigation, yes. And there was an inquest over the . . ." He cleared his throat. "Forgive me for being indelicate, your grace." He gave her a kindly yet still efficient look.

Kate's chin trembled slightly but she nodded. "Go on. I want to hear everything."

"There was an inquest over the body," Abernathy continued.

She clenched her jaw. "And?"

"Now I will lead an investigation on your behalf. I shall call the witnesses, record their statements, and take note of anything else relevant to the case."

Kate shook her head. "But I've already been charged, haven't I? I wouldn't have been arrested otherwise."

James leaned forward in his chair and met her eyes. "Yes, you've been charged. The coroner's jury named you in their verdict."

"And not only that . . ." Mr. Abernathy's voice trailed off. "Although it doesn't exactly matter."

Kate snapped her head around to face the barrister. "What? Not only what?"

Abernathy's voice was matter-of-fact. "In addition to the coroner's jury's verdict, there's been a warrant sworn against you."

Kate's mouth fell open. "By whom?"

Abernathy glanced at James. He nodded.

"By Lady Bettina Swinton," Abernathy said.

Kate's hand flew to her throat. "Lady Bettina swore a warrant against me?"

"Yes, it seems she's convinced of your guilt."

"Wait. Why was Lady Bettina there?" James asked, shifting forward in his seat.

Abernathy put up a hand. "We'll get to that," he

assured James. To Kate, he said, "But Lady Bettina's oath doesn't mean there won't be a full investigation. The lady herself will be questioned."

Kate pressed her fingertips to her temples. "What else do I need to know?"

Abernathy placed a hand on the stack of papers. "The House of Lords has already been notified of the verdict and the warrant, else, as you indicated, you would not have been arrested."

She expelled her breath. "So, what's next?"

Locke returned with the tea tray then and set about serving the three occupants of the study.

"The grand jury must indict," Abernathy said, reaching for his teacup from the butler.

"And then?" Kate's hand trembled a bit as she took her cup.

Abernathy pushed his saucer onto the desk in front of him. "If Parliament is in session, the lord chancellor will request the appointment of a lord high steward. All peers will act as judge and jury."

"And if the House is not in session?" Kate replied.

Abernathy gave a curt not. "Then the trial shall be held at the Court of the Lord High Steward, and he will act as judge and the peers as jury, except, of course, for the bishops."

Kate glanced at James. "Why not the bishops?"

"The bishops may be members of the House of Lords, but they do not take part in any case where the sentence might be death," James told her.

"I see," Kate replied quietly. "And my penalty, if I am found guilty?"

Abernathy quickly shook his head. "Your grace, I do not think you should worry about that at this time. I—"

Setting her teacup on the desk, she closed her eyes.

She clutched at the arms of the chair until her knuckles went white. "Please, Mr. Abernathy. I need to hear you say it."

Abernathy straightened his shoulders. Another curt nod. "As you wish, your grace." He cleared his throat yet again. He glanced at James. "The penalty is death by burning."

A shiver ran through Kate. She hung her head.

"But there are many options," Abernathy hastily continued. "We may plead down to manslaughter on provocation . . . self-preservation."

"I wasn't provoked," Kate whispered softly. "And there was no self-preservation. I didn't do it." She glanced up at Mr. Abernathy and, for the first time, James saw real fear in her pretty blue eyes. His chest felt tight.

Mr. Abernathy pushed up his spectacles on his nose. "I understand, your grace, and please believe, I shall do everything in my power, absolutely everything, to prove your innocence."

"Thank you, Mr. Abernathy. I trust you will. Now." She lifted her chin. "What do you need from me? To help?"

Abernathy pulled out another swath of papers from the middle of his stack and grabbed up a quill. "I need you to tell me everything you remember about that day."

CHAPTER 9

Kate took a deep breath and exhaled slowly. She'd known this moment would come. The moment when she'd have to relive it all, the horrific details of the morning George had died. She'd dreaded it, yes, but she'd been mentally preparing herself. She'd have to face this again, in court. The first time would be the most difficult, however. She already knew that much. She turned to face Mr. Abernathy and swallowed the lump in her throat. "Very well. I'll tell you everything."

"Including . . ." Mr. Abernathy glanced away a bit hesitantly. "To be frank, the rumor is that you and your husband had a row that day. If that is indeed true, I must insist upon the details."

Kate nodded.

Lord Medford rose from his seat. "I'll leave you two."

"No, my lord," Kate replied, looking up at him. "Please stay. You have every right to hear this after the assistance you've provided me. Unless, of course, you'd rather not."

"Are you certain?" he asked, meeting her eyes.

She glanced away. A single nod. "Yes." For some unknown reason his presence comforted her.

Lord Medford settled back into his seat. He motioned to Mr. Abernathy. "Proceed."

The barrister cleared his throat. His hand grasping the quill hovered over the parchment lying on the desktop in front of him. "Your grace? Is it true that you and his grace argued the morning of his death?"

Kate bit her lip but she returned the older man's stare. "We did argue. That is true."

Abernathy scribbled on the paper. "And the nature of your argument?"

She paused, opened her mouth, and then closed it again.

"It's all right, your grace," Lord Medford said. "We understand how difficult it must be for you to say these things."

Kate felt a bit bolstered by his encouragement. She closed her eyes, trying to remember. She blew out a breath. "The previous evening, my husband had informed me that he refused to grant me a divorce." She opened her eyes again.

Abernathy merely nodded, as if a duchess announced every day that she intended to divorce her duke. The man continued busily scribbling. "You had asked his grace for a divorce?"

"Yes." She squeezed her clammy hands together in her lap.

Mr. Abernathy scribbled more. "When had you first mentioned a divorce to his grace?"

"I'd written to him, the week before. I'd been waiting for George to come to the Abbey and discuss it with me."

More scribbling. "And that's why he was there?"

"Yes."

Abernathy looked up from his paper. "And he didn't come alone?"

"No." She gulped and her throat ached. "Lady Bettina, his . . . his mistress, was with him."

James pounded his fist on the desktop, and the teacups bounced. The duchess and Abernathy turned to stare at him. Damn it. If that ass Markingham weren't dead, James would like to land a punch squarely on his jaw right now. How dare the cad bring his mistress with him to discuss his marriage with his wife?

Abernathy returned his attention to the duchess, his hand poised over the parchment once again. "Did anyone else accompany his grace?"

Her eyes searched the ceiling. "His valet, Tucker, was with him as well."

Abernathy kept his eyes trained on the paper while he busily wrote. "And what did your husband say to you?"

"He said . . ." She swallowed again. "He informed me . . . that he and Lady Bettina were in love."

James cursed under his breath.

Abernathy didn't look up. "But he refused your request for a divorce?"

She nodded. "Yes. As you know, the grounds for divorce are very . . . delicate and he refused to consider it."

Abernathy cleared his throat. "And did you argue with him about the divorce that evening?"

She looked out the window, her eyes staring as if she were reliving what must have been a horrendous night. "No, not that night. I was . . . in shock."

"Shocked that he refused to grant you the divorce?" Abernathy clarified.

"Yes. And that he told me he was in love. It made no

sense to me that he wouldn't want the divorce if he could be rid of me. You see, he'd . . . he'd been unfaithful many times before but he'd never been so bold as to tell me he was in love with any of them."

James clenched his fist. If Markingham were as big an ass to everyone else as he was to his wife, no doubt he had a steady queue of people wanting to murder him.

Abernathy nodded. "What happened later that night? Did you see his grace, or Lady Bettina?"

Kate cleared her throat. "I did not. I spent the evening alone in my bedchamber. I asked my maid to bring me my dinner there."

"And you didn't see either one of them again until the next morning?" Abernathy continued.

"That's correct."

Abernathy paused for a sip from his teacup. "So, the next morning, when did you see them again?"

Kate also took a sip with a shaky hand. "I didn't see Lady Bettina again until . . . after . . ." She glanced away.

"And his grace?" Abernathy asked evenly.

Her voice was high, strained. "He came to say goodbye. He told me he never wanted to see me again. He said he was returning to London and wouldn't be back until I'd vacated the Abbey. He wanted me to move to a small property he owns near Carlisle. To be out of his way, once and for all, I suppose."

Abernathy's wrinkled hand shuffled across the parchment. "And that's why you fought?"

"Yes." She closed her eyes and pressed two fingertips to one lid. "I told him I was leaving, that I would seek a divorce with or without his consent. That I intended to come to London, to live here."

Abernathy frowned. "And he wasn't pleased with that?"

She shook her head frantically. "No. He yelled. Told me that he forbade it."

"And what was your reply?" Abernathy scribbled furiously.

"I yelled back. I told him I didn't care anymore what he wanted me to do. I was through taking orders from him. I'd spent the last ten years alone in the country, without him, without anyone, and I was going to leave." She was shaking, trembling, and James could tell how much the experience had cost her. His heart wrenched for the woman who'd had to remain hidden in the country, alone for so long. But then Lily's words from a few days ago came back to taunt him. *I give you one week of dealing with the duchess before you're assisting with her defense.* Damn it, he didn't want to care. Didn't want to get involved. He shouldn't have stayed in the room to hear all of this.

Abernathy faced the duchess head-on. "Several people overheard your argument that morning, did they not?"

She nodded. "I've come to understand they did. But at the time I had no idea anyone was listening, though it doesn't surprise me. We were not attempting to keep our voices low. We were both extremely agitated."

Abernathy pushed his spectacles up on his nose once more. "Yes, your grace. My apologies, but we're nearly finished. However, this next part may be rather difficult for you."

She took a deep breath and folded her hands in her lap. "I'm ready, Mr. Abernathy."

"Your grace," Abernathy said. "Did you say anything else to your husband that morning that those listening would have taken . . . amiss?"

She wrung her hands with a vengeance. "I did."

Abernathy paused to dip the quill back in the inkwell. "What did you say?"

Kate straightened her shoulders. "I said I'd see him dead before I remained married to him."

CHAPTER 10

If the duchess's statement shocked Abernathy, he betrayed his surprise by neither word nor deed. "Why did you say that, your grace?" was all the barrister asked. The man was skilled at his job, James had to admit, quite skilled.

Kate buried her face in her hands. "I didn't mean it. Not literally at least. I was so ashamed, humiliated, angry. I reacted out of fear. But I didn't mean it. And I certainly never would have done it."

Mr. Abernathy laid down his quill, reached over, and placed his hand atop hers. "I understand, your grace."

James watched the exchange through narrowed eyes. He didn't know what to make of it. She wasn't crying but she was distraught. She seemed strong but she also appeared vulnerable. She was either a bloody brilliant actress or the most unlucky woman in the kingdom, and damn it, James couldn't tell. He'd always prided himself on being able to sum up people quickly, make decisions about their character, their integrity. But the duchess remained a mystery to him. A beautiful mystery.

She expelled a long breath. "Oh, they might as well just burn me now. I know my story sounds just dreadful."

"Stay strong, your grace. You're doing an excellent job," Abernathy replied.

The duchess's jaw clenched. "Please, Mr. Abernathy, do not call me 'your grace.'"

The barrister nodded. "Very well. Now." He grabbed up his quill again. "After your argument, your husband left the room?"

She tugged at her bottom lip with her teeth. "Yes, I assume he went to his own bedchamber."

"And when did you . . . see him next?" Abernathy asked.

She rubbed her forehead. "It was less than an hour later. I wanted to ask him when he planned to leave. I should have sent a servant."

Abernathy made a note. "Did you go to his bedchamber to apologize?"

She shook her head and straightened her shoulders. Her voice was steady, calm, direct. "No. I did not."

James's gaze snapped to her face. He respected the hell out of that answer. It would have been so easy for her to say yes. It might have made her look a bit less guilty. Instead, she held her head high and told . . . the truth. She hadn't gone to Markingham's bedchamber to apologize. And from what James had just heard of the man's treatment of her, he couldn't blame her.

"Forgive me, but I must ask," Abernathy continued, eyeing the duchess carefully over the rims of his spectacles. "What did you see when you entered your husband's bedchamber?"

"Take your time," James added, watching her closely.

She was quiet for several long seconds, and James saw the tears she was valiantly trying to quash shimmering in the blue depths of her eyes. "I knocked," she whispered, holding up her fist as if she were back there in front of the door to Markingham's room. "Quietly at first and then more loudly. There was no answer."

"Go ahead," Abernathy prompted, in a calm, steady voice.

She shook her head slightly, and one red-gold curl came loose from her bun and fell to her cheek. "And then I don't know why, but something . . . something made me decide to open the door, to not turn away and assume he'd already left."

A nod from the barrister. "Yes."

Kate expelled a shaky breath. "I turned the handle and opened the door. I pushed it open and stepped inside."

"What did you see?" If Abernathy was anything like James, he was holding his breath too.

"It was cold in the room. Dark. I had to blink to focus, to see anything."

"Yes." Abernathy nodded.

Kate's voice shook. "There he was." The far-off look was back in her eyes. James was certain she was reliving every awful moment of it.

"He was lying on the floor. Twisted, bloody." She cupped her hand over her mouth.

"He was dead?" Abernathy prompted.

"Yes." She mumbled through her hand. Her voice cracked.

"You're sure." Abernathy's eyes bored into her.

The duchess remained in a trance of memory. "Yes. I walked over to him, so carefully, so slowly. 'George,' I called. 'George.' He'd been shot in the chest. I . . . I couldn't believe it." She shook her head frantically.

"You hadn't heard a pistol fire?" Abernathy asked.

"No, no, I hadn't. I'd been in my bedchamber which was on the other end of the floor but I never heard anything like that."

Abernathy jotted a note. "When you entered the room, did you see the pistol?"

"Yes." She nodded. "It was on the rug in front of him."

"Did you touch it?"

"No." She shook her head frantically. "No, I didn't want to touch it."

"But you . . ." Abernathy audibly gulped. "You touched him?"

A single nod. "Yes. I touched him. I fell to my knees. I cradled his head."

Abernathy sat up straighter and met her eyes. "Forgive me, but I must ask. Did you love your husband?"

"No." The single word seemed to echo off the wooden bookcases. Tears fell freely down her face now. She shook her head. "I didn't love my husband. I don't think I ever did." Her eyes were like wet velvet, sparkling with tears. "But I never . . . never wished him to die and certainly not like that. And when I think about his poor mother being told . . . We had no love lost between us, the dowager and I, but I just can't imagine losing a child." Her voice cracked and her chest heaved.

Mr. Abernathy reached out and squeezed her hand. "I'm nearly through. You're doing well. Just a few more questions. What happened next? How were you discovered?"

She shook the tears away and wiped at her eyes. James leaned forward and offered his handkerchief. She took it with a small nod of thanks.

"Lady Bettina," Kate said. "Lady Bettina came into the room. She looked . . . horrified."

"Did she say anything?'

Another nod. " 'What have you done?' She screamed it. 'What have you done!' "

"And after that?" Abernathy prompted.

"The entire household came rushing in, all of the servants."

The barrister scribbled another note on the parchment. "And the magistrate came soon after?"

Kate bit her lip. "Yes. One of the servants must have summoned him. I still don't know for certain."

"Did the servants say anything?" Abernathy asked.

"They defended me. They said I couldn't have done it."

"All of them?" Abernathy prompted.

"Well, Mrs. Anderson, the housekeeper, and Edwards, the butler. My maid, Virginia. They were all in shock, of course, but they knew I couldn't have done it."

"Did they say that to the magistrate?" Abernathy asked.

"I think so. Oh, I don't know. It all was such a blur to me."

"One last question."

"Yes?"

"Who do *you* think murdered your husband?"

The duchess shook her head slowly. "I've had nothing to do but think about that question for weeks now. Believe me, it's on my mind every moment."

"And?" Abernathy prodded, and James leaned forward too, suddenly extremely interested in her answer.

"I just don't know. I don't know who would have wanted him dead. Not Lady Bettina, surely, and the servants never seemed unhappy with him. He was never there to make them miserable. I honestly don't know who shot my husband, Mr. Abernathy. All I know is that it was not me and I'd take my own life before I unjustly accused another person."

Abernathy set down his quill. "That's enough for today. Thank you for telling me your story."

Kate hastily wiped at her eyes with James's

handkerchief one more time. "If you gentlemen don't mind, I think I may just go lie down for a bit."

"By all means," they both said simultaneously, standing while she stood.

After Kate left the room, James lowered himself back into his seat, crossed his arms over his chest, and stared at Abernathy. "Do you think she's telling the truth?"

Abernathy's expression was blank. He plucked the spectacles from his nose, folded them neatly, and slipped them back inside his coat pocket. "It's not my business to determine whether she's telling the truth, my lord. It's my business to defend her. And I intend to. Vigorously."

"Yes, but what do you *think*?" James insisted, eyeing the barrister carefully. Bloody hell, he was beginning to sound like Lily. But Abernathy was a solid judge of character and he intended to hear the man's opinion on the matter.

Abernathy gathered his papers and tucked them back into his bag. He stood and moved toward the door, before turning to face James. "I think that if she's not telling the truth, she's doing an awfully good job at lying."

CHAPTER 11

It was the music that woke him. The haunting strains of Beethoven's "Moonlight Sonata" played by a deft hand on the pianoforte in the ballroom. James raised himself on his elbow, shook off his sleep, slipped out of bed, and pulled his dark green robe over his shoulders. Securing the belt tightly around his waist, he made his way into the ballroom on the second story.

Kate was there, with a brace of candles barely glowing in front of her pretty face. She played the instrument with her eyes closed.

James cleared his throat. "You're very talented," he said, and his words echoed across the cavernous space.

She immediately stopped, hitting the last note incorrectly. She snapped open her eyes. "My lord!"

"Please don't let me stop you." He moved closer along the cold marble floor, recognizing that she too was wearing her nightclothes, including a robe. "It's lovely." But he wasn't sure if he was talking about the music or the vision of her in her robe, her luxurious hair down around her shoulders, her scrubbed-clean face simply breathtaking.

"I'm so sorry to have wakened you," she said, ducking her head. "I couldn't sleep. I'd hoped it wouldn't be too loud with the doors closed."

He moved toward the pianoforte and rested his forearms on the back of the instrument, meeting her gaze over the top of it. "I'm a notoriously light sleeper, I'm afraid." He smiled at her. "Besides, I'm glad to have heard it. I love that piece."

She blushed and it was enchanting. "It's my particular favorite," she admitted. "I haven't played the pianoforte since I was . . . arrested. I used to play every day at Markingham Abbey."

He furrowed his brow. "Your time at Markingham Abbey doesn't sound like it was particularly happy, your grace."

Kate's blue eyes flashed. "Please don't call me that."

James frowned. "I noticed yesterday, you asked Abernathy not to call you that either. You don't like your honorific?"

She shook her head and the red-gold curls bounced along her shoulders. "No. I never have."

He tipped his head to the side. "Why?" he asked quietly.

"It's an odious title. As if I'm somehow better than everyone else. Your grace. Your grace. Your grace. I've grown to detest it."

James eyed her carefully. "I don't understand."

"I'm not a duchess," she whispered, meeting his gaze with the deep pools of her eyes. "I'm just a girl who married a duke."

James nodded. Somehow that made sense to him and somehow she never ceased to amaze him. Before they'd met, he'd expected her to be all superciliousness and attitude. Instead she reminded him of a lost soul.

She tossed her head slightly as if shaking off the seriousness of their conversation. "I suppose it's completely inappropriate for us to be here together like this, wearing nothing more than our nightclothes." She stared at his chest and then her cheeks flushed a lovely shade of pink.

James glanced down to realize his robe had opened a bit and a sliver of his bare chest was visible at the top of the robe. He smiled, propping his elbow on the top of the pianoforte and resting his chin in his palm. "Seems a bit late to be worried about appropriateness. I hate to say it, but nothing about our relationship is appropriate."

She blushed again, and James was momentarily regretful of his words. He stood up straight. "I mean to say, nothing about our interactions is conventional."

"Yes." She smiled softly but didn't meet his eyes. "I suppose you're right."

Silence fell between them before Kate spoke again. "May I ask you a question, my lord?" She fidgeted with her hands.

He grinned again. "Ah, now that is hardly fair. If I am not to call you 'your grace,' you cannot be so proper as to call me 'my lord.'"

She gave him a mischievous smile that made his heart beat faster. "I didn't realize you weren't fond of your title."

"Oh, I am," he replied. "But I insist. If we're going to be inappropriate, we may as well call each other by our first names. I'm willing if you are."

She nodded. "Yes, absolutely. Please call me Kate."

"And you may call me James," he said, stepping back and executing a bow.

"Very well. May I ask you a question, James?"

He grinned at her. "I owe you an answer, I believe."

She rested her fingers on the ivory keys of the piano but did not move them. "Why did you bring me here? To your home, I mean. You must own many properties."

"I do," he replied. "Several in fact. Here and in the countryside."

She bit her lip. "Then why not place me in one of those houses?"

James rested his elbows on the back of the pianoforte again. "I couldn't ensure your safety in my other houses."

Her brow immediately furrowed. "You brought me here to keep me safe?"

"Does that surprise you?"

She nodded this time, her curls bouncing again, and James had to keep himself from reaching out and touching one of them. The one that rested against her soft cheek. "Yes."

"Why?" he asked.

She shrugged slightly. "I assumed you wanted me here to keep an eye on me. To ensure I don't run off."

He grinned at that. "Do you intend to run off?"

She shook her head and squared her shoulders. "No. I shall face my fate."

James watched her closely. She was telling the truth. He could sense that about her. She *would* face her fate. He'd thought many things about her since he'd met her but cowardice wasn't in her. Whatever else her faults might be, Kate Townsende had courage. Real courage. The kind of courage that would face a death sentence. The kind of courage that would stand up to an unkind husband bringing his mistress into her home. The kind of courage that would ask for a divorce and face public censure and ruin in an effort to live an authentic life.

"When we left the Tower . . . how did you . . . ?" She cleared her throat. "I saw you salute the guard."

He stared off into the dark ballroom. Ah, so she'd noticed that, had she? A keen observer was the duchess. She reminded him a bit of . . . himself actually. He turned his head back to face her. "When I was very young, just out of university, I bought a commission. I served in the army for two years.

Kate gasped. "You have no siblings. Your father must have been beside himself with worry."

He slid up his hand to cover his mouth and hide his smile. And it seemed the duchess had done a bit of research on him too. *Well played.*

"It's true. I have no siblings. And my father and I, we . . ." He glanced away and narrowed his eyes in the darkness, searching for the right words. "Suffice it to say we rarely agreed on anything. Including my desire to serve in the army."

She pulled her hands away from the keys and rested them in her lap. "I'm . . . I'm glad you made it out safely."

He cracked another grin. "So am I."

She returned his smile and then, "One more question," she said softly.

James inclined his head. "Yes?"

"Why do you run a printing press? It cannot be because you need the money."

Ah, there was that naïveté again. A woman born into the world of the *ton* would never mention money so blithely. But Kate was also perceptive. Damned perceptive. "You're right on that score," he answered. "It's not about the money."

"Then why?" She'd cocked her head to the side and the glow of the candles against her hair made it look like spun gold. He swallowed. She smelled like strawberries. He wanted to . . . taste her.

James groaned and ran his fingers across his face. She'd asked a good question. Why indeed did he run the press? For the challenge? The fun of it? The hint of scandal he'd never allowed himself in his "real" life? All of those answers were true but there was something else. Something he didn't know the duchess well enough to reveal.

"Do you relish scandal?" she asked breathlessly.

"No, actually. Order, rules, truth. Those things have always been important to me. I am a storyteller of sorts. But above all I relish the truth."

She glanced away. "But you don't think I'm telling it."

James set his jaw. He couldn't afford to feel sorry for her. Couldn't afford to continue to wonder whether she'd actually killed her husband. Lily was right. He had a long history of trying to "fix" everything and Kate was not about to become his new project. Besides, getting close to a woman who had a death sentence on her head was pure folly. He pushed himself away from the pianoforte. "I think, whatever your story, it will sell a great many pamphlets."

CHAPTER 12

James woke the next morning at his usual hour. With the help of his valet, he shaved and dressed. After he returned from his daily bout of fencing at the club, he breakfasted and made his way to his study. Themis followed him. Her tail wagging, she lay on the rug next to him.

James tried to concentrate on the paperwork on his desk but the scenario from the night before kept replaying itself over and over in his mind.

Kate had asked him if he'd brought her here to keep an eye on her. Yes, partially, but mostly because he had to ensure she was safe. If the public discovered she was staying in a Mayfair town house, they'd rip the bloody walls down around them, and James would be responsible for her being hurt or possibly killed. He couldn't allow that. No, keeping her as close to him as possible was the best defense and he intended to do so, right here.

But there was another reason if he were being honest with himself. One that made him shift in his chair, rather guiltily. Despite what he'd told himself last night, he wanted to be around her to get a sense of whether she was truly innocent. Did she kill Markingham or not? All external evidence indicated that she did. But she seemed so soft and sincere, as if she couldn't harm a bug. There was something so incongruous about the woman herself and the charges that had been brought against her.

James tossed his quill onto the desk and scrubbed his hands across his face. And why was he so bloody attracted to her? He'd lived the life of a monk. True, he'd had the occasional liaison here and there with a discreet widow, but he was hardly a profligate. He prided himself on being discerning. Meaningless intimate encounters didn't interest him. And love had hardly been anything he'd been interested in either. He was a confirmed bachelor. But bachelor or no, Kate was making him feel things that had been dormant for . . . too long. Much too long. And it was entirely inappropriate. Good God, the woman had just lost her husband and was accused of murder. She should not be forced to endure James's unwanted attentions. How many times had he stopped himself from reaching out and touching her hair last night? Not to mention her smell, a mixture of strawberries and soap . . . was slowly driving him mad every time he was in her presence. No. He'd keep his hands to himself, however difficult that proved to be. He was a gentleman after all. He couldn't help his physical reaction to her, but he could bloody well help whether he acted upon that attraction, and he had absolutely no intention of doing so.

A sharp rap sounded at the door and James glanced up. Themis did too.

Locke entered and bowed to James. "My lord, two callers have arrived."

James clenched his jaw. Callers? Who? He must keep Kate's presence in the house a secret. Where was she?

He must speak with Mrs. Hartsmeade about ensuring that Kate would not be seen when visitors arrived.

"The Marchioness of Colton and the Countess of Ashbourne are here," Locke's deep voice intoned.

James let his shoulders relax. Lily and Annie? Nothing to worry about. "Tell them I'll be there shortly."

The butler cleared his throat. "They are not here to see you, my lord."

James looked twice, his brow furrowed. "Not here to see me?"

"No. They are here to see her grace."

James leaned back and folded his arms over his chest. "They are, are they?"

Locke gave a curt nod. "Yes, they insist upon it."

James shook his head. Lily and Annie were incorrigible. Only they would have the nerve to call upon a prisoner in a house where she wasn't even supposed to be. "By all means, show them to one of the salons and notify her grace."

Kate made her way to the blue salon, her palms sweaty and her heart racing. She stood outside the door and took a deep breath. She was about to meet with peeresses, ladies of the social class with whom she should have been rubbing elbows for years. Instead, the only peeress she'd ever met was her husband's mother, and that lady had detested Kate on sight. Oh, and Lady Bettina. And a more awful woman Kate had never known. Kate pushed her hands down her skirts in an attempt to dry her palms and quell her nerves. Hopefully the Marchioness of Colton and the Countess of Ashbourne were not as awful and high-handed as her mother-in-law had always been or as haughty and cold as Lady Bettina.

James had told her that these two ladies were close friends of his, and they knew Kate was staying with him. Apparently, he trusted them completely. But could she? Were they only here to stare at her? Would they take jibes at her? Ask her why she insisted upon putting their friend's home and life in danger?

Very well. There was no help for it. If these two were going to ridicule her, she might as well step inside and get it over with.

She reached out a trembling hand, pushed open the door handle, and stepped inside. Two young women sat on the settee in the middle of the room, chatting to each other and laughing. As soon as Kate stepped inside, they both immediately stopped talking and looked up at her.

"Why, your grace," the older of the two—who was a breathtaking beauty—said, plunking her hands on her hips. "There you are."

Kate blinked. She wasn't sure how to react. The lady's voice had been friendly enough, but Kate still wasn't sure if these two were allies or foes.

"Come sit," the lady continued. "It's insufferably rude of Medford not to be here to introduce us and surprising, to be sure, because usually the man is so prompt. He didn't earn the moniker Lord Perfect for nothing." The beauty winked at Kate, and this time there was no mistaking. Whoever she was, she was friendly indeed. "But come and we shall introduce ourselves and have a much better time chatting together than we'd have with a stuffy old viscount around."

She stood and held out her hands to Kate, and Kate made her way forward. "Officially, I am the Marchioness of Colton," the lady said. "But you must call me Lily." Another wink and Kate expelled her breath. Oh, how wonderful. They would not stand on ceremony. There would be no "your graces" here.

"And this is my sister, the Countess of Ashbourne," Lily continued.

The younger woman stood, reached out, and squeezed Kate's hand too in a terribly friendly gesture. "Just call me Annie, please," she said. Annie was nearly as pretty as her sister with dark brown hair and soft brown eyes. Both ladies were so the opposite of what Kate had expected, she wanted to sigh with relief. Instead, she became exceedingly conscious of the fact that she hadn't said anything yet and the two lovely sisters were staring at her with expectant looks upon their faces.

"I . . . I'm Kate." Ooh. She should have been a bit more formal. She pinched the inside of her arm. "Please do not call me 'your grace,'" she blurted next, and her fear that the sisters would think she was mad was quickly dispelled when both of them smiled widely at her. "Absolutely not. We wouldn't think of it," Lily said. "Now, come and sit." Lily motioned to the settee.

Annie leaned over and said in a conspiratorial voice, "Locke is bringing tea and cakes, and I'll let you in on a secret if you have not already discovered it yourself. Medford has the *best* teacakes."

Kate didn't bother trying to hide her smile. Peeresses who seemed as devoted to teacakes as she? Oh yes, Kate could become friends with these two ladies, she was quite sure of it.

"It's very nice to meet you both," Kate murmured, hoping she didn't sound like a fool.

"We want you to know right away," Lily said, "that we do not for one moment think you are guilty. I had the, ahem, misfortune of meeting your husband and I have to believe there were a great number of people who wished him dead."

Kate bit her lip and did her best to hide her smile. "I see. Thank you for that."

"But I must ask, my dear," Lily continued. "Is it true you'd asked him for a divorce?"

Kate took a deep breath. There was something about these two, their openness and friendly demeanors, that made her feel safe answering the question. "Yes. I'm afraid so. Ours was a very unhappy marriage."

Lily watched her with sympathetic violet eyes. "It must have been truly awful for you."

Kate let out a sigh of relief. Two peeresses who would not censure her for wanting a scandalous divorce either? The sisters truly were special.

"Well, I don't blame you," Annie said. "We're quite happy that you'll have an opportunity to write your story for Medford."

Kate's eyes went wide. "You know about Lord Medford's printing press?" She wanted to kick herself again for asking the question. Of course they must know, why else would they think she was here? But the question had just flown from her mouth.

"Oh, we've known for quite some time," Lily replied with a wink.

"And you're not . . ." Kate lowered her voice. "Scandalized by it?"

"Oh, certainly not," Lily replied with a laugh and a quick shake of her dark head.

Annie laughed too. "Oh, now we shall be forced to tell her our secrets, Lily."

Kate looked back and forth between the two of them, knowing her eyes must be wide as the teacakes. "*Your* secrets?"

Lily gave her a conspiratorial grin. "Yes. You see, you happen to be sitting next to the authors of *Secrets of a Wedding Night* and *Secrets of a Runaway Bride*."

"No!" Kate's mouth fell open. She clapped a hand over it.

Annie's face wore a catlike smile. She nodded resolutely. "Yes."

Lily settled into the settee and kicked out her legs in front of her, in what Kate assumed was a most unmarchionesslike style. "Guilty. So you see, you are about to join our illustrious club. Although *our* pamphlets were anonymous of course," she finished with another wink.

"I promise not to tell anyone it was you," Kate said. How marvelous that these ladies were so open and friendly with her, trusting her with their secrets so completely. It seemed too much to hope for, really.

"I must say, I'm a bit surprised," Kate murmured.

"Whatever for?" Annie asked.

"James . . ." She cleared her throat. "Lord Medford doesn't seem entirely convinced of my innocence, but both of you—"

Lily tossed a hand in the air. "Oh, ignore Medford. He fancies himself a businessman. And we don't always see eye to eye. Knowing Medford, I'm surprised he hasn't taken over your defense himself and seen to it that you're acquitted by now."

Kate's blush heated her face. Lily must have noticed it. "He has, hasn't he?" she asked, plunking her hands on her hips again.

Kate bit her lip and nodded. "Mr. Abernathy, the barrister, was here, at Lord Medford's request."

Annie nodded. "Now that sounds like our Medford."

"Yes," Lily agreed. "He's a fixer. Always putting things to rights. It's just in him. He cannot help but rescue a damsel in distress."

Kate shook her head. "Oh, but he's not trying to save me . . . really. He just wants his pamphlet and—"

"Do not believe that for one moment," Lily replied. "First of all, look at you, you're absolutely breathtaking, and secondly, Medford may seem calculating, but he isn't. Not at all. He couldn't be if he wanted to. He'll do anything in his power to help you, Kate. Truly."

Kate couldn't help her blush again. The marchioness had called her breathtaking. And coming from a lady who looked much like a goddess herself, that was a true compliment. But Kate wasn't about to argue with Lord Medford's close friend about his intentions. He'd made it clear that the pamphlet was all he wanted from her and she clearly had a much different relationship with him than his friends did, which stood to reason, of course.

Locke carried in the tea tray just then and Annie clapped her hands, changing the subject. "Oh good. Cakes!"

They waited for Locke to slide the tray onto the low table in front of them, serve the tea, and retreat from the room before Lily spoke again. She turned to Kate. "So, Medford tells us that you want to enjoy yourself while you're here."

Kate gulped. When she put it that way, it sounded positively indecent. Oh, how could these ladies think she wasn't guilty if she was such an awful wife that she wanted to enjoy herself while her husband lay dead in the ground? "You mustn't think badly of me for saying that," Kate answered. "It's just that . . . I may not have much time left." Her voice trailed off for a bit and then she said softly, "It's complicated."

"Oh, we don't judge you. Not one bit," Lily replied. She reached over and placed a hand over Kate's and squeezed. "I cannot imagine how difficult it must be for you. How frightening. Besides, I was once a widow with very few choices. I know how difficult it can be for a woman in our Society. I could never judge you."

"Thank you for that," Kate replied, swallowing the lump that had unexpectedly formed in her throat.

Annie delicately picked up a cake from the silver tea

tray and dropped it onto her saucer. "Tell us. What is it that you wish to do, Kate? What is your fondest dream?"

Kate plucked a cake from the tray too, then she laughed. "Oh, I fear you'd think me quite silly if I told you."

"Oh, please do," Annie replied with a conspiratorial grin just before taking a sip of her tea. "I am ever *so* fond of silliness."

"Yes, tell us," Lily prompted, swiping a teacake of her own. "You wouldn't believe the silliness the two of us can get up to if given half the chance." She motioned toward Annie.

Kate smiled at that. The sisters seemed like such lovely ladies. They would have been the types of women she could well have been friendly with had she been a part of the world her husband had inhabited. If things, everything, had been different. As it was she wouldn't know them very long. She shook her head and swallowed the second lump that formed in her throat over that thought. She pressed her lips together and faced the marchioness and the countess. "Very well. The truth is, I should like very much to visit a farm."

Annie blinked rapidly. "A farm?"

Lily joined in the blinking. "A farm?"

Kate glanced away, wondering briefly if she could hide under the settee. "Oh, I knew you would think it was silly."

Annie shook her head. "No, no, not at all. I was just making sure I had heard you correctly. I don't think I ever met a duchess who wanted to visit a farm."

Kate blushed. "I know, it's ridiculous, but you see, I was raised on a farm and I miss it. The animals, the meadows, the fields, the barns."

"I don't know that I've ever been to a farm," Lily

said, taking another nibble from her cake. "It shall be an adventure for us, Annie. Though I cannot believe the meadows are much to look at in winter. But we shall make the best of it."

Annie nodded rapidly. "Oh yes, a farm sounds absolutely lovely. You must show us what a farm is like, Kate."

Kate furrowed her brow. "What do you mean?"

"Now who is being silly?" Lily asked. "We mean we intend to take you to a farm."

Kate's heart beat rapidly. "Do you truly think we could sneak off to a farm?"

Lily handed her another cake. "Consider it done."

CHAPTER 13

When Abernathy returned that afternoon to meet privately with James in his study, the news was not good.

"It appears it shall be a difficult case, my lord," Abernathy announced. "More difficult than we first imagined, I'm afraid."

James sat forward in his chair, bracing his forearms on the desk, and shook his head. "That's saying something. What's happened?"

Abernathy cleared his throat and pulled his ubiquitous stack of papers from his bag. The stack hit the desktop with a loud *thunk,* and Abernathy tapped the papers with a finger. "I've reviewed all of the evidence gathered at the inquest. The witnesses' statements are most damaging. A number of the servants, including his grace's valet, and Lady Bettina Swinton overheard the argument between the duke and the duchess just before he was killed."

James furrowed his brow. "What specifically did Lady Bettina say?" Ever since he'd heard Lady Bettina was involved he'd been suspicious. Lady Bettina was a beautiful young widow who'd made overtures to James a time or two. She was a bit of baggage that was usually up to no good. A woman who went from protector to protector in the peerage, always vying for gifts and money and power. Yes, James knew Lady Bettina, and he didn't like her. Not one bit.

Abernathy fished in his coat pocket and pulled out his spectacles. He perched them on his nose and regarded a single sheaf of parchment that he'd pulled from the stack. "Lady Bettina essentially said what her grace already told us. She heard the duke and the duchess arguing. Then, about an hour later, she went to check on him and found her grace on the floor with his dead body, the pistol on the floor next to them and the duke's blood all over her hands and clothing. Curiously, Lady Bettina did not hear the pistol shot either."

James winced. "It's not good, is it, Abernathy?"

Abernathy shook his head. "I'm afraid not, my lord."

"What else did you discover?"

The barrister consulted his paperwork. He pulled out another sheet and scanned the parchment up and down, a frown on his face. "The valet, the housekeeper, and at least one housemaid overheard the argument. The butler says he did not. All of them entered the room when they heard Lady Bettina's scream."

James expelled his breath. "And what did Kate say, when they found her?"

Abernathy flipped the page. "They all said the same thing. Her grace said nothing. She was perfectly silent, just staring at her husband's body."

James's jaw went tight. If Kate were innocent—and it was such a big if—that moment must have been horrendous for her. Unimaginable. His stomach clenched in knots thinking about it. But she was caught literally red-handed. Was there any doubt she'd done it?

"I suppose it's a good thing that she remained silent," James replied.

Abernathy nodded. "Yes. It can only be good for an accused person not to incriminate herself any further. If she'd confessed, of course, there would be no hope of defending her. Though as it stands now . . .". The barrister's voice trailed off.

"There's very little?" James replied. With a deep sigh, he leaned back in his chair and pressed his fingers to his temples where a sharp headache had begun to form.

"Yes," Abernathy replied. "I'll be honest. There's very little."

James's gaze met his. "I know you'll do your best, Abernathy."

The barrister plucked the spectacles from his nose and tucked them back inside his pocket. "I will, my lord."

"Did you learn of any reasons why any of the other occupants of the house might have wanted to kill Markingham?" James asked.

"Not one," Abernathy replied, steepling his fingers over his chest. "The servants all seemed quite loyal and happily employed by the family. Lady Bettina didn't appear to have a reason to commit murder, nor to stand to gain financially in any way by his death."

James let his hands drop from his forehead and narrowed his eyes. "No other possible motivation?"

Abernathy shook his head. "His grace's mother was at the dower house nearby that day, but by all accounts, she dearly loved her son and was napping at the time the murder occurred. Her servants have confirmed that."

James gripped the rosewood arms of his chair. "What about Markingham's heir? Who stood to gain the title upon his death?"

"I looked into that too, my lord. The heir is Markingham's cousin. His father's younger brother's son. A Mr. Oliver Townsende."

"I've heard that name." James nodded. "Where was Mr. Townsende that day?"

"At his town house in London, I'm afraid. Also confirmed by his servants. But don't worry, I intend to investigate that more fully . . . and immediately."

"What about his wife?" James asked. He was reaching, he knew, but a Society-minded wife might have a motive for murder after all.

"Mr. Townsende is not married, my lord. Though I daresay as the new duke, he's become a great deal more eligible."

James expelled his breath. "I don't envy him."

"Neither do I."

James leaned back in his chair and scrubbed his hands over his face. He felt tired all of a sudden. "Was there anything else, Abernathy? Anything at all?"

The barrister cleared his throat. "Yes. I confirmed, through several sources, that Lady Bettina and his grace were, indeed . . ."

James raised a hand to spare the poor man from his misery. "I understand." James expelled his breath.

So, Markingham did have a mistress. It wasn't just Kate's conjecture or attempt to deflect the scandal. And somehow Markingham had had the nerve to bring his mistress to his wife's home and inform her that he was in love with the other woman. Parading his new love in front of Kate, all while denying her her freedom. James clenched his fist. The bloody cad. Markingham's behavior sickened him.

On the other hand, such a set of circumstances did seem like something that might well push a woman scorned over the edge. Perhaps even to commit murder.

Either way, James needed to discover the truth. He'd begun his association with the duchess with the sole intention of getting his pamphlet written and turning Kate back over to the authorities to determine her fate. But now he had to know. He had to. Was she guilty or not?

Abernathy gathered up his papers and dropped them back into his bag. "My lord, everything I've discovered so far is based purely on the magistrate's investigation, his notes. I intend to conduct my own investigation next. There may well be more information that has yet to be uncovered."

James considered everything that had happened with Kate since he'd met her. The moment she'd named her terms he should have walked away. Lord knew it had been ludicrous to even entertain the notion of taking her into his house. But there had been something about her plea, something that had awoken an emotion long dormant in him. She wanted to live, she'd said. To enjoy herself. And Lily and Annie were right. It was possible that Kate was innocent, that she would be put to death for a crime she did not commit. If so, and her last wish was to live out her final days in the semblance of normalcy, James had to admit that made sense to him.

And the very nature of her plea had intrigued him. Wanting to live. Live. God, had he ever had that thought? Perhaps when he was very young. Before he'd realized what his father had expected of him. But James had learned at an early age that life wasn't about enjoyment. It was about duty and honor and studies and business and commitments. It fascinated him, however, that the last wish of a dying woman would be to live.

He eyed the barrister. "The duchess has the blackened reputation of Napoleon himself. Even if you conduct your own investigation, this will be very difficult, won't it, Abernathy?"

"Very difficult indeed, my lord," Abernathy replied solemnly.

James leaned back in his chair and turned his eyes toward the ceiling. He had a very clear delineation in his life. The man who owned the printing press, engaged scandal, and enjoyed a good tale. And the viscount who courted the *ton*'s favor and who had a pristine reputation second only to Wellington himself. And he had every intention of keeping it that way.

But first he had to discover the *truth*.

He leaned forward and braced his elbows on the desk again. He met Abernathy's eyes, and gave the barrister a stern stare. "I want you to hire a runner, Abernathy. The best Bow Street has. Spare no expense. I want to know every detail of what happened that day."

CHAPTER 14

Kate sat on the sofa in the library, her feet curled under her. She was writing on a small table that had been pulled up in front of her by one of James's ever-so-helpful footmen.

She stared blindly at the paper in front of her. The pamphlet.

She sighed, twirling a curl around her finger. Writing the pamphlet was proving more difficult than she'd imagined. And she'd never expected it to be simple. She smoothed her hand over the pieces of parchment in front of her. The ink had long since dried. But it just wasn't right. Not yet. None of it. She'd started and stopped a dozen times already, crumpling up the insufficient words, and tossing them into the rubbish bin.

She'd begun by telling her story that day. She'd begun by relating her feelings. She'd begun by attempting to explain why she and Markingham had never suited. All of the stories, hopelessly inadequate. Though all of them true. That's what James wanted . . . the truth. But which truth? Which one should she tell? Which one was right?

She sighed and rubbed the back of her neck with ink-stained fingers. How exactly did one explain one was not a murderess? Or, more correctly . . . how did one explain one was not a murderess when faced with a mountain of incriminating evidence to the contrary? Every word she'd written seemed hopelessly inadequate.

A knock sounded at the door and she let her hand fall away from her neck, her heart nearly pounding out of her chest. She hadn't yet become accustomed to the fact that she was no longer at the Tower. A knock on the door there might mean anything from she was being taken to trial to she was being put to death. The constant fear hadn't left her.

Her pounding heart soon slowed when she called, "Come in," and glanced up to see James stroll into the room. The man had one hand shoved in his pocket, his dark hair was perfectly in place as usual, and a hint of a smile played upon his firm lips. Kate glanced away. He was too good-looking by half. She pinched the inside of her arm. It was positively indecent of her to have that thought. Oh God, perhaps she deserved to be burned at the stake for her disloyalty to her poor dead husband. But then she thought of Lady Bettina Swinton spending the night at her house, flaunting her relationship with George, and Kate couldn't quite conjure the guilt she was supposed to feel over being disloyal to the man even though he was dead.

She sucked in her breath, doing her best to ignore the clean masculine scent that accompanied James into the room. She swallowed and turned her attention back to her parchment. "My lord?" she said, picking up her quill and feigning interest in her work. "Do you need something?"

He stopped a few paces in front of her. "I've come to ask you something, Kate."

He took a seat in a chair across from her and she looked up at him. A too serious look rested on his handsome face.

"What's that?" she asked hesitantly, dropping her quill, and studying his face closely.

"I was speaking with Abernathy—" James began.

Kate shook her head frantically. "We've been over this. I don't think—"

He leaned forward and braced his elbows on his knees. "Leave it to me to worry about it then."

She glanced away, tears unexpectedly burning the backs of her eyes. "That's not your occupation, my lord. Or your concern."

"Tell me, Kate." He paused. "Is there anything? Anything at all that you remember?"

She took a deep breath and met his eyes. "I've thought about it so many times. So, so many times. I replay the entire morning over and over again in my mind." She pressed her fingertips to her temples. "In addition to George, the only people in the house were myself, Lady Bettina, and the servants."

"You're sure of that?"

She nodded. "As sure as one can be in a large estate. We certainly had no other visitors."

He watched her carefully. She could feel his hazel eyes on her. "Do you think Lady Bettina could have done it?" His voice was tight, authoritative.

Her fingers dropped away from her temples, and she searched the ceiling, resting her palms on her knees. "I suppose it's possible, but I don't know why she would. It makes no sense. And they did seem to be . . . in love." She sucked in her breath. That last part had been difficult for her to say, he could tell. Damn it, he'd like to lay his fist into Markingham even now.

James's voice was clear and calm. "Perhaps they had a fight. One you didn't know about?"

She shrugged, meeting his eyes again. "It's possible. Anything's possible. But the only thing I remember . . ." She looked away, out the dark window. "The only real thing I remember . . . was coming into that room . . . and . . . seeing him." Her throat worked convulsively.

James reached out and squeezed her hand. It was so small and cold compared to his. "It must have been horrifying," he whispered.

She blinked away more tears and turned to face him again. "I'm afraid I can be of little help. That is all I remember. And all I know."

"That's enough, Kate. Thank you. I shouldn't be asking so much of you."

"If I remember anything, I'll tell you immediately," she assured him.

"Thank you." He glanced away briefly. "Now to discuss a more pleasant topic." He leaned back in his chair and gave her a smile that made her heart do a little flip. The stubble was back on his chin and cheeks this late at night, and she was doing her best to ignore it.

"What topic is that, my lor . . . James?" She cleared her throat.

He crossed his booted feet at the ankles and rested his hands on his thighs. "You said you wanted to live. That was the bargain, was it not? Annie and Lily assure me your trip to the countryside is being planned as we speak. What *else* would you like to do?"

She smiled. "Now *that* I've been thinking about and I believe I've decided." She bit her lip, a bit hesitant to admit to him the other thing she'd been wanting. But if he didn't laugh her out of his home over the desire to visit a farm, this next thing would probably not surprise him one bit. She took a deep breath. "I want to dance at a ball."

James blinked and his hands dropped to his sides. "A ball?"

She nodded. "Yes. I only attended one ball in my life, before I was married. It was so beautiful and perfect. It was the last time I can remember being happy. Wearing beautiful clothing and enjoying myself. Dancing and laughing and not having a care in the world. I know it's winter and I know we cannot have guests and moonlit gardens and champagne on the balcony, but oh, James, I want to dance."

James gave her a conspiratorial grin that made her heart beat faster again. "If it's a ball you desire, my lady, a ball you shall have."

CHAPTER 15

When Mrs. Hartsmeade and two maids arrived in Kate's bedchamber that afternoon armed with pins, scissors, thread, and fabric, Kate didn't know what to make of it.

"His lordship has instructed us to make you a ball gown," Mrs. Hartsmeade announced.

"A what?" Kate asked, turning in a circle while Louisa measured her waist.

"A ball gown, your grace," Louisa replied with a bright smile.

"His lordship says he regrets he couldn't have the finest seamstresses from Bond Street come to work on your gown, but he couldn't risk the . . . well, you know." Mrs. Hartsmeade glanced away.

Kate nodded. "It's certainly very nice of him and all of you, but I don't need a real ball gown—"

"No, your grace, he insisted upon it. He picked out the color himself. This gold." She handed the swath of lovely satin fabric to Kate. " 'It'll bring out the highlights in the duchess's hair,' he said. Though I doubt he'd like it if he knew I repeated such a thing to you." Mrs. Hartsmeade smiled, and Kate swallowed and pressed her hand to her belly where butterflies had just taken flight.

"He said that?" she asked, feeling like an eighteen-year-old about to make her debut again.

"He did," Louisa reassured her. "I heard him."

Kate bit back her smile. She reached out and gingerly touched the gold satin. It was the most beautiful fabric she had ever seen. Why, she couldn't have picked better herself. "Then, by all means, let's make me a ball gown."

By the time the afternoon was over, Kate and the three servants had giggled themselves silly deciding upon all the details of the gown including the décolletage. "Lower," Kate had insisted, making Louisa blush. She was being improper, no doubt, but this might well be her last chance to dance with a handsome man at a ball in a low-cut gown. And she wanted to live after all.

By the time Mrs. Hartsmeade ushered Louisa and the other maid from her bedchamber, the gown had been entirely designed, was well on its way to being made, and Kate had smiled more than she had in an age. She threw herself on her bed and hugged her pillow. A ball. She was going to attend a ball. And with the ever-so-dashing Lord Medford. She kicked her legs against the cool sheets and squealed into the pillow.

It was two days later before the gown was complete. Kate had spent those two days in a completely unsuccessful attempt to write the pamphlet. She'd spent time reading Lily's and Annie's pamphlets over and over again, hoping one or both would spark some idea for her. Make her come up with some formula for success. Both of their pamphlets hinted at scandal and had a bit of a warning tone, but Kate couldn't imagine how hers ought to be. It would not be a confession. Nor a plea for mercy. She just wanted it to be . . . honest. Just what James had asked of her. To tell her story, in her words. But what if no one believed her? What if the pamphlet was not a top seller as James had predicted? What if copies were burned in the street? Burned . . . She gulped. She couldn't think about that. She must do her best.

Mrs. Hartsmeade came into the study on the second afternoon to announce the ball gown's completion. She and the girls had worked day and night to sew the fabulous garment and after a few fun fittings, they were ready to declare it finished.

"It's beautiful," Kate said, touching the wide skirt reverently, tracing her fingers along the delicate fabric.

"His lordship asked me to give you this." Mrs. Hartsmeade handed Kate a piece of parchment sealed with wax. Kate widened her eyes and grasped the piece of paper, ripping it open and scanning it quickly. It was an invitation. To Viscount Medford's ball. The man had thought of everything.

"And you are the guest of honor, your grace," Mrs. Hartsmeade said with another quick wink.

Kate bit her lip, also biting back the little squeal of happiness that rose to her lips.

She playfully curtsied to the housekeeper. "Please tell his lordship that I shall be most delighted to attend."

Kate stood in front of the looking glass in her bedroom, butterflies in her stomach again, and a tentative grin on her face. She felt like Cinderella. Certainly her first ball gown had never been this grand. She twirled in a circle. They'd made her wide skirts, reminiscent of the turn of the century in France, with a tight, corsetlike bodice and long sleeves that ended in points on the tops of her hands. It was a lovely gown and Kate felt like a dream in it, petticoats and all.

Louisa had put up her hair in a chignon with a few wisps pulled out to frame her face, and somehow Mrs. Hartsmeade had secured a pot of rouge and Kate dabbed the stuff on her lips and her cheeks and even the smallest bit between her daring décolletage. *Live. Live Live.* She sung to herself.

She took another look in the mirror and sucked in her breath. She didn't have any jewels, true, but that was perfectly all right. It wasn't a real ball. She stared at her reflection. Would Lord Medford think she was beautiful? Oh, why was she even thinking such a thought? It didn't matter. This entire night was just for fun. Nothing more, nothing less. It was not as if James were a suitor and she a young innocent looking for a husband. In fact, the situation could not be more opposite. She was an accused murderess who had forced the man to throw a pretend ball for her. No, this was not a night for moonlit gardens and stolen kisses. It was freezing outside and she was a prisoner, she thought with a wry smile.

Apparently, she could romanticize anything. She sighed. No sense in waiting any longer. She wanted to dance. She smoothed her eyebrows with her fingertips and gathered up her voluminous golden skirts. Mrs. Hartsmeade had even brought her delicate golden slippers that Lord Medford had apparently purchased for her on Bond Street. He must have set the gossipmongers' tongues wagging with that purchase. Or wait. Perhaps he'd sent Lily or Annie to do it. That would make much more sense. And those ladies seemed so kind and thoughtful. No doubt the sisters had picked out the beautiful little slippers with the golden bows on the tips.

Kate moved to the door to her bedchamber and reached out to pull the handle just as Louisa came barreling through. "Oh, your grace, beg your pardon." The maid bobbed a curtsy. She was holding something behind her back.

"Did you forget something, Louisa?" Kate asked.

"No, that is to say . . . *I* didn't." She had a curious sparkle in her eye.

Kate couldn't help but smile. "What is it?"

Louisa pulled a midnight-blue velvet case from behind her back and presented it to Kate with both hands. "It's from his lordship, your grace. He wanted to be sure you wore them tonight."

Kate gingerly took the velvet case and flipped it open with her thumb. "Oh my!" There, nestled inside the cream silk lining, was the most beautiful set of sapphires in a necklace she'd ever seen. They were large, round, and sparkling. And there were matching ear bobs. "He said they'd bring out your eyes," Louisa said, fluttering her own eyelashes.

Kate was sure her cheeks were turning pink and her chest felt so tight she couldn't breathe.

"Oh my goodness, Louisa. These are the most beautiful things I've ever seen. Quick. Help me put them on." She hurried back over to the looking glass and held up the wisps of hair that would be in the way while Louisà took the sapphire necklace and fastened it around her neck.

"I feel like squealing," Kate admitted, bobbing on her tiptoes. "But I shall refrain."

"Duchesses squeal?" Louisa asked from behind her with wide eyes that reflected at Kate through the looking glass.

"I don't know about all the duchesses, but duchesses who were raised on farms do." She winked at the maid and Louisa gave her a wide, conspiratorial grin.

"If there was anything for a duchess to squeal about, I'd certainly say these jewels qualify," Louisa replied.

"I couldn't agree more." Kate took two very deep breaths and exhaled.

"I've noticed you do that, your grace," Louisa said, motioning to Kate with her chin.

"Do what?"

"Take two deep breaths every so often."

"Oh, that," Kate replied. "Yes, my mother taught me that. 'There's nothing two deep breaths won't cure,' she always said. Especially nerves."

"You're nervous?" Louisa asked, wide-eyed again.

Kate laughed and turned to face the maid. "Why, yes, of course. Isn't every young woman nervous before a ball?"

Louisa glanced down at her hands. "I wouldn't know. I've never been to ball."

Kate winced. She pinched the inside of her arm. Of course the maid hadn't been to a formal ball before. What possible occasion would she have had to go to one?

"I'll tell you what, Louisa, come to the ballroom later, wear your best dress, and I'll ask Lord Medford to dance with you."

Louisa's eyes looked as if they'd pop from her skull this time. "No, my lady. I absolutely could not!"

Kate laughed. "Why, of course you could. Why not?"

Louisa's chin trembled. "Because it's completely improper."

Kate waved a hand in the air. "Oh, who cares about being proper? Besides, I'm a duchess and I've invited you."

Louisa looked up at her through long lashes. "Do you truly think . . . Lord Medford wouldn't mind?"

"I'm sure he'd be delighted. I had neighbors in the country who used to host servants' balls once a year. I'm sure he's heard of such a thing before."

"Yes." Louisa bit her lip. "I've heard of it too, but we've never done it here."

"First time for everything," Kate replied. She glanced at the clock on the mantel across from the bed. "It's nearly ten o'clock now. Come at midnight."

Louisa grinned from ear to ear. "I might just peek in and see how it's going . . ."

"Come in, Louisa. And dance. I insist upon it. If Lord Medford won't dance with you, I'll dance with you myself."

Louisa laughed outright at that, and Kate patted her shoulder.

"Now I must hurry," Kate said. "Mustn't keep Lord Medford waiting. Thank you for everything." She squeezed the maid's hand and quickly hurried over to the door. She pulled the handle and made her way into the corridor.

Kate nearly flew down the hall, rounded the marble balustrade, and made her way as elegantly as possible to the ballroom. Locke stood at the entrance to the room wearing his finest livery. Her eyes went wide when she saw him. What was the butler doing there?

"Miss Kate Blake," he announced. Kate was delighted. He'd called her by her maiden name. He hadn't introduced her as the Duchess of Markingham, didn't call her "your grace," and was it her imagination or did the man wink at her when she walked past him into the ballroom?

The moment she stepped through the door, Kate caught her breath. She pressed her hand against her middle and took in the scene that lay before her. The entire ballroom was transformed. It had been decorated as if an arbor had come to life inside. Flowers lined the walls, vines had been brought in, hanging greens were everywhere. Why, the man must have raided every conservatory in the land. Where he'd managed to get beautiful fresh flowers in the middle of winter she'd never know. But they were there, all sorts, including red, red roses. Her very favorite. It looked exactly like a . . . moonlit garden. Just what she'd requested. Unexpected tears stung the back of her eyes. No one—never her husband, certainly—had ever done anything quite so . . . nice for her before.

There was a refreshment table off to the far right, and a group of musicians stood behind a wooden screen tuning their instruments.

Kate glanced around breathlessly. She was in the middle of a dream. She was sure of it. A movement from the other side of the room caught her eye.

There he was, standing in the middle of the dance floor, surveying the ballroom, a single red rose twirling between his fingers, his other hand in his pocket. He was wearing impeccably tailored black evening clothes, superfine trousers, a black overcoat, and a shirtfront so white it nearly blinded her. His cravat was tied in a perfect knot, but most intriguing of all was the look he wore on his face. So handsome he took her breath away. Kate quickly glanced down to compose herself. Then she turned her face up again and smiled.

He made his way over to her slowly and she curtsied. "My lord."

He bowed. "My lady."

He pulled his hand from his pocket and held out his arm to her. She stepped closer and slid her hand through, marveling at the feel of his warm muscles through his coat. She took a deep breath.

"You are breathtaking," James said, handing her the rose. "I thought you might like this."

"Roses are my favorite," she murmured, noticing that he'd plucked away the thorns. She twirled it in her gloved hand and brought it up to her nose to inhale its sweet scent.

"I remember," he murmured. "I've been sending them to your room every morning."

Her eyes went wide. "That was you? I thought it was merely a coincidence." Her chest felt tight again.

"Nothing is a coincidence," he said. And then, "The sapphires bring out your eyes."

She sucked in her breath and touched the lovely necklace with the hand that held the rose. "Thank you so much for allowing me to wear them," she murmured. "They are beautiful."

His arm dropped away and he turned to look at her with a furrowed brow. "Wear them? They were a gift."

Her eyes met his and her breath caught. She couldn't allow him to give her such an extravagant gift. It was exceedingly inappropriate. Not to mention that she hadn't much occasion to wear jewels nor would she in the future . . . But it was exceedingly kind of him just the same. She opened her mouth to speak. "I cannot—"

"I hope you're not thinking it improper of me," he replied, as if reading her thoughts. "We're far past improper."

She snapped her mouth shut. And smiled. She couldn't help herself. "I was actually thinking . . . I wouldn't need them . . ." She couldn't finish that thought. She looked down at the marble floor.

He slipped a finger under her chin and tilted up her face to look at him. "Let me worry about that. Tonight is for . . . dancing." He let his hand fall away, and Kate knew a moment of regret.

She glanced away, feeling self-conscious all of a sudden.

Twirling her rose between her fingers again, she

gestured to the musicians with her hand. "Why are they hidden?"

"I couldn't allow them to see my guest, could I? The music might be a bit strained but it's a precaution we must take."

As if on cue, the music started, and a beautiful song began to play. "Shall we?" He offered her his arm again.

"Which dance?" Her brow was furrowed.

"Ah, I see I shall have to teach you to waltz."

She shook her head. "Waltz?"

"Yes, it's all the rage. The Prince Regent introduced it at a ball last summer."

Kate reached out and slid her gloved hand over his sleeve again. James's arm was so warm and hard and muscled and, oh, she mustn't think such things. Apparently, the waltz involved a bit more . . . intimacy than the dances she remembered from so long ago. He showed her the steps and she did her best to concentrate upon remembering them. But she found it rather difficult with his hand on her waist and the feel of his strong shoulders under her fingertips.

James plucked the rose from her fingers and tucked it behind her ear, then he took her into his arms.

And they danced.

"You are a perfect dancer," she said, concentrating on the steps and trying not to think about how well his broad shoulders filled out his evening coat.

He flashed a grin. "Perfect?"

"What? Did I say something funny?"

"No." He shook his head. "It's just that my epithet is 'Lord Perfect.'"

"Ah, so I've heard."

He arched a brow. "Who told you?"

She pressed her lips together. She couldn't very well

tell him she'd been asking a possibly treasonous prisoner about him. But then she remembered, Lady Mary wasn't the only one who'd mentioned it. "Lily told me."

Both of his eyebrows shot up this time. "Did she?"

"Yes."

"And did she tell you why?"

Kate laughed. "She didn't have to. I've seen your house, your study, your desk, your paperwork, even your hair. Oh, and your cravat."

"What's wrong with my cravat?" he asked with a mock frown.

She giggled. "Nothing! That's my point. Everything about you is perfect. Including this ball," she breathed. "It looks like a fairy tale in here."

"I'm glad you like it," he said, not taking his eyes from her face.

Her voice shook a little. "Do you dislike your epithet?"

He sighed. "I used to be proud of it."

"Used to?"

"Yes."

"And now you're not?" She cocked her head to the side.

He narrowed his eyes for a moment as if lost in thought. "Perfect is a dangerous word. Sometimes being perfect isn't a choice."

Kate was still contemplating that cryptic answer when he asked, "Are you enjoying yourself?"

She gave him a self-conscious little smile. "Yes, immensely. I've always adored dancing but had little occasion to do so."

"I'm sorry we can't do more of the country dances and the quadrilles without more dancers."

"It's perfectly all right," she said. "I find I am quite

enjoying the waltz." *A bit too much*. Kate wouldn't mind if *every* dance were a waltz.

She breathed in deeply and closed her eyes for a moment. "I hope I remember tonight forever."

" 'For it is the beginning of always,' " he replied.

Kate caught her breath. The Dante quote had always been one of her favorites. And James had said it. Something about that made her heart wrench. She kept her eyes focused on his perfectly tailored jacket, trying to blink away the unexpected tears that had sprung to her eyes.

They danced three more waltzes before James led Kate over to the refreshment table. With a bow, he offered her a glass of champagne, and she plucked it eagerly from his fingers. "We may not want to drink this on the balcony, given the temperature tonight, but we can *pretend* we're outside," he said.

"Thank you, my lord," she replied with a curtsy.

"Oh, we're back to using titles tonight?"

"No," she breathed, taking a long sip of champagne. "I just want to pretend. I want to pretend I'm eighteen again, and you're a beau, and we're courting at a ball."

His smile made her knees weak. "Exactly why I asked Locke to introduce you as Miss Blake."

She grinned at him. "I thought as much. Thank you for that. It made all the difference."

He touched a curl that had fallen against her neck, and the warmth of his hand on her skin nearly made her knees buckle.

"So," he said. "*If* we were courting and we were at a ball, I would endeavor to get you alone with me."

She laughed a little laugh. "And if I had a fan, I would slap you with it playfully."

"Is that all?" He arched a brow, and Kate had to glance away. She was becoming a little too good at pretending tonight.

"I don't believe you. You're much too much of a gentleman to attempt such a thing as getting me alone with you." She laughed again. But her laugh was cut short when he tugged her gloved hand and led her into a secluded spot behind one of the nearby vines and sets of flowering bushes. The music still played but they were entirely alone for the moment.

"Don't count upon it." His voice was low.

Kate swallowed. Hard. He smelled like soap and the barest hint of sense-tingling cologne. She wanted to touch him. The thought came out of nowhere and stole her breath. But he was just playing with her. Teasing. Trying to give her the experience she'd asked for at the pretend ball. Wasn't he? She squared her shoulders. Perhaps there was only one way to find out.

"Now that you've got me alone, my lord, what do you intend to do with me?" Where she had conjured the nerve to say *that,* she would never know. Must be the champagne. The tiniest amounts of the stuff had always made her a bit bold. *Must get more champagne.*

He stepped closer and his eyes sparkled. They looked positively emerald in the shadows. "What does any gentleman want to do when he's alone in a secluded alcove with a beautiful lady?"

Her voice faltered. "I . . . s-suppose he would try to . . . steal a kiss." She touched her fingertips to the sapphire necklace. "But you . . . you would never be so improper."

He leaned over and pulled the champagne flute from her numb fingers and set it on the ledge of the wainscoting next to them. She watched him as if in a trance. He leaned down. His cheek brushed hers. He whispered in her ear. "As I said earlier, we're far past improper." He tugged her into his arms and his mouth swooped down to capture hers.

Kate's head fell back and her arms went wide for a moment. This couldn't be happening. She was not being kissed by Lord Medford. Handsome, dashing, perfect Lord Medford. She hadn't thought for a moment he'd actually go so far as to kiss her. She'd wished for it, certainly, but the man was far too proper to—Very well, no he wasn't. And she was about to take full advantage of that fact. *Live. Live. Live.*

She slowly allowed her arms to travel up his rock-hard chest and wrap around his shoulders. She lifted up on tiptoe to meet his mouth. His was hot, demanding. His body leaned into hers and pushed her back against the wall. He pressed into her, and she moaned. He ravaged her lips, kissing her in ways she'd never even known a man could kiss a woman. The only other kisses she'd received had been George's tentative ones while they'd been courting and then his impatient ones when they'd been married, but none of them compared to the full onslaught of the senses she was experiencing now.

James's mouth owned her, shaped her lips, explored her mouth. Then moved to her cheek, her temple, her earlobe. Her eyes rolled back in her head. She moaned. She wanted to rub herself against him. Wanted to pull him on top of her, wanted to—

"You're so beautiful, Kate," he whispered in her ear.

She could pretend, couldn't she? That he was a beau and she was eighteen again. Why not?

"You smell like roses, and oh God—" He left off when she pressed her breasts to his chest and met his mouth again. He pulled away, moving down to kiss her throat, nuzzling at the delicate spot where her jaw met her neck. "That ball gown has been driving me insane all evening."

Kate shuddered.

James moved up again and pressed his forehead to hers. He expelled his breath and closed his eyes, cradling her hands in his.

Kate looked up through kiss-drugged senses. In the back of her mind it vaguely registered that a clock somewhere within the house was striking twelve. Twelve. Midnight.

Midnight!

She'd invited Louisa. The maid would arrive at any moment. "James, there's something I must tell you."

She pulled away, out of his arms.

He turned to look at her, guilt and resignation etched upon his handsome face. "There's no need, Kate. It's my fault, I shouldn't have—"

She shook her head. "No. You don't understand. I promised Louisa you'd dance with her tonight. At midnight."

CHAPTER 16

Kate closed her bed chamber door behind her, leaned back against it, and sighed. The gold ball gown shimmered in the dark of her room, and she took a moment to twirl in a circle. Her skirts billowed around her, and she smiled to herself. What a night. The waltzing, the champagne, the . . . kissing. It was amazing. All of it. But what about the kissing? Certainly James had only been responding to her taunt that he would never be ungentlemanly. Hadn't he? Or perhaps he only wanted to make her feel desired. Either way, he'd seemed to regret it afterward. Feeling as if he'd taken advantage of her, perhaps? But he *had* made her feel eighteen again. And alive. And that was a gift for which she could never repay him.

If only circumstances were different. If only she *were* eighteen again. If only she were not . . . herself. A woman accused of murder. A social outcast.

James was a man with his life completely in order. A seat in Parliament, a thriving business, plenty of money, a perfectly run household, and a score of other properties. He didn't need her making a mess of his affairs. And that's exactly what she was . . . a mess.

And he . . . he was wonderful. She had to admit that much. He'd acted the perfect gentleman as soon as Louisa had arrived. The maid had tentatively stepped through the ballroom door. She was wearing a simple cotton gown and looked so nervous that Kate's heart went out to her. She was obviously afraid her employer wouldn't take kindly to her intruding upon their ball. But James had happily danced with Louisa. He'd treated her like a true lady, like a princess even. He'd bowed to her and offered his arm and in the end he had called in Locke to make it a foursome so they could dance a few country dances all together. It had been one of the most wonderful, magical nights Kate had ever experienced. Better even than the other official ball she'd attended, for that one hadn't ended in a kiss from a handsome gentleman.

Oh, she knew she was being positively insane. Imagine how outraged the *ton* would be if they discovered the murderess Duchess of Markingham was hidden away in a Mayfair town house kissing Lord Perfect. They'd come burn her themselves. She shuddered. She should be mourning her husband not kissing a viscount. She knew that. Knew it well. But she just couldn't follow the rules of a Society that was about to sentence her to death.

Oh, how would she ever explain all of this in her pamphlet? It would never sound right. Never come out the way she meant it to. And she had to question how much she even wanted to finish writing the thing. As soon as she was through, James would return her to the Tower. Wouldn't he? Oh, he'd have to. It's not as if she could stay with him indefinitely. That would be entirely improper. His words from earlier in the evening flashed through her mind and a rush of heat passed through her body. "We're far past improper," he'd said, just before he— She shuddered.

She crossed over to the small writing table in the corner of her room and stared down at the first words of her pamphlet that lay scribbled on the parchment. "The mind is its own place and in itself, can make a Heaven of Hell, a Hell of Heaven."

She sighed, tracing her finger along the quote. Seemed Milton knew exactly what he'd been talking about. The mind could make a hell, indeed. But tonight, tonight it had been a heaven.

Kate rang for Louisa to come and help her remove her gown. She expelled her breath, promising herself she'd stop her insane fantasies about James Bancroft. No good could come from being attracted to him. It was not as if a viscount could fall in love with a murderess. Even if a miracle happened and she was acquitted, there could be no future for them. His reputation would be tattered to bits by an association with her. And besides, marrying one nobleman had led to nothing but heartache and tragedy for her. She couldn't afford to take a chance with another one. No, it would be best for both of them if Kate stopped having impossible dreams that couldn't come true and concentrated instead on finishing her pamphlet. That was the bargain, was it not? Her pamphlet for an opportunity to enjoy herself. And with James she had enjoyed herself. A bit too much.

James slammed shut his bed chamber door behind him, the wood reverberating. He cursed savagely, resting his hands on his hips. Damn it. What in the hell had that kiss been about? Correction. Those kisses—multiple. Something about Kate's beauty and niceness. Something about the dancing and the candlelight. No, that was no excuse. There was no excuse. He'd acted like a total cad. Fine. She was not an innocent. She wasn't eighteen, and they hadn't been at a come-out ball. She was a woman on trial for her life, living under his roof because he'd made a bargain with her. But it didn't sit well with him that he'd taken advantage of her. Damn. Damn. Damn. He'd just have to make it up to her . . . somehow.

He tugged viciously at his cravat, unwinding the garment from his neck and flinging it into the corner of the room. He breathed heavily, letting the fabric sit there for a moment before he stalked over and yanked it up. What had he told her? Sometimes being perfect wasn't a choice.

That was the bloody truth. Only he hadn't been perfect tonight, had he? Far from it. Christ. Wasn't this always the struggle he'd had? His perfect pristine exterior warring with the way he *wanted* to be? The perfectionistic side of him had earned him perfect marks in school, a perfect reputation, and the rebel in him made him purchase a printing press and publish scandalous pamphlets. It's what caused him to fling his bloody cravat in the corner. And it's what compelled him to go retrieve it.

He scrubbed his hands across his face and groaned. What the hell was Kate to think of him now? She was a widow, damn it. Albeit an unconventional one. But he bloody well knew better than to kiss a recent widow, not to mention someone who essentially was working for him, and on top of it all, just *happened* to be accused of murder. *Bad. Bad. Form.*

James yanked his shirt over his head with both hands. He closed his eyes. All right. He could admit it to himself. He was attracted to her. Insanely attracted to her. So attracted that he'd forgotten all about his self-imposed monklike celibacy and pulled her into his arms. He'd wanted to do a hell of a lot more than kiss her, actually. He'd wanted to rip the flower from her hair and the bodice from her gown. He'd wanted to—

He clenched his jaw. Damn it. He was getting hard again just thinking about it. Thank God for Louisa. There was no telling how long that craziness with the kissing would have lasted if the maid hadn't arrived.

James folded his shirt and placed it in the wardrobe. He wouldn't call for his valet. He was too wound up tonight. He sat on the edge of the chair next to his bed and shucked his top boots. He stood up, unbuttoning his breeches, and pulled them off too.

He needed to sleep. A good night's sleep always helped. *If* he were able to sleep tonight. Too many nights he'd lain awake thinking of the beauty who slept down the hall from him. That was it. He was going mad. He'd seen a pretty face before, even incomparably lovely faces. They hadn't been enough to turn his head. Hell, Lily and Annie were beauties, but he had nothing more than brotherly feelings toward them both. What was it about Kate that made him toss out his gentlemanly code and forget every rule of conduct that had been burned into his brain since childhood? What was it about her that made him want to forget about his enforced celibacy and pull her into bed and make endless love to her all night long? He couldn't possibly *be* more inappropriate. Kate might be a murderess, for God's sake. She was the outcast of the *ton,* the entire town actually. Even if she were acquitted somehow, magically—which he highly doubted—it was not as if they could have a future together. Being with her would make him an outsider from his life, Society, everything he'd ever known. True, he'd made money by publishing scandal, but few people knew about that, and he bloody well didn't want to be in the center of it himself.

No. He'd do well to remember why he'd met Kate Townsende in the first place. She was writing a pamphlet for him. That was all. She'd asked for his protection, and he'd asked for her story. It was a business transaction, nothing more. He bloody well wasn't about to jeopardize his life and livelihood over it. It was true he was known for wanting to fix things, help people, and he was doing that by hiring Abernathy and the Bow Street runner. But it had to end there. Kate was merely an author whose story he wanted. He must remember that.

Even if it killed him.

CHAPTER 17

It was just past sunrise when Lord Colton's magnificent coach arrived in the alley behind James's town house. Kate slipped out the back door with a cloak over her head, her face covered. Despite the heavy coat, the winter wind whipped along the bits of skin she had exposed. She rubbed the tip of her icy nose with her gloved hand. The coachman standing next to the conveyance quickly helped her inside, and the door closed behind her with a solid thump.

"You made it," came Lily Morgan's cheerful voice as soon as Kate sat back against the seat cushions.

"We're so glad to have you," Annie Holloway added with a bright smile.

The curtains on the windows were quickly pulled. Kate glanced around. The three women were alone inside the coach. "Are we the only ones going?" Kate asked, trying to keep the disappointment from her voice at the prospect that James wouldn't be there too.

"No. We're just taking separate coaches in case anyone follows us out of town. Besides, it certainly would be cramped in here with six of us. The men will follow us in Medford's coach."

Kate smiled and nodded, suddenly feeling joyful again. She would be spending an entire day in the country on a farm . . . with James. It was silly, she knew, and she couldn't explain why she suddenly had butterflies in her stomach, but the fact remained that they were there, winging around giddily and reminding her she didn't know the last time she'd been so . . . happy.

"It's going to be so cold," Kate said, biting her lip.

"Nonsense," Lily replied. "It shall be bracing." But even as she said it, she handed Kate a wool blanket that Kate quickly spread across her lap.

"Absolutely," Annie added, from beneath her own wool blanket. "We'll make the best of it."

Kate smiled at the sisters. "It's nice of you to pretend . . . for my sake."

The coach took off with a solid jolt, and Kate leaned back against the seat, a smile on her face. She'd never imagined she'd make it to the country again and, cold or no, she intended to enjoy herself.

"Now, while we're on the way," Annie began. "Tell us, we're positively on tenterhooks to know . . . what is it like to live with Lord Medford?"

Kate blushed, thankful for the darkness in the coach on this early morning to hide the pink that must be on her cheeks. "Whatever do you mean?'

"We just cannot picture him living with a woman," Lily replied. "It's quite a phenomenon actually."

"Yes." Annie nodded. "How does he act? What does he do? I mean, I'm sure he's a perfect gentleman, but—"

"Of course he is," Kate responded, perhaps a bit too quickly. "And he's been so kind by indulging my little whims."

"Ooh, like what?" Lily leaned forward, bracing her arms on her lap.

Kate couldn't help the slow smile that spread across her face. "He threw a ball for me the other evening."

Annie's jaw dropped. "A what?"

"A ball." Kate giggled.

"With just the two of you?" Lily asked, bouncing back against the seat again, her eyes wide.

"Yes, well, the two of us and Louisa . . . and Locke."

Lily's pretty violet eyes grew even wider. "Who is Louisa? And Locke? The butler?"

Kate pulled the blanket closer to her face and tucked it under her chin. "Louisa is the maid. I promised her James would dance with her. You see, she'd never danced at a ball before and . . . Oh, the two of you must think I'm an awful ninny."

"Nonsense. I think it sounds absolutely divine," Annie said, tucking her blanket under her chin.

"I just cannot imagine Medford dancing with a maid and the butler. He's usually so . . . proper," Lily said.

"Oh, he didn't think a thing of it. He's not a snob at all," Kate said.

"Oh no, not a snob, dear. I'd never think that. He's just very accustomed to . . . following rules," Lily replied.

"I still say it's divine." Annie sighed.

"I agree." Lily's face wore a wide grin. "And just the sort of thing our Medford needs." She winked at Kate.

Kate furrowed her brow. "What do you mean?"

"Don't tell me you haven't noticed," Lily replied. "Medford's a bit . . . how shall we say . . . ? Ordered? Orderly?"

Kate smiled shyly. "I have noticed that everything is in its place in that house, if that's what you mean."

"Yes, you've never seen such order," Annie replied.

"Though he hosted my debut ball there and I must say it was absolutely lovely. Perfect actually." She laughed.

"It was," Lily agreed, nodding.

"The ball he hosted for me was lovely too," Kate said with a dreamy look surely in her eye, but she wasn't so much remembering the ball as the kiss afterward.

"Did Medford dance with Louisa?" Lily asked.

"Absolutely," Kate replied.

"I knew it," Annie said. "Medford's a capital fellow. I mean, he owns a printing press for goodness' sake. He's not about to say no to dancing with a housemaid."

Kate giggled at that. "He didn't. And here I thought it was my plain roots that made me think it was a good idea."

"It's an excellent idea," Lily replied. "Absolutely excellent."

The three women spent the morning talking, laughing, and telling stories. By the time they arrived at their destination more than an hour later, Kate was feeling as if they were old friends. A pang of loneliness beat in her chest. But they weren't old friends, and they wouldn't be. She might spend a few pleasant hours with these nice ladies but they would be separated soon by prison and—she gulped—possibly worse. And even if she were not found guilty, it was not as if Lady Lily and Lady Annie would remain friends with her. A former duchess with a blackened reputation including murder charges and a thwarted divorce? Why, just being seen with her could ruin them. No wonder they'd taken the extra precaution of bringing two coaches to the countryside.

The coach pulled to a stop and Annie let the coachman help her down before turning back around to address Lily and Kate. "You two stay here. I'll ensure no one is about. We can't have anyone seeing you."

Kate nodded but felt hideously conspicuous. She was putting her new friends in danger by asking them to accompany her on this trip. Even though they were taking precautions to keep her identity and location a secret, there was always the possibility that someone might see her and trace her back to James's house.

"Where exactly are we?" Kate asked Lily after Annie left.

"We're on a farm outside Jordan's estate," Lily replied. "We asked the owners to allow us to come and stay for the day. They were going to town today as a matter of fact and won't be here. It's perfect."

Kate clapped her hands. Leave it to the efficient sisters to plan everything so well.

Only a few minutes later, Annie returned and motioned for them to follow. "They've got the barn all ready for us," she said. "And there isn't another soul for miles."

"Excellent," Lily replied, and the coachman helped the other two women down the steps. Just as Lily had predicted, the wind in the country was bracing, but Annie quickly explained the plan. "We decided we would stay in the barn, mostly, to escape the cold, but if you'd like to build a snowman or something, just say the word." She giggled and Kate returned her happy smile.

"The barn will do nicely," Kate said. "I'm already freezing."

"And there's a surprise for you too, Lily," Annie added with a wink.

"What?"

"A litter of piglets was born in the fall. Two of the babies are still with their mum."

Lily squealed and Kate finally had an answer to her question. Apparently highborn ladies squealed when they were happy too. She suppressed her smile.

"You'll have to excuse me, Kate. I love animals of all sorts. Especially baby ones," Lily said with a laugh.

"Oh, I've always adored piglets," Kate said. "Where are they?"

"Follow me." Annie motioned and Kate and Lily stepped behind her toward the barn. If the men's coach had already arrived, Kate didn't see it anywhere. She had to pinch the inside of her arm to keep from asking Annie where James was. He'd arrive soon enough, she told herself. And in the meantime, why, there were piglets.

They stepped inside the barn, and familiar smells immediately surrounded Kate: hay, animals, wood. She breathed it in. She'd never thought she'd miss the smell of a barn. But she did. She desperately did.

A movement off to the side caught her attention. Kate looked over and immediately froze. The men were already there. James leaned against a stall, his boots crossed at the ankles, looking particularly handsome in fawn-colored buckskin breeches, a white lawn shirt, and a midnight-blue wool overcoat. The man looked wonderful in a cravat and topcoat but he looked even more ravishing in less formal attire.

"There you are," called a handsome man whom Kate didn't recognize. "Lily, did Annie tell you there are piglets here?"

"She did, Jordan," Lily called back. "And I cannot wait to see them."

Ah, so the handsome man was Annie's husband. A very nice choice, indeed.

"They're here," Jordan replied, gesturing to the stall next to where the three men stood.

Lily, Annie, and Kate edged closer and all three leaned over to look inside the stall. The mama pig was curled up in a pile of hay in the back of the stall snuggling her two little piglets.

"That may be the cutest thing I've ever seen," Lily whispered. "They're still so tiny."

"Apparently, they're a special breed that doesn't get very big," Jordan added.

"Don't even think about it," the third handsome man warned, arching a brow. He had to be Lord Colton, and he was just as good-looking as his wife was beautiful.

"What?" Lily asked innocently, pushing the tip of her slipper into a bit of hay. "And this, by the way, is my husband, Kate. The Marquis of Colton, but you may call him Devon."

"And this," Annie Holloway said, "is my husband, the Earl of Ashbourne, or just Jordan."

Kate curtsied. "Very nice to meet both of you. Please call me Kate." She glanced up at the four of them. My, but these were good-looking people. The Marquis of Colton was tall, dark, and handsome, and his friend the Earl of Ashbourne had silver eyes that were positively breathtaking. But despite the attractive company, Kate's entire being was riveted to the third equally good-looking man in the barn. James.

The other two men bowed to her while James remained leaning against the stall door. She didn't look at him. She swallowed. Was he remembering their kiss the other night too? She hadn't seen him since then. Hadn't spoken to him. And now their being together was positively . . . awkward.

Annie winked at Lily. "Seeing these piglets, Lily, I know you're thinking exactly what I'm thinking."

Kate turned back to listen to the conversation.

"And that is?" Jordan Holloway asked his wife.

"That there are two of them. Lily and I could each take one."

"I should have known that's what you were going to say," Jordan replied with a grin, smacking himself on the forehead.

"I am not about to take a pig into the house," Devon said. "We've already got a raccoon."

"And *we've* already got a fox," Jordan added.

Kate shook her head. Surely they were jesting. And she had no idea what a raccoon was. But she couldn't take her eyes off the cute little baby pigs.

"Not to mention, I doubt pigs make very good pets," Devon continued.

Lily opened her mouth to speak but Kate interrupted. "Actually, they make excellent pets."

All four of them turned to look at her.

"They do?" Annie asked.

Kate nodded. "Yes. The little runt there reminds me of the pig I had when I was a girl."

"You had a pig?" James asked, pushing his shoulder off the stall door and walking toward her. She did her best to ignore the rush of heat his voice sent up her spine.

She nodded. "I did. A little pink one named Margaret."

"See," Annie said to her husband. "Kate's had a pig and says they do make good pets."

"Excellent pets. You can train them just like any dog, and they're quite loyal." Kate sighed. "I'd give absolutely anything to have a pig again."

James gave her an inquiring look. Oh dear, what he must think of her. A duchess with a pet pig, what was next?

Annie lowered her voice. "Let's let the mama feed

her babies, and we'll have breakfast. It should be all set up in the little cottage down the pasture."

The group made its way out of the barn and across the fields, the brisk wind whipping along their hair and cheeks. Annie led them to the copse of trees on the edge of the forest where a small whitewashed cottage stood nestled among the evergreens. The cottage reminded Kate of the ones that had been sprinkled along the lands where her parents' home had been. A wave of homesickness hit her. It was so nice of these people to bring her here. To give her this experience. How could she ever repay them?

Annie ran ahead and opened the door to reveal a fire burning in the fireplace, warm and cozy. A picnic lunch had been set out on a large tabletop, six mismatched wooden chairs sat around it. Their little group piled into the house, shed their cloaks, and quickly took their seats. Lily and Devon sat together, Jordan and Annie sat together, and in the space remaining, Kate and James managed to squeeze together at the end of the table.

Jordan poured wine into wooden cups for all. "It's a bit early for spirits but perhaps this might serve to warm us up." He grinned widely.

"Tell us, Kate," Annie asked as she filled plates full of cheese, eggs, meats, and bread and passed them around to everyone. "What was it like living on a farm as a child?"

Kate smiled widely. "It was . . . magnificent. Always something to do, always something happening. But nothing as grand as the lives I'm sure you all led." She held up the wood cup and gestured to the small room in which they sat. "Of course, I lived in my parents' house which was a bit more formal, but I visited all the farmers constantly. This cottage is not more grand than the ones I used to frequent as a child."

Lily waved a hand in the air. "We were raised at a grand estate, to be sure," Lily replied. "But there was never any money for anything. My father gambled it all away. No doubt we would have been happier in a home like this."

Kate bit her lip. She'd never considered such a thing. She'd always assumed all of the people who lived in large luxurious homes were wealthy. Lily's words made her stop and think. Kate had had a happy life as a child and money hadn't been what made it happy. Not at all.

"You didn't have brothers and sisters?" Annie asked. "That seems so sad. I don't know what I'd do without Lily." She reached over and squeezed her sister's hand.

Kate smiled at the friendly gesture between the women. "No." She shook her head. "I wasn't lucky enough to have siblings. It was just my parents and I. But we had scores of animals to keep us company."

"Like pigs?" Devon asked her, smiling.

"Precisely." Kate nodded. "I talked my mother into letting me take in one of the pigs that was born on the farm."

Jordan cleared his throat. "If you don't mind my asking, how did you ever . . . that is to say . . . how exactly did you . . . become a duchess?"

Annie slapped her husband's sleeve and gave him a warning look, but Kate laughed. "I don't mind one bit," she said, taking a sip of wine. She could feel James's eyes upon her, watching her, waiting for her answer. "I met my husband at a country dance."

Annie's eyes were wide. "A country dance?"

"Yes." Kate took another bracing sip of wine.

"And he just asked you to marry him?" Lily replied breathlessly, leaning forward.

Kate nodded. "Yes. It all happened very quickly."

"Oh, how romantic," Annie replied. She elbowed her husband playfully. "I wish our courtship had happened quickly."

"No. You two took your time," Devon replied with a laugh.

"Ironic," Annie retorted. "Coming from the man who took five years to marry his wife."

Devon lifted his wine glass playfully as if proposing a toast. "Better late than never."

Lily raised her glass too. "I'll drink to that."

Annie sighed and turned her attention back to Kate. "I still say it's romantic that you met the duke at a country ball, and he asked you to marry him."

Kate nodded. "Yes, I . . . I thought I was very much in love." She could still feel James's eyes upon her, but she couldn't look at him. He'd been so quiet. Barely spoken since they'd all arrived. Was he angry with her? Did he wish he were somewhere else? Was coming out to the country a silly waste of time for him when he could be doing things like planning his next pamphlet or attending to business in his study?

"You weren't always in love?" Annie asked, and she quickly yelped when her sister elbowed her in the side. "Ouch. What?" Annie rubbed her side.

"Don't ask Kate such a thing," Lily replied. "You've put her in an impossible position. She cannot answer that."

Kate shook her head. "No, no. I don't mind. The truth is, I learned quickly after my marriage began that love wasn't all that I thought it to be."

Annie reached out a hand and covered Kate's. "Oh, but love is the most wonderful feeling in the world."

Kate smiled wanly. "I suppose. If it's the kind of marriage that you and Lord Ashbourne have." Ashbourne inclined his head. "Or you and Lord Colton, Lily." Devon smiled at her.

"It's all about finding the right person to marry," Lily replied.

Annie shook her head sadly. "There are many people who marry for connections or to fulfill a duty."

Kate nodded. "Yes, but my husband and I were supposed to be marrying for love. Sadly, we realized, it wasn't love at all. We were completely incompatible."

Lily reached out and put her hand over Kate's this time and squeezed. "You were very young."

"Yes," Kate said.

"I do hope you still believe in love," Annie added.

Kate glanced away. She wasn't about to tell them, but love scared her more than almost anything in the world. The promise of love had kept her in an unhappy marriage for ten years and now had her facing a sentence of death. Oh, how her life would have been different if she'd found a husband like Lily's or Annie's. They were very lucky women indeed.

James spoke, his voice tight. "Love is a luxury many cannot afford," he said in a clipped voice.

Lily nudged at James's sleeve. "Present company notwithstanding, I hope you mean to say."

"Of course." He inclined his head and took a long draught from his cup.

Annie slapped her palm on the tabletop. "Oh, here we are, Kate, we promised you a grand time and we're making you sad, bringing up the past. Let's speak of happier things."

By the time the morning was over, Kate was rosy from the two glasses of wine she'd had. No doubt her face was pink from the laughter she'd enjoyed, and her cheeks ached from all the smiling she'd done. She should be in mourning. She should be in prison. Oh, none of it made any sense, but she'd just had the most wonderful time in all the world. She'd gone back to a farm, if only for one day, and it would have to last her the rest of her life.

They rode horses, played in the snow, watched the sheep roam the fields, and played with the baby piglets once they were awake from their nap and their mama was otherwise occupied with her lunch.

And thankfully, James became less distant. He helped her build a snowman, raced her across the fields during their ride, and scooped up the tiniest piglet, handing it to her to allow her to hold the little thing. Kate smiled at him shyly but not before glancing over and noticing that Lily and Annie had taken note of the solicitous way James was treating her. It made her cheeks heat, but she couldn't help but beam at him. Being in his company made her heart race. She cuddled the baby pig and cooed to her. "If you were mine, I would name you Margaret the Second," she whispered.

"An illustrious name." James grinned at her, before gently taking the piglet and laying her back in the hay next to her brother and her mama.

All too soon, their party prepared to return to London. The three ladies walked arm in arm back toward the coaches that had been brought around. They stood together in the barren snow-covered meadow. This time, Annie led them to James's coach and Kate entered first. Lily stuck her head in.

"Remember to keep the windows closed," Lily warned, pulling at the curtains from her vantage point.

"And keep your hood up when you get out of the coach," Annie added, from outside.

Kate shook her head. "Aren't you coming with me?"

"No, we thought we'd all ride back to my house together and let you and Medford share the coach to his," Lily said.

Kate gulped.

CHAPTER 18

Minutes later, James and Kate waved good-bye to their friends and soon the coach was in motion back to London.

James watched her carefully from across the seat. It was dark in the coach with the shades still drawn.

Kate's neck worked as she swallowed convulsively. "Surely we can keep the shades open while we're in the country like this," she said, pulling back one of the curtains. "There's no one to see us here."

He shrugged. Was she suddenly shy to be alone with him? Had her hand trembled earlier when he touched her? All he could think about was how beautiful and vulnerable she looked today and how lovely she'd been when she laughed. He was glad she was able to laugh. This trip to the countryside had been a good idea. He desperately wanted to make her laugh again. He'd started the day attempting to keep his distance, remembering their kiss at the ball. He'd been tortured by it for the last two days. He'd decided it would be much better for both of them if they remained apart, and he'd meant to do so, honestly. But when the coach had arrived this morning to take them to the country, he hadn't been able to refuse to go. So he'd decided to ride in a different coach on the way there, assuming it would make things easier. And once they'd arrived, he'd watched her, surreptitiously, unable to keep his eyes from her. And then they'd had a wonderful morning, laughing, riding, playing in the snow. He couldn't remember having had fun like that even when he was a child. And it was so easy with Kate. He couldn't keep from smiling and laughing around her. He knew Annie and Lily had been watching him closely, but it didn't matter. He'd promised Kate fun while she wrote the pamphlet for him and, by God, he intended to keep that promise. He smiled to himself thinking about her reaction to the piglet.

"Tell me something," he said. "Did you really have a pig when you were a child?"

Success. She laughed, and it was a musical sound. "I did."

"As a pet?" he continued.

"Yes, she lived in the house and everything. She was a very small pig," Kate clarified. "But a pig just the same."

James couldn't help but smile at that. He tried to picture a young Kate chasing a pig around the house. But he couldn't picture her as a child. He couldn't picture her any way other than the lovely woman she was, sitting across from him, self-consciously pushing a lock of shimmery golden-red hair behind her ear and glancing up at him from behind velvety black lashes.

"Please tell me something," she said in a saucy tone to which James was immediately drawn.

He nodded. "As you wish."

"What exactly is a raccoon?"

His laughter shook the coach. "It's a furry little

animal that's sort of black, gray, and white with a long striped tail. Looks as though it's wearing a mask. Quite common in the Americas or so I've heard."

"Do Lily and Annie really have a fox and a raccoon?"

He grinned at her. "Yes and no."

At her questioning look he continued. "Annie has a fox all right, but the raccoon is really just a dog that looks like a raccoon. Her name is Bandit."

Kate laughed. "Oh, I see. And here I thought I was being improper with my pet pig."

He shook his head. "No, you're in excellent company actually."

"I'm glad to hear that." She paused for a moment, biting her lip. "James, may I ask you something else?"

He nodded. "Of course."

"Why did you seem so standoffish at the farm today?"

He glanced out the window. "Did I?"

She bowed her head and plucked at the folds in her skirt. "You know you did."

He leaned to the side and braced an elbow on the seat cushion. "The truth is . . . I'm feeling guilty for kissing you."

Her jaw dropped. Apparently, she hadn't expected him to be quite that . . . forthright. "Guilty? Why?"

"I had no right."

Her voice was soft. "There were two of us in the ballroom that night, James. It wasn't just you."

"I know, but—"

"I feel guilty too," she murmured.

His eyes narrowed on her. "Why?"

"You've asked me to write for you, not to distract you with dancing and . . ."

He shook his head. "You distract me just sitting there,

but that's no excuse for me to behave like a total jack-ass and—"

She sat up straight. "But you didn't. You didn't act like an ass at all."

"Didn't I?"

"No."

"Thank you for that," he said. "I shall endeavor to keep my hands off you and allow you to write in peace."

Was that a look of disappointment on her face? Oh, now he was guilty of wishful thinking. Fool.

Kate glanced away and tugged on her curl again. "Do you think Lily and Annie like me?"

He sobered. "Yes, they do. Very much."

"They seemed a bit hesitant when they asked about George, and I just—"

"They weren't sure whether you're in mourning. It's an odd situation."

She cringed. "To say the least. I know. I hate to make them feel uncomfortable, and I know I should be mourning, but I just cannot. George and I . . . we barely knew each other and the fact was I hadn't seen him in at least five years. How can I grieve for someone whom I didn't even know?"

"Believe me, I understand."

"Do you?" she asked.

James scrubbed his hand through his hair. He wasn't about to explain to her how he understood, but he did. He simply nodded.

Kate glanced out the window. "And the worst part is, George and I didn't even have that unconventional of a marriage. I'd say it was more normal than anything."

James shook his head. "Most wives are not left in the countryside to rot while their husbands gallivant around London if that's what you mean."

She laid her head back against the seat cushion. "Perhaps not, but many married couples spend long amounts of time apart. Though I suppose the divorce and the murder make us entirely unconventional." She tried to laugh but tears shone in her eyes.

"Kate." James's voice caught. He leaned forward.

She glanced out the window. "I am sorry he died that way. I'm sorry and I'm angry. Angry with him for being such an ass and angry at myself for how I reacted, and angry at whoever did it and allowed me to take the blame. There's a murderer out there, James. A murderer."

He clenched his jaw. "I know."

James set about making the rest of the journey full of lighthearted discussion and jests. Kate kept remembering the way he'd said, "You distract me just sitting there." The words made her go hot and cold at the same time. She tried to shove them from her mind, but they came back to make her smile again and again.

He had her laughing the rest of the way, and by the time they arrived at his town house, Kate had forgotten to pull up her hood or close the curtains in the coach.

She gasped and quickly tugged on the hood as they descended the steps. She glanced about surreptitiously. A few people hurried past the alleyway. A couple of horses ambled past the mews on the corner. Kate kept her head down and hurried up the stairs onto the back porch.

James cursed under his breath. Damn it. He should have been paying closer attention. Should have ensured she'd covered her head when she'd alighted from the coach, but he'd been so entranced by her, by their afternoon together.

"You don't think anyone saw me, do you?" she asked as soon as they were inside.

James shook his head. "No. I don't think so," he replied in his most reassuring tone. But if anyone had, it was too late.

CHAPTER 19

Kate sat curled up in her favorite spot in the library, writing the pamphlet. Themis lay at her feet. Kate tapped the nib of her quill against the parchment. It was easy enough for her to record the details, but that's not what she wanted to convey. She wanted to convey her sense of sadness, sense of horror when she'd found George lying on the floor that morning. Explain why she went to him, cradled his head, tried to save him. And that she wouldn't, couldn't—no matter what had happened between them—have killed him. Because murder was not in her heart.

Of course, even if she were able to convey her innocence, it didn't mean anyone would believe her. She'd have no way of knowing. All she could do was try. Tell her story as honestly as she could and hope at least some among the haughty *ton* believed her.

She thought about her mother-in-law, the dowager duchess of Markingham. "Not fit to shine your boots," she'd told her son when he'd introduced Kate to her all those years ago.

"George is momentarily turned by your pretty face,"

she'd sneered to Kate when George had left them alone to become acquainted. "But rest assured he'll return to his senses." Kate winced at the memory. Unfortunately for everyone, neither of them had come to their senses before the wedding took place. And her mother-in-law had continued to detest her with a shocking virulence.

It had struck Kate to the core. But she'd been so naïve believing their supposed love would conquer all. She'd spent years trying to court the woman's favor, all to no avail. Finally, she'd given up. She hadn't seen the dowager in years, even though the lady lived only a mile away from Markingham Abbey in her dower house. Kate had realized finally that George's mother had been right. A match between a duke and a dairy maid (as his mother was fond of calling her) was a hideous idea. Absolutely awful. And now she could only imagine the dowager duchess's pain . . . and anger. In addition to hearing the news that her beloved only son had been murdered, she believed the murderer was her own detested daughter-in-law. Oh, Kate hadn't blamed the woman for hating her in years and now she certainly couldn't. Her heart wrenched when she thought of the awful pain George's mother must be going through now. Losing a child was completely unnatural. And to lose him in such a way . . . unimaginable.

Kate laid down her quill on the parchment and rested her head in her hand. Her thoughts turned to George again. Poor George. He hadn't deserved to die that way, a bullet to the chest. And he'd seen whoever had killed him, Kate was sure of it. He'd seen the face of his murderer with those cold, staring eyes.

Kate dug her fingernails into the palms of her hands. Oh God. Who had done it, and why? She'd gone to her room, begun packing her things. She'd decided to leave him for good. He might have refused to grant her a divorce, but she'd refused to remain under his roof.

She'd decided she'd live on the streets rather than spend one more day a prisoner at Markingham Abbey. Her whole marriage had been a sham, and she would no longer spend another day dead. For that's what her life had become, a living death.

Dead. The word stopped her cold. George's body, lying on the carpet. George was dead. But she had been too. For years. Just in a completely different way. She shuddered.

She shook her head. Who would have killed George? Lady Bettina? That made no sense. The two had been wrapped around each other. That lady had flaunted her relationship with George in Kate's face, in her own house. Lady Bettina supposedly loved George. But who else?

Perhaps someone had sneaked in. George's cousin? The next in line to the dukedom? She'd only met Oliver a few times, and he seemed perfectly nice, but she supposed it was possible. People had been killed for lesser things than a dukedom.

One of the servants? She couldn't imagine which one. Aside from George's valet who was gone with him to London most of the time, the other servants were people she'd come to know, come to rely upon. Her only friends really. And she saw no reason why any of them would want George dead. He was their provider. Their employer. She'd never heard any of them speak ill of him.

She scrubbed her hands over her face. Mr. Abernathy had assured her he'd be investigating every possibility in great detail. She could only hope he found something . . . anything.

The door to the library opened just then, snapping Kate from her reverie. Mrs. Hartsmeade walked in in her usual brisk, efficient manner. "Oh, your grace. I didn't know you were here. My apologies, I'll come back another time."

Themis leaped up and ambled over to get a pet from the housekeeper who clearly adored her.

"No, Mrs. Hartsmeade, please stay," Kate called, eager for any small bit of company to distract her from her thoughts.

"I was just going to get a book I sometimes consult for removing stains from linens," the housekeeper explained, patting Themis on the head.

Kate nodded. "Please don't let me stop you."

Mrs. Hartsmeade made her way to one of the bookshelves on the far wall, pulled a tome from the stack, and turned around. She made her way over to the settee where Kate sat. "Is there anything I can get you, your grace?"

Themis curled up on the rug near Kate's feet again.

"No, no, I'm quite all right," Kate replied.

Mrs. Hartsmeade smiled and turned to leave when Kate stopped her. "Wait. There is one thing . . ."

Mrs. Hartsmeade stopped and turned back around. "Your grace?"

Kate cleared her throat. "Won't you . . . wouldn't you . . . that is to say. I'd like it if you'd sit and talk to me for a bit, Mrs. Hartsmeade."

Mrs. Hartsmeade's blue-gray eyes went wide. "Your grace?"

Kate bit her lip. Oh, she was making a royal cake of herself in front of James's perfectly ordered servants, wasn't she? "It's just that . . . well, I'm lonely, Mrs. Hartsmeade. And my housekeeper at Markingham Abbey, she used to sit and talk with me sometimes."

Mrs. Hartsmeade gave her a kindly smile. "I understand . . . but . . . I hardly think it's appropriate if I—"

"It's not," Kate admitted, shaking her head. "But I won't tell anyone if you won't."

Mrs. Hartsmeade smiled conspiratorially at that and looked around. "Since you put it that way, how can I resist?"

"Excellent!" Kate cleared a spot on the settee next to her and Mrs. Hartsmeade hesitantly settled in, the book propped upon her lap.

"What would you like to speak about?" Mrs. Hartsmeade asked.

"Let's see." Kate tapped her chin with her fingertip. "How long have you been in Lord Medford's employ?" She pushed her paper and quill aside on the table in front of her and pulled up one foot to tuck it beneath her.

"Since he was a boy," Mrs. Hartsmeade replied. "In fact, I was the maid to his father, the former viscount."

Kate blinked. "You knew James's father?"

The housekeeper nodded. "Yes. For many years."

Kate leaned closer. "What was he like?"

Mrs. Hartsmeade shook her head emphatically. "Oh no. I couldn't possibly gossip about his lordship, your grace. No. No. No."

Kate gave her an innocent look. "I'm not asking you to gossip, Mrs. Hartsmeade. Just describe him."

The housekeeper appeared to be a bit mollified. "Well, he was tall, dark. Looked a great deal like the current Lord Medford though not quite as handsome."

Kate nodded. "Go on. What was he like?"

A frown covered Mrs. Hartsmeade's face. She glanced over her shoulder. "I do hate to speak ill of the family, your grace, but the current viscount, he's a sight better man than his father ever was."

"Really?" Kate leaned closer still. She couldn't help

it. She wanted to know every detail. James had already mentioned that he and his father had been at odds. But was there more to it than that? Perhaps *he* should be the one to write a pamphlet.

Mrs. Hartsmeade nodded. "Yes, the former viscount, he was very hard on our Lord Medford. Always insisting he get perfect marks in school, maintain a perfect reputation. Wouldn't allow him to bring shame or scandal on him. Obsessed with scandal that man was." The housekeeper clucked her tongue.

"So that's why James is so . . . particular?" Kate said slowly, tapping her finger against her jaw.

"Yes," Mrs. Hartsmeade said, nodding. "Every morning, the former viscount would inspect the work Lord James did for his tutors. If he found so much as a spot of ink, the slightest smudge, the boy would be forced to start completely over again before he had his breakfast."

Kate reached down and patted Themis on the head. "He sounds positively dreadful."

"Oh, he was. And I do hate to speak ill of the dead, but . . . Well, Lord Medford's always been so hard on himself. Harder on himself than even his father was. If the old viscount was an exacting master, Lord James is twice as exacting . . . on himself."

"I see." Kate's mind drifted off. It stood to reason that James's insistence on perfection, his reputation as Lord Perfect, was well earned, but there was another side to him, a rebellious side, the side that owned a printing press and harbored a supposed murderess.

"What about his mother?" Kate asked.

Mrs. Hartsmeade sighed. "It's an awfully sad tale to be sure, but his lordship never knew his mother. Died in childbirth, she did."

"So that's why he has no brothers or sisters," Kate murmured.

"Indeed," Mrs. Hartsmeade replied with a shake of her head. "I often wonder how his lordship would be different had his mother lived." She expelled her breath and clutched at the book on her lap. "Though I expect it does no good to wonder."

Kate wondered too. "I'm glad he's had you, Mrs. Hartsmeade." She reached over and squeezed the housekeeper's wrinkled hand.

Mrs. Hartsmeade smiled at that then suddenly sat up straight, dropping the book to the floor. "Oh, your grace, please don't tell his lordship I told you these things. He'd dismiss me immediately for being so improper."

Kate leaned down and retrieved the book. She handed it to Mrs. Hartsmeade with a smile. "Is he such a hard master, then?"

The housekeeper took the book and settled back into her seat. "No, no. Not at all. He's the soul of generosity with all of us. He demands the best from us, yes, but he always rewards hard work, and he rarely gets cross. He's a wonderful employer, your grace. That's the truth."

"But you wouldn't want to anger him?"

"No. Never. I'm very loyal to his lordship, your grace."

"Don't worry, Mrs. Hartsmeade. We never had this conversation."

CHAPTER 20

Something crashed through her window. Kate, immediately roused from her slumber, bolted upright in bed. Her heart pounded wildly, a scream silenced on her lips. She glanced frantically around the room.

Smoke.

Fire.

Amid the shattered glass in the center of the room, a large chunk of wood was burning.

They were under attack. This time she did scream.

She pressed the back of her hand to her mouth, biting it fiercely. She scrambled up, tossing the sheets aside, the smoke from the burning wood already making her eyes water. She raced over to the broken window, and a bit of glass on the floor sliced open her foot. She grabbed at it, clenching her jaw. What was that noise? A glance out onto the street revealed a mob of people screaming and yelling, throwing things, and chanting.

"Murderess. Murderess. Murderess."

Kate covered her mouth with her hand to stifle her scream. They were coming for her. They would kill her. And they were destroying James's house. Oh God. She never should have come here.

She must escape. But first she must ensure James and the servants were safe. She turned to run. The long hem of her white nightgown caught on her bleeding foot, and she stumbled. She fell to the floor, the smoke clogging her lungs. She coughed fiercely.

The door to her room blasted open with a sharp crack. Kate's head snapped up. James strode through the smoke and debris, his face a mask of anger. He looked like an avenger.

He should toss her to the mad crowd, Kate thought for an awful second. It would be one way to be rid of her and her disruption to his life.

"You're bleeding?" He motioned to her foot and the bloody hem of her night rail.

"I'm fine," she answered.

He ripped a blanket from the bed, tossed it over her, and pulled her to her feet with a gloved hand. Once she had her footing, he wrapped the blanket around her, spun her into his arms, and pulled her forcefully from the room.

"I've already seen to it that the servants and Themis are safe with the neighbors, the fire coaches are coming and the guard has been called. Come with me," he commanded in a voice that brooked no debate.

Kate nodded. Eyes burning, still coughing from the smoke, she followed him from the room. He led her by the hand. They hurried down the back staircase and out a side door that adjoined a small fenced yard. James's horse was there, already saddled. He boosted her up and swung up behind her. Fear clutched Kate's heart in its frenzied grasp. She barely felt the freezing cold night air. All she could hear were the frantic screams of the mob, see the reflection of the orange haze of fire from the corners of her eyes. *Please. Please. Let this be a dream.*

A sharp yell sounded from the front of the house. Kate turned to see a smaller group of the mob that had broken apart. The men ran to the side yard, yelling, hissing, throwing things. "There they go!" they yelled, trying to catch the attention of the larger group, but the chaos was such that only a handful of the others heard. James tugged the reins and guided the horse in the opposite direction. They bolted out of the side yard, down the back alley and past the mews. Several of the mob members chased them on foot, but they were soon lost behind them as James and Kate galloped through the cold light-gray morning streets. They took two sharp turns and eventually came to a stop in the back of another fine town house. James swung down quickly and pulled Kate with him, holding her in his strong, warm embrace. He quickly ushered her inside.

The next hour was a blur. They had arrived at the Marquis of Colton's town house. Arrangements were made to borrow a coach to travel to James's country estate.

Kate sat huddled in a corner on a chair, a bigger blanket wrapped around her. Lily busily treated the cut on Kate's foot, wrapped a bandage around it, and provided her with a pair of shoes and some stockings. Then she packed Kate a bag, ensuring she had enough warm clothing for the trip, and soothed her with a cup of hot tea.

"How did they find you?" Lord Colton asked James.

James's face was a mask of stone. "I suspect someone must have seen us return from the farm yesterday."

Colton nodded grimly.

Lily's eyes were filled with tears. "I'm just glad the

two of you and all the servants and Themis got out safely, but oh, James, your beautiful house."

James didn't answer. Kate fought the tears that filled the backs of her eyes. James's hair was mussed, his face darkened with soot, his eyes were red-rimmed. He'd never looked more of a mess. He'd never looked more handsome. She could only imagine the state of his perfect house at present. Oh God, what had she done? Just her mere existence had placed him and his possessions in danger.

She closed her eyes. She couldn't think about any of that now. She was safe. James was safe. That's all that mattered at present.

Kate finished her tea, and Lily helped her clean up with a warm cloth. Within minutes, Colton's coach was prepared, and James and Kate were ushered inside with a bundle full of clothing and food to last them for their trip to Hamphill Park.

The coach door slammed shut, and Lord Colton called to the coachman to be under way. The coach took off at a fast clip, and Kate was jolted back against the velvet cushions. No, this was no dream. She was on her way to James's country house. They'd been chased out of town by an angry mob.

They rode in silence for the first hour, both too shocked and tired to say much. Kate leaned against the pillow Lily had given her and tried to sleep. But all she could think about was James's beautiful house, his beautiful life, and how it had been destroyed because of her. The mob knew she'd been staying with him, and his reputation would suffer. If they dug around enough, they might even discover he owned the printing press.

"Your house," she finally murmured, her voice cracking.

"Pardon?" came his reply.

"Your beautiful, perfect, orderly house, destroyed." Tears clogged her throat. "Oh, James. I'm so sorry."

"It's just a house, Kate."

"But you love your house."

"Don't worry about that. Get some rest."

She lifted her head from the pillow and met his gaze. "How can I not worry about it? Your life, it's in chaos now, because of me."

James pinned her with a penetrating stare. "Kate, my decision to take you in was just that, *my* decision. I knew the dangers and the possible consequences."

Kate rubbed her eyes with her balled fists. "But you couldn't have thought this would really happen. The pamphlet cannot be worth it to you."

He rested his head against the back of the velvet squabs. "Let me worry about that."

She pressed her head to the pillow and forced herself to close her eyes. "I cannot help but think your life would be so much simpler if I had never come into it."

His voice was steady, calm, clear. "I'm beginning to think simple isn't as wonderful as I'd once believed."

CHAPTER 21

James's country estate was even more splendid than his town house had been. Nestled in a quiet valley in Oxfordshire, the manor was surrounded by trees, ponds, and miles and miles of fertile ground. It was an enormous home on hundreds of acres, encompassing beautiful gardens, trees, a lake, and a park. And the entire thing was every bit as orderly and perfect as the town house had been. More so, if that were possible.

The interior of the house was absolutely grand, resplendent with priceless antiques, fine fabrics, thick new carpets, and brass finishings. The grand hall displayed an impressive array of portraits of the Medford ancestors. The library contained an enormous assortment of leather-bound tomes all well ordered inside gleaming mahogany shelves. The salons were outfitted in lovely matched wallpapers, luxurious curtains, and the finest furniture. The corridors were all spotless marble, and the foyer itself took Kate's breath away with its wide, sweeping staircase and dazzling chandelier.

Upon Kate's arrival, a nice maid ushered her into a suite of rooms that was no exception to the finery. Her bedchamber was absolutely spectacular, decorated in violet with soft curtains and a comfortable bedspread embroidered with tiny flowers. She soon learned that every morning, a small vase of the little flowers appeared on her bedside table.

It didn't take her long to find her favorite room in the house, the music room, where she discovered, to her delight, a grand pianoforte. And with a house as big as this one, she could play as much as she liked in the middle of the night, and she doubted anyone would hear her.

She took her meals in her bedchamber at first. She knew she was being a terrible coward, hiding from James, but he couldn't want to see her and be reminded of what she'd done to his life. She didn't encounter James until they'd been there two days. He came around a corner just as she was about to enter the library. She nearly knocked into him.

"Pardon me," she said in a rushed tone, her cheeks heating as soon as she'd realized exactly whom she'd nearly toppled over.

"No, it was my fault," James replied. He bowed to her.

Kate wrung her hands and watched him. Why was it so awkward between them now?

James cleared his throat. "I trust you've been . . . well. Is your foot healing?"

She nodded quickly. "Perfectly. Thank you. How have you been?" Ugh. An asinine question. She pinched the inside of her arm for asking it.

"Busy," he replied noncommittally.

"Doing what?" She was obviously committed to the asinine today.

His stance relaxed a bit. "Making the arrangements for the town house to be rebuilt, for one thing."

She wanted to sink through the floor. Of course

that's what he'd been doing. "Did you hear anything? About the damage, I mean?" She twisted her hands together nervously.

"Yes. I received a letter . . . from Locke. Apparently the mob dispersed soon after we left. The night watchmen called out the guard to help them control the crowd and the fire was put out as quickly as possible."

"I see." She nodded. "I suppose that's . . . good." Good. What a horribly inadequate word.

His voice grew sober. "Kate. I don't want you to worry. I've been writing letters to my friends in Parliament and elsewhere."

She swallowed. There could only be one reason for him to write such letters. "I'd be lying if I said I haven't been holding my breath," she admitted. "I've been so afraid the lord chancellor will insist I return to the Tower."

"I've been granted permission to allow you to stay in the country . . . with me. In fact, I was coming to look for you just now, to tell you as much."

Kate expelled her breath in a rush. She couldn't help it. She closed her eyes briefly too. "I'm so relieved."

He gave her an encouraging smile. He turned to leave and Kate's hand shot out of its own accord and grabbed at his sleeve, stopping him.

He faced her again, his look inquiring. "Yes?"

She snatched her hand away. "It's just that . . . James . . . I . . ." She glanced down at her slippers, unable to push the words past the lump in her throat.

"What is it, Kate?"

"Do you want me to go . . . back to the Tower, I mean?" She had no idea how she'd managed the nerve to ask that question but she had to.

James smiled at her. "You've still got a pamphlet to write, do you not?"

She nodded jerkily and he continued down the hall.

Kate leaned one hand against the wall after he'd gone. That wasn't exactly the answer she'd been expecting . . . or hoping for. True, she'd been worried that the lord chancellor would demand she return to the Tower, but she'd been equally worried that James would want to rid himself of her. The money from the pamphlet couldn't possibly make up for the destruction of his home. Yes, he'd told her that had been his choice, but she couldn't help feeling guilty about it.

If he did want to send her back to the Tower, he hadn't said so. But he was too much of a gentleman to say it. "You've still got a pamphlet to finish," he'd said. Oh God. She did. No doubt he wanted nothing more than for her to finish writing as quickly as possible and leave.

Kate let her hand drop from the wall and squared her shoulders. She would do that for him. Finish her work. She might have placed him in danger and destroyed his home, but she would not linger and cause more trouble. No, she would complete the pamphlet as quickly as possible and extricate herself from James's life. She owed him that much. She didn't want to think about how sad she would be, returning to the Tower, alone, unhappy. But she was already taking advantage of James's kindness, and she refused to do so any longer. She just needed to finish her pamphlet and do her story justice.

On her fourth day in the country, Kate stopped outside the door to James's study, her palms sweaty, her stomach in knots. The country butler had just informed her of Mr. Abernathy's arrival. Apparently, he and Lord Medford requested her presence in the study. She'd raised her hand to knock but clenched her fist and let it drop to her side again. Fear gripped her. There was no telling what Abernathy would say. By now, perhaps he was convinced that she had murdered George. Perhaps he would even tell James that. Perhaps they were calling her in to accuse her. James would tell her he was sending her back to the Tower posthaste. Living in constant fear had become normal for her. But now, each day brought its own new set of worries. She'd dreamed the last two nights about fire and mobs, being burned at the stake. She'd woken in a sweat, heart pounding, James's name on her lips. James would save her. Wouldn't he? He had the last time.

She closed her eyes briefly and squared her shoulders. She must face whatever the barrister said with courage. *Courage. Courage. Courage.* She'd repeated the words to herself so many times over the last few weeks they had begun to lose all meaning. She swallowed the lump in her throat and rapped her knuckles against the door.

"Come in," James called.

She pushed open the door and walked inside, shutting the heavy oak portal behind her. A quick scan of both men's faces told her little. Their countenances were blank. They rose to greet her, however, and Abernathy held out the chair next to his in front of James's desk.

"Your grace," he said, bowing.

She nodded. "Mr. Abernathy." She tried to get the words "Good to see you" past her dry lips but they wouldn't move.

She dropped into her seat, scanning James's face. Handsome as usual, but without a hint of what they were to discuss.

"Very well, Abernathy," James began in a businesslike voice. "Now that Kate is here, tell us how the investigation is going."

Abernathy cleared his throat and shifted in his chair. "The case is progressing, my lord."

Progressing? That was vague. Kate concentrated on breathing regularly.

James leaned back in his chair and steepled his fingers. "What exactly have you learned?"

Abernathy pulled something from his coat pocket. "The runner is investigating everyone, including Lady Bettina and his grace's valet. Here is his card." He tossed a small piece of paper on the desktop.

Kate sat up straight, her gaze shooting to James's. "Runner?"

Abernathy nodded. "Yes, Mr. Horton, the Bow Street runner Lord Medford has hired to investigate your case."

Kate braced her hand on the arm of her chair. The room felt as if it were twirling. "You hired a runner?"

James nodded once and returned his stern gaze to Abernathy.

Abernathy spoke in a measured tone. "Mr. Horton has spoken to the servants multiple times and gone to Lady Bettina's town house twice. He's indicated he has some interesting news to share when next we meet. I have an appointment scheduled with him in London on Friday."

Kate's breathing was coming in fast pants now. Her heart beat a staccato rhythm in her chest. Interesting news? What did that mean? Friday was far too long to wait.

"Has there been any information about the grand jury?" she managed to choke out, twisting her skirts in her hands.

Abernathy regarded her down his long nose over the rims of his ever-present spectacles. "It's to be convened after the holidays, your grace. Right after the new year, after Twelfth Night."

James nodded. "So we have only until then to gather the rest of the evidence and complete the investigation?"

"Yes, my lord, but Mr. Horton has agreed to work day and night, even over Christmastide if he must. With the amount of money you've given him, he—"

James cleared his throat and gave Mr. Abernathy another stern glare. Abernathy snapped his mouth shut and cleared his throat too. "Yes, well, quite right, all of that is neither here nor there."

Kate glanced back and forth suspiciously between the two men. James was spending a fortune on her defense? Oh God. The thought made her elated and completely anxious at the same time. She'd had no idea he'd hired a Bow Street runner to investigate. And apparently he hadn't wanted her to know. He hadn't mentioned it to her. Perhaps he did believe in her after all. She bit her lip. But what if Mr. Horton didn't find anything? Or what if after his investigation was complete, he came to the conclusion that she was guilty? She shook her head. "I don't understand. What exactly does Mr. Horton hope to discover?"

Mr. Abernathy turned to face her. "Why, the identity of your husband's murderer, of course."

CHAPTER 22

Themis had been retrieved from the neighbors' house in London, placed inside a coach, and sent to the country. She was now lying curled up on the floor at Kate's feet while Kate made her own little comfy spot in the estate library that had become her new workspace. She stared at the scribbled-on pieces of parchment that lay strewn all over her lap and the sofa.

She'd made a vow, a vow to finish the pamphlet as quickly as possible, and today she was feeling quite proud of herself for she'd made headway. She'd decided to write from the heart. Be honest. Write the truth. And the truth was that while she'd felt hurt, rejected, and scared, while she'd been angry with her husband and unhappy in her marriage, never, never in all of her imaginings had she ever thought about killing him. That was the truth, and she meant to tell it, and the devil take the consequences.

There was a sharp knock just before the door opened, and Kate glanced up to see James stroll in. Her heart melted. He took her breath away, so clean-shaven and straight-backed. His close-cropped dark hair perfectly in place and an always pleasant look upon his face.

"Am I interrupting?" he asked, and Kate had the urge to toss her quill and parchment aside and shout, "Absolutely not."

"I can come back later," he continued.

"No, don't leave!" The words escaped her lips with a bit more emphasis than she'd intended. How unfortunate. She pinched her arm.

He moved forward into the room. Themis lifted her head and wagged her tail. James called the dog over to pet her. "You're writing?" he asked Kate.

"Yes." She swallowed. "James, I—"

He put up a hand. "No need to—"

She pushed the quill and paper aside. "There is a need. Please let me say what I must say."

"Very well." Still standing, he propped a booted foot on the stool in front of her.

Kate screwed up the courage that had been flagging ever since the fire. "I'm sorry, James. So sorry for the trouble I've caused you. I've turned your whole life upside down and—"

"We've been over this. There is no need to apologize."

"I must," she said, glancing down at her hands. "I was the one who insisted you take me in. I should have just agreed to write the pamphlet in the Tower, not put you in danger. You offered me money and a venue to tell my story. That should have been enough."

"Kate, I cannot blame you for wanting to be free."

"I didn't need to insist upon going to the farm. That was foolish of me. Someone saw us returning. I heard you tell Lord Colton. I'll never forgive myself for what I've done, hurting you."

"Kate, if anyone is at fault here, it's me. I should have been more aware that afternoon when we returned from the country. It's my fault you were seen. I agreed to your terms, knowing the danger. The pamphlet is something I wanted, something I asked for. You've nothing to apologize for."

She hung her head. "Yes, but how much money will the pamphlet have to make you to pay for the cost of your ruined town house?"

"You let me worry about that. I just want to keep you safe."

His words tugged at her heart. This man, he trusted her. He believed in her. He'd . . . "You hired a runner for me," she said softly.

"Yes."

"Why?"

Pulling his boot from the stool, he shifted on his feet, bracing them apart. "You didn't seem inclined to do so on your own."

"You think I'm innocent?"

His jaw was tight. "I want to have the answers. Mr. Horton will see to it that the truth comes out."

Tears burned the backs of her eyes. "But you wouldn't have hired him if you were convinced I was guilty."

His voice was low. "I don't think you're guilty, Kate."

She glanced away, uncertain how to respond, biting the inside of her lip to keep from crying. "I'm nearly done with the pamphlet."

He nodded.

"I just can't help but think—" She stopped and twisted her fingers.

"Think what?"

"You've such an opportunity, James. To help people."

He narrowed his eyes on her. "What do you mean?"

"Your press, the pamphlets."

"I don't understand."

"I'm privileged. I'm famous, well, infamous. All of

London wants to know what I have to say. I've been given the chance to tell the truth, share my story. But I can't help but think of all the others."

"The others?"

"Yes, all the other prisoners who've been wrongly accused. There must be scores of them, hundreds. No doubt Newgate is filled with them. Especially women who've been accused of something they haven't done. They'll never get the opportunity to tell the truth."

"They will have their day in front of a judge."

"Yes, but they can't afford things like Bow Street runners and no one will ever know the truth if they are sentenced to die horrible deaths. There are no pamphlets for them."

"Unfortunately, the justice system does not always mete out justice."

"I cannot stand to think of the wrongly accused who have no one to fight for them."

"I can understand your concern, but for now I am only worried about you. Let Abernathy and Horton finish their investigation and then we can discuss the others." He turned to go.

"James?"

He stopped, turning his head to the side. "Yes?"

"Why do you believe in me? My innocence, I mean?"

He straightened his stance. "Perhaps it's because I know what it feels like to be innocent and accused of killing someone."

CHAPTER 23

Wearing a spring-green gown, Kate slid into the chair next to James at the dinner table that night. He'd left earlier. Stalked out of the library just after he'd made that amazing statement about knowing what it was like to be innocent and accused of killing someone. He hadn't given her a chance to ask any questions. The accusation couldn't have been public knowledge. She would have read about it in the papers. There'd be whispers. Rumors. Lady Mary would have mentioned it. His reputation wouldn't have been so pristine—well, prior to his association with her at least. No, there hadn't been a hint of scandal around the man. He was obviously harboring a secret, however. What was it?

She took a sip from her wine glass and cast her glance over the beautifully set table. She traded the solitude of her room for his company at dinner. Their meals together had become the bright spots of her day. She'd been enjoying their interludes, looking forward to them. That thought scared her more than she cared to examine. But she refused to leave here tonight without learning what James had meant by his cryptic statement in the library earlier.

A toasty fire crackled in the hearth while the cold wind whistled against the windows outside. The smell of the burning logs and roasted meat permeated the air. It was positively cozy in the dining room tonight. Would it be the last time she'd ever feel cozy?

Kate salivated when the footmen served roasted beef with watercress. The dinners James's French chef cooked were absolutely delightful, so much better than the meals at her husband's estate. She took up her fork and knife and began with relish.

James glanced at her. "How did the writing go today?"

Kate bit her lip. Apparently, they would begin with innocuous conversation. Very well. But she was loath to tell him that she was nearly finished with the pamphlet. She would never be so sneaky as to lie and tell him it wasn't done when it was, but she had to admit, despite her vow to finish as quickly as possible, she'd been procrastinating and daydreaming a bit when she should have been writing. She glanced away. She'd been dreaming of him, actually. But she wasn't about to tell him so. Her heart ached. James was the sort of man she might have fallen in love with ten years ago, had circumstances been entirely different. Of course the circumstances were not different, but it didn't hurt to daydream, did it?

"Very well, actually," she answered noncommittally, taking a bite of the delectable beef from the plate in front of her.

"I'm pleased to hear it." He smiled at her.

Oh God, if only he knew what she'd been thinking. She glanced down at her plate and stabbed her fork into her watercress.

Two hours later when the dinner plates had been cleared, Kate pushed out her chair and stood to go. She dropped her napkin onto her chair. Somehow they'd managed to spend an entire evening together, and she hadn't been able to summon the courage to ask James what he'd meant earlier. And now she was about to leave him. This was always the most melancholy time of the evening. James usually went back to his study to read or work, and she went back to her room or the library to write and to do her best to forget how lonely she felt, how awful things were.

"Thank you for yet another lovely dinner," she said with a weak smile, turning toward the door.

"Kate." The tone of his voice stopped her. There was something about it. Something different.

She turned back toward him. "Yes?"

"Would you . . . would you care to have a drink with me, in the study?"

"Would I . . . ? Why, yes I would!" She smiled at him brightly.

"Excellent." He extended his arm toward her and she moved forward and took it, so happy to have a reprieve from her maddening thoughts for one evening at least.

They walked down the hall discussing their very favorite parts of the meal they'd just enjoyed. James stopped in front of the doors to the study and pushed them open with one hand. "My lady." He bowed, allowing her to precede him into the room.

"Thank you," she answered, laughing.

The room was dark, save for a brace of candles resting on an end table. James saw her settled on the sofa before striding to the sideboard and pouring two glasses of Madeira. He returned to the settee, sat next to her, and handed her one.

"Thank you," she said, taking the glass from his strong, warm hand. "It's been an age since I drank Madeira."

"Me too, actually." He winked at her.

She took a long draught and closed her eyes, letting the wine play across her tongue. Madeira. The fine Portuguese wine so popular during the war with France when French wine had been in short supply. She'd savor it. It might well be the last time she'd ever drink it. *Live. Live. Live.* The words scattered across her brain. They used to comfort her, but now they haunted her. James's town house would still be standing if she hadn't tried to live, live, live.

James expelled his breath. "I don't want you to worry," he said. "About the case, I mean."

She snapped open her eyes. "Worry?"

"I could tell you were upset when Abernathy was here. Horton is the best Bow Street has to offer. He'll discover the truth."

She took another small sip of wine. "I wish that could comfort me."

"I know it must be difficult, Kate."

She met his gaze. "Even if he discovers the identity of the murderer, he'll have to prove it."

James nodded. "He will."

"How can you be so sure?"

"I have confidence."

She reached out and touched his sleeve. "Thank you, James. For your faith in me. You don't know what it means."

"No need to thank me."

It would be the perfect time to ask him about his statement from earlier. She met his gaze. She opened her mouth. Oh, her blasted nerves failed her again. Perhaps because she didn't really want to know. She trembled and looked away at a portrait on the wall near the fireplace. She couldn't discuss her case anymore. *Courage. Courage. Courage.* Those were her new favorite words. She'd repeated them over and over to herself, but what was she now? A coward. Disgusted with her own inability to ask the man in front of her a simple question, she had to change the subject. "Who is that man?" she asked, pointing to the portrait.

"My father."

Kate took another look at the picture, basing her opinion of the man on what Mrs. Hartsmeade had told her about him. He was handsome, to be sure, but there was something angry and cold about him. He looked like the kind of man who would chastise a little boy for marring his schoolwork with a speck of ink. He was all dark cold eyes and grim countenance.

"When did he . . . die?" she asked haltingly.

James's voice was flat. "Over ten years ago now."

"Around the time I got married," she murmured, raising her glass to her lips again.

He cocked his head to the side. "I suppose so."

"You were young when you inherited your title," she said.

"Yes."

"Were you very sad, to see your father die?" Ugh. She winced. Why had she asked that? She pinched her arm. "I'm sorry, James," she hurriedly added. "Of course you were. It's just that—"

"The answer is no," he replied quietly. "And I just realized that you're one of the only people in the world to whom I can admit that."

Her mouth formed an O. "What do you mean?"

"You know what it's like to feel as if you're supposed to mourn someone when you don't."

She glanced away, rolling the wine glass between her palms. "Your father treated you badly?"

"I wouldn't say that exactly. He always hated me, though."

Kate gasped. One hand flew to her throat. "No. You don't mean that."

He nodded grimly. "I'm afraid I do. But don't worry. He had good reason to hate me."

Her brow furrowed, Kate searched his face. "How can you say that? He was your father."

Setting his wine glass aside, James stretched his long legs in front of him and braced his elbows on the settee behind him. "I have learned in my life that those two things are not mutually exclusive."

"Why did he hate you?" The words slipped from her dry throat.

He paused, then sat up and took a long draught of his wine. "Because I killed my mother." His voice was sadly matter-of-fact, tinged with a hint of guilt.

Kate nearly dropped her glass. That was it. What he'd been referring to earlier. "No! James! What do you mean?"

He smiled a humorless smile. "The occasion of my advent into this world was the same as my mother's exit. My birth caused her death."

Tears filled Kate's eyes. "Surely your father didn't blame a baby—"

A wry smile touched his lips. "Officially, of course not. But I felt it in everything he ever said to me, every word, every deed. He loved my mother very much and . . . I killed her."

Kate set her glass aside. She wanted to reach out and touch James, comfort him. Instead, she dug her fingertips into the flesh of her palm. "But that's insane."

He sighed. "I won't argue that point."

"He was hard on you."

"He demanded perfection from me. And that's exactly what he got." His voice trailed off. Another draught of wine. "Lord Perfect."

"You wish you were different?" she asked hesitantly.

"On the contrary, I am never happier than when everything is perfectly in its place. I was always an excellent student." His voice was without irony but was traced with anger.

Kate eyed him carefully. "Would your father have approved of your printing press?"

James raised his brows. "Why, Lady Kate, you surprise me. You've uncovered my secret."

She furrowed her brow. "It's no secret. I always knew you had a printing press."

He shook his head. "*That's* not the secret. Not the real one at any rate."

"What's the real one?" she asked, holding her breath.

He stared off beyond the brace of candles into the shadowy darkness of the room. "The real secret is that my printing press is my only form of rebellion. To answer your question, my father would absolutely hate it."

"Rebellion? I don't understand. Your father's not even here to see it."

"It doesn't matter." James affected a mock voice. "A gentleman makes money from his land management. A gentleman does not go into common business. And a gentleman, at all times, under all circumstances, distances himself from even the *hint* of scandal."

"Your father hated scandal?"

He raised his wine glass. "Precisely."

"And that's why you own a printing press?"

"Not just any printing press. A wildly successful

one. Wildly successful because of the content I publish. Very, very scandalous content."

She smiled. "When I first met you, I wondered if you did it to make money."

He gazed at the ceiling. "Ha. Money's easy. I have money."

"I've come to realize that." She glanced around at the fine furnishings that adorned the room in which they sat.

"I do it because my father would hate it." James tipped back his glass and drained it in one final maneuver. "But I'm not sure I even want that anymore."

"So you never made amends with your father? Before he died, I mean?" Kate asked carefully.

James shook his head. "We came to a peaceable understanding, I suppose. But we were never close. He never once told me he was proud of me."

"Oh, James, I'm so sorry."

"Don't be," he replied. "It's been a great many years now and I've learned to live with it."

Her heart fluttering in her throat, Kate turned to face him. "You said you thought I was the only one who understood what it's like to not mourn someone when you should."

"Aren't you?" There was a hint of sarcasm in his tone.

She glanced away, tears filling her eyes. "It's true. When I think about George I'm sad, yes. He didn't deserve to be murdered no matter what the reason. But I'm not sad because I miss him. I'm sad because of what my life became after I married him. I'm awful to admit it, but I'm sad . . . for myself."

James set his empty glass on the table next to him and moved closer to her. "I admire your honesty, Kate."

She shook her head frantically. "You shouldn't. It's

perfectly horrendous to feel the way I do. I'm sorry for myself, not my dead husband."

"But you didn't kill him."

She met his gaze, the tears spilling from her eyes, her voice catching. "Do you really believe that, James? Do you?"

He groaned. "Kate, if I didn't believe that, I wouldn't have hired the runner."

He pulled a handkerchief from his pocket and offered it to her. She gingerly wiped away the tears on her cheeks. "Tell me something, James. What do you want? What do you *really* want?"

He ran a shaking hand over his face. "Kate, I thought you knew by now. What I want, what I really want . . . is to fix everything."

CHAPTER 24

Kate dropped her gaze from James. She dropped the handkerchief into her lap and ran her hands along her skirts, smoothing them. "Fix everything? Is that what you want or what you're compelled to do?"

He smiled at that. "Is there a difference?"

"Yes, a big one."

He regarded her down the length of his nose. "May I ask you a question, Kate?"

She turned back and nodded. "Of course."

"Why didn't you and George have any children?"

She closed her eyes, briefly. "We tried . . . at first." She swallowed and bit the inside of her cheek. "For several weeks of our marriage. It was awful, but . . . I did my duty. When it was obvious that I wasn't with child, George tired of me. He told me he had mistresses to spend the night with, he wanted me to bear him a son."

James winced.

"He left for London soon after. We argued constantly whenever we saw each other, though he rarely came home, and when he did . . . we never . . . He didn't touch me again." Oh God, her face must be bright pink.

James nodded. "And that's why you wanted the divorce?"

She closed her eyes briefly. "I was so unhappy. I knew it would cause a horrendous scandal but I truly believed George would see the benefit. Frankly, he couldn't have an heir any other way. We'd long since stopped pretending we would ever spend the night together again."

James's gaze pinned her. "You never took a lover, did you, Kate?"

She gasped. Her hand flew to her throat. "Of course not. I would never betray my husband."

"I'm sorry I asked that," he said a bit sheepishly. "The papers implied that you wanted a divorce because you had a lover."

She sighed. "If it would have helped obtain the divorce, I would have said that I did," she replied. "I would have done anything to provide him the grounds upon which to divorce me. I offered to allow him to bring a crim. con. suit."

James sighed. A crim. con. suit. One of the few acceptable reasons for divorce. Of course, it hinged on the *wife* being an adulteress. No mention of the husband. An unfair law to be sure. "I must admit I didn't know George well. We didn't frequent the same club, and he rarely attended Parliament, but he sounds positively detestable."

Kate nodded. "He was."

James leaned toward her. "Do you regret not having children?"

She breathed a shaky breath and stared ahead of her, her eyes not focusing. "I've thought about that so many times in the past few weeks. And I have to say, for the first time since I married, I am glad I haven't given birth. Oh, I wanted children at first, to be sure. I felt like a failure for being unable to produce an heir, but now, now that I'm on trial for my life and George is dead . . . I'm glad I didn't bring innocent little lives into this world to suffer due to the fate of their parents."

He touched her hand. "I understand, Kate. I do."

She smiled wistfully. "Though, perhaps if I'd produced an heir, the entire situation would never have happened to begin with. Perhaps George would have loved me, would have stayed with me." She shook her head. "Oh, I know that's not true. And I couldn't have stood it if he touched me again. It was . . . awful."

"I'm sorry it was so bad for you, Kate." His voice was soft.

Her breath caught when she met his eyes. They were nearly emerald and regarding her with such warmth, heat.

James set his wine glass on the table next to hers. "You know it's not always like that, don't you?"

Her voice caught. "Like what?"

"Awful."

She shook her head.

"If you were my wife, you'd never call it a 'duty,'" he breathed just before his mouth moved closer to hers.

Kate swallowed, her breaths coming in short little pants. "I believe that."

And then she was in his arms.

James's lips met hers, tangled with hers, teased hers. Kate moaned. His lips were at her ear, her cheek, her chin, they moved down her neck and nuzzled at her décolletage.

His fingers made quick work of the back of her gown,

and the fabric fell away from her breasts. Next, her stays came undone. Apparently, James knew exactly what he was doing when undressing a lady. She shivered.

"Let me touch you, Kate," he whispered.

"Yes," she breathed.

Her breasts sprang free, and Kate sucked in her breath. No man had ever seen her naked before, save for her husband. It felt wrong to be doing this in the middle of the library. Wrong, but delicious. And when James's mouth moved down to her nipple and bit and tugged, she ceased thinking at all. *Live. Live. Live.* The words sang in her head. Sharp pangs of desire zinged to the private spot between her legs. She held his dark head against her breast. She'd never felt such utter longing before. Never closed her eyes like she did now and just allowed herself to . . . feel.

James shifted on the settee. He pulled her underneath him and lay atop her. His hips were moving of their own accord against her, and she answered his thrusts. She couldn't stop if she'd wanted to. He pulled up her skirts to the tops of her thighs and jerked her legs around his waist.

Kate's eyes flared wide. Her head fell back. She moaned in the back of her throat. And then his head moved to her breast again, and she ceased thinking entirely. His lips teased her, bit her, drove her wild. George had never done this. He'd barely even touched her breasts, let alone sucked on them. She was half mad with wanting. James's strong, sure hands tugged at her skirts. And then her dress was gone, a heap on the floor in a matter of seconds. She should be embarrassed or ashamed. She was neither.

"Take off your clothes too," she demanded, pulling at the buttons to his breeches.

He shook his head emphatically, his eyes, dark green now, staring into her soul. "I can't."

"Why not?" she moaned as his mouth came back to play with hers.

"If I do, I won't be able to stop."

She reached for his breeches again, but he moved his hips away, and Kate stopped all protest when he moved down on the sofa, plucked at her stockings, and pulled them down. Oh God, what was he doing?

Kate shuddered. Any of the servants might come in at any moment, but for the life of her, Kate couldn't bring herself to care one bit. All she wanted was to feel James's hands and mouth on her. Touching her, branding her, scorching her skin. She'd never felt anything like this passion that flared between them. If she were going to be put to death in a matter of days or weeks, she wanted to feel more. *More. More. More.*

His hot breath was on the inside of her thigh, and Kate gasped. She wanted to die. She never wanted it to end. He couldn't possibly mean to . . .

No.

But the next feeling was the tip of his fire-hot tongue probing at a spot between her legs that was so sensitive, so wet, so hot. She shuddered and reached down to grab his head. She couldn't let him do this. It was . . . indecent . . . wasn't it? Oh God, was it? Then, suddenly, she hoped not, or more specifically didn't care. All she knew was that she never wanted him to stop. His mouth left her briefly, and she whimpered only to have his finger come up to play in the springy hair between her legs. He parted her with his fingers, and then his tongue was back, licking her, sucking at her, making her feel things she'd never known she was capable of feeling. She clutched at his shoulders. "Yes, James, please," she begged.

He licked her, in tiny little laps, over and over. His tongue moved up and down on her with such precision and skill. She was convinced she would die of happiness, of feeling, was convinced she couldn't take any more. But then, just when she thought she might burst apart into a thousand tiny pieces, he stopped. "No!" Kate cried out, and then his finger was there, thrusting into her, up and down, making her hips buck uncontrollably beneath him.

"James, I don't think . . . I can't . . ." She twisted her hands in her own hair, half mad with wanting him.

"Shh," he whispered against her thigh. "Don't be frightened, Kate. I want to make you feel good."

Oh God. She wanted to feel him inside of her, filling her, completing her, moving inside of her, making her his. She'd never experienced such lust before, and she never wanted it to end.

"James, please." She pushed her hands down and tried again to grab at his hips to undo the fastening to his breeches. He moved away again, but this time she moved lower and clasped him, through his breeches. She wrapped her fist around him and squeezed. His eyes closed tightly and his mouth fell open. He gasped. "Kate, don't."

"It's not fair," she whispered against his mouth. "I want to touch you."

His head was thrown back. He looked as if he were in abject misery or ecstasy, possibly both, and Kate rubbed him up and down while he groaned.

"Let me make you feel good, Kate. Let go."

She squeezed him again, and he shuddered but she did let him go, reluctantly, but only because she didn't know what else she could do if he refused to allow her to remove his breeches.

And God help her, she wanted to see what else he was about to do to make her feel good.

His breathing slowed and his finger came back to play with her again, and she shuddered. He pushed his finger inside of her and slowly removed it, again and again. Her head moved back and forth fitfully on the cushions of the sofa. He watched her face, his eyes smoldering.

She clutched at his shoulders. "James, please."

He moved back down her body and the tip of his tongue returned to lick her in the spot that made her eyes roll back in her head. She begged him, pleaded with him, felt his strong jaw moving against her, possessing her.

"Kate, just let go," he whispered huskily, his breath a hot brand against her thigh.

His finger entered her again and stroked unfailingly. He moved the tip of his finger inside her and touched her in a place that made her toes curl and her thighs quiver. "Oh God. James!" Kate shuddered, and her entire body exploded into a mass of shuddering ecstasy. Whatever that man had done, wherever he was touching, it was a spot so perfect it made her want to cry. She rode a wave of shimmering perfection, clinging to his shoulders, holding him, while she cried out his name.

It was several moments before Kate returned to earth. James had just made her feel something beyond extraordinary. She bit her lip. James Bancroft, it seemed, was gifted at more things than just printing presses and perfection. And on the subject of perfection. Now *that* had been perfect.

But for some unknown reason, she couldn't stop the tears that pooled in her eyes. "James," she whispered, as he held her and then helped her to retrieve her gown and right her clothing.

"Yes, Kate?"

"That was . . . amazing."

He smiled at that.

"It makes me sad though . . ."

His head snapped around to face her and he must have seen the tears in her eyes. "Are you unhappy, Kate? Did I hurt you?" He looked so earnest and worried that her heart wrenched.

"No. No, of course not. It was the most incredible thing I've ever felt. But I . . ." She clenched her jaw. Oh God, how could she bring herself to say this to him?

"What? What is it, Kate?"

"It's just that . . . with George I never . . ." She glanced away. "I never experienced anything like that and I . . ."

He nodded and clasped her hand. "Yes?"

She steeled her resolve and closed her eyes. She would just have to come out with it. "It just makes me think you've been with a great many women to have learned how to do that, and that thought makes me sad for some reason."

His soft laughter made her crack open one eye to look at him. "What's funny?"

"A gentleman never tells, of course, and I'm not about to discuss such subjects with you, but let's just say I'm hardly a rake, Kate."

She shook her head and searched his face. "You aren't?"

"No. Not at all."

"But how did you know how to—" Oh, that was it. Her face was probably mottled purple by now.

She'd already pulled on her gown again, and he'd refastened the buttons in the back. She was busily smoothing her skirts when he glanced at her.

"I admit I have some experience, of course, but quality is always better than quantity as far as I'm concerned," he said with a wink.

She couldn't help but smile at that. "But Lord Colton and Lord Ashbourne are your good friends, and their reputations—" She twisted her hands together. She couldn't bring herself to say more.

He arched a brow. "Let's just say there are many things Colton and Ashbourne and I do not have in common, and rakishness happens to be one of them."

She bit her lip. "I know that I don't have any right to be jealous of the other women you've known, James. But I am."

He pulled her close and let her head rest on his shoulder. He stroked her hair and her cheek. "Kate, believe me when I tell you, you have nothing whatsoever to be jealous of."

Kate smiled against his shoulder. It made no sense, but that statement made her ridiculously happy. And the way he was cradling her made her feel another host of emotions she didn't want to examine at present.

Oh, she knew she shouldn't be doing these scandalous things with him in the library or anywhere else for that matter, but she'd enjoyed and adored every single moment of it. She'd like to do it again, actually. Though she couldn't bring herself to tell him that. She wanted him to make love to her. Be her lover. She could admit that to herself now. And she would tell James too. When the time was right. But he'd barely allowed her to touch him tonight, and she doubted he'd break all his self-imposed rules and make love to her. For now. But she intended to make it difficult for him to resist.

The man was a master of all things, and he certainly knew his way around a woman's body. Good God, what he'd made her feel. She could weep now just thinking about it. Oh, how she longed to spend the entire day in bed with him. She smiled to herself. She'd heard stories about women who greatly enjoyed their marital rights. But they seemed more like characters out of folklore to her. Lies told to unsuspecting brides to make their wedding night seem less ghastly, or stories invented by their mothers to keep them from going out of their minds with worry. But now, now, Kate wondered. Perhaps the right groom could make a wedding night better than the folklore even. And in her case, she hadn't even needed a groom. She hid her smile behind her hand. She'd asked Lily once whether her pamphlet was true. *Secrets of a Wedding Night* was all about how horrendous a wedding night could be. It had frightened a great many young women. When Kate had inquired about it, Lily had merely given her an engaging smile and her famous wink and said, "I wrote that before I spent the night with Devon." It had confused Kate at the time, but now she knew exactly what Lily meant.

Kate's body was still feeling all sorts of happy little twinges and pings as James helped her right her final bits of clothing and escorted her to her room. She briefly thought about trying to invite him into her bedchamber but decided against it. She had been scandalous enough today, no use courting more trouble. Yet. Instead, she sighed, and slipped through the door, humming a tune she hadn't hummed since she was eighteen.

"Good night," she murmured, turning back to James and giving him a sly look over one shoulder. It was official, that man was too handsome for his own good. And so, so good at . . . ahem . . . things.

After James saw Kate safely to her bedchamber, he made his way to his own room, cursing himself mentally in five different languages. His cock was throbbing unmercifully. He might just explode in his breeches. He hadn't felt like this since he was . . . a lad, damn it. What the hell was he doing? Very well. It was obvious that he could not. *Could. Not.* Keep his hands off that woman. He shouldn't even try. He wanted her with a madness he had no idea how to combat. His every thought was consumed by her now that he'd touched her so intimately, tasted her, watched her beautiful perfect face as she'd come . . . Oh God, he couldn't help himself. He was going to make love to her if she stayed under his roof. He wouldn't be able to stop himself. Especially not if she tried to touch him again. It had taken every single ounce of self-control he possessed to keep her from unbuttoning his breeches and grasping his naked cock. And oh God, he'd wanted her to. *Really* wanted her to. He ached now just thinking about it. He needed a bloody cold bath. He needed a good bout at fencing. No. He needed to lose himself between her perfect pale thighs.

Damn it. What he needed to do was get her finished pamphlet and keep his distance. Some lunacy had just forced him to admit to her what compelled him. He did want to fix everything. Every bloody injustice in the world. Right every wrong. Make up for the one thing he could never fix. He squeezed his eyes shut. But damn it, he might not be able to fix this. Even if Kate were innocent, Abernathy would have to prove it, just like she'd said. And the evidence against her was overwhelming. She might well be going to her death in a matter of days, and what sort of a bloody cad took liberties with a woman who was about to die? He'd never forgive himself.

He threw open the door to his bedchamber. It cracked loudly against the wall. He called savagely for his valet. The younger man came nearly running down the hall, breathing heavily by the time he entered the bedchamber. "Yes, my lord?"

"Draw me a bath," James commanded in a thunderous tone. "A cold one. Now!"

CHAPTER 25

Lily came barreling at James through the front door of the estate, Annie close on her heels. "Medford, how are you?" She buzzed around him like a solicitous bee, checking him for any sign of damage.

Kate stopped short at the landing to the stairs. She couldn't help but listen. After their interlude last night, she'd begun to feel close to James. So close. But now she was being detestable and eavesdropping. She should step out and greet Lily and Annie, but for the life of her she couldn't force her feet into action. Instead, she remained hidden at the bottom of the stairs.

James laughed. "I'm fine. All in one piece as you can see."

Kate surreptitiously leaned around the wall to see them.

Annie squeezed James's hand. "I was so frightened when I heard, Medford. Thank God you all made it out safely."

"The servants are fine," Lily told him. "Half are staying with me and half with Annie until we can get your house repaired."

James shook his head. "First of all, you didn't have to come all the way out here to tell me that and, secondly, you didn't have to take in the servants. You know I have several properties in London. They can take their pick. But I do appreciate your concern."

Lily shook her head vigorously. "I wanted to take care of them, poor dears. Besides, Mrs. Hartsmeade has been a joy to have around the house. Though she says she misses Themis terribly. Bandit and Leo have attempted to cheer her."

James laughed again. "I'm sure. Thank you for seeing to Mrs. Hartsmeade."

"My pleasure, of course," Lily replied.

"So, tell me, why have you come all this way?" James asked. "If I know the two of you, it's because you're up to something."

Annie shrugged. "We've come to see how you're doing, to visit."

"And to warn you," Lily added.

Kate sucked in her breath. Warn him? Warn him about what?

James shook his head. "I knew it was something. But a warning sounds quite dire."

"It is dire," Lily answered, plunking her hands on her hips.

"We've been to see your town house," Annie announced.

James winced. "How bad is it?"

Lily shook her head. "It's not good. Not good at all."

"It's not completely destroyed, however. They were able to stop the fire before it spread throughout the house. There is smoke damage but it's not a complete loss," Annie added.

James let out his breath. "That's something."

"James." Lily placed her hand on his sleeve. "You're frightening me. I'm worried for you, and Devon is too."

James arched a brow. "I'm sure Colton is quite worried for me," he said, his voice dripping sarcasm.

"Be serious. He is."

Annie nodded. "Jordan is too. He said as much."

Lily wrapped her arm around James's, and the three began to walk toward one of the salons. Kate slipped back against the wall so they wouldn't see her.

Lily's voice carried down the corridor. "Your penchant for always trying to fix everything is getting you in real trouble this time."

Kate pressed her hand to her chest. She couldn't breathe.

"What am I trying to fix?" James asked.

Lily lowered her voice. "Why, Kate, of course. I mean, we believe she is innocent, but you cannot save her, Medford. You must leave it to the courts."

James's reply held an edge. "I'm under no false impressions that I'm a barrister if that's what you mean."

Annie piped up. "We just know you, Medford. And we know how kind you are. Yes, you may have started all of this for a pamphlet, but Jordan says you've hired a runner."

James sighed. "Remind me to thank Ashbourne next time I see him for telling you that."

"We're serious, James," Lily continued.

They paused outside the salon door. Kate struggled to regulate her breathing, but popped her head around the corner to continue to listen. She might as well hear the rest now that she'd already turned into the type of dreadful person who listened to private conversations.

"You are in real trouble this time," Lily added. "Your town house is a shambles and your reputation is in danger. You should hear what they're saying about you on the streets. Have you seen the papers?"

James nodded slowly. "Believe me. I know what they're saying about me."

"You've always prided yourself on your reputation," Annie said. "Are you sure this entire affair is still worth it to you?"

James straightened his cravat. "I'm having the house repaired as we speak."

Lily tossed a hand in the air. "Fine. But what about your reputation?"

He grinned at them. "If I was that worried about my reputation, I wouldn't own a printing press."

"Be serious," Lily insisted.

"But it's not just the house and your reputation, Medford," Annie added. "It's more than that. You're placing yourself in real danger. Someone may try to hurt you, try to kill you. Perhaps the same person who killed the duke."

James opened the door to the salon then, and the three of them filed inside. He called to the butler for tea. Kate slipped back around the wall as the butler made his way to the kitchens so he wouldn't see her.

When the salon door shut behind them, Kate expelled her breath and let her hand slide down to her belly. She felt ill. Physically ill. Lily and Annie had just perfectly expressed every single fear she'd had since she and James had come to the country together. She was ruining his life. And not only that, she was putting it in danger. Yes, he may have wanted the pamphlet, may have started all this to make a profit, but he hadn't expected things to turn out the way they had. He hadn't known how much danger he'd been placing himself and his property in.

Kate had been selfish too. Taking so much time to

write the pamphlet when she could have finished by now. If she'd been gone before the trip to the farm, James's house and reputation might not have been destroyed. No. She had no right to stay. No right to be here any longer. Money or no. Pamphlet or no. It was time to leave. For James's sake.

Kate pressed her fingertips to her temples. She would never spend the night with James now. She knew it. That had been a foolish dream. One that she'd cherished, but foolish nonetheless. It was never meant to be. She must go upstairs, pack the few belongings she still possessed, and leave. She would always be grateful to James for giving her these past days of freedom but she could not, would not, endanger him any longer.

CHAPTER 26

James stood outside the towering heap of what had once been his town house. The freezing wind whipped along the street front. He pulled his cloak around him more tightly and pushed up his collar. The smell of burned wood and the lingering scent of smoke permeated the air. James expelled his breath. Yes. This mess had once been his home. Now it was half rubble. Lily had been right. The first floor was still relatively intact, but the top floors were burned out. All the windows were shattered and mud and debris had been tossed all over the structure. He stared at the building and shook his head.

His town house. His refuge. The place where every speck of dust mattered. He smiled wryly to himself. None of that mattered now, did it? There was far more than a speck of dirt involved here. He groaned. If someone had told him a fortnight ago that he'd be standing here now, staring at the burned-out remains of his house, why, he'd probably have had an attack of nerves. But now, a strange sense of calm came over him. It was just a house. Kate was facing down a death sentence. He couldn't imagine that fear. In comparison, the idea of rebuilding his home was barely more than an inconvenience. What did a home matter, compared with one's life?

Kate. She thought it was her fault that this had happened, but it was actually his. If he'd been more careful that afternoon when they'd returned from the farm, they wouldn't have been seen. He'd let down his guard, and he had only himself to blame.

He kicked a piece of stone with his booted foot. It skipped off the mud in the roadway and settled with a decisive click on a pile of burned wood. He turned and hoisted himself into his waiting carriage. "Abernathy's office," he directed the coachman.

Twenty minutes later, James lowered himself into the seat in front of Mr. Abernathy's desk.

"Give me some good news," James said. "I'm exhausted. I traveled through the night to get back to town for this meeting today."

"Have you seen it yet?" Abernathy asked with a strained look on his face.

"The town house? Yes." James nodded. "But not to worry, my solicitor has already seen to it. The repairs will begin soon."

"Glad to hear it." Abernathy shuffled a mass of papers on his desk and pushed his spectacles up on his nose. "How is her grace?"

"As well as can be expected given the circumstances. What news from Mr. Horton?"

Abernathy frowned. "None, unfortunately. He canceled our meeting Friday, sending a note saying he had to return to Markingham Abbey for a bit more investigation. I hope he'll have something solid by the time he returns."

James sat back in his chair and crossed his heel over his knee. "And the court system?"

"The lord chancellor has scheduled the first hearing for just after Twelfth Night."

James nodded. "What about the court of public opinion?"

"I assume you've read the papers. It's not good, though there are some who've staunchly defended you."

James shrugged. "I expected as much."

Abernathy cleared his throat uncomfortably. "There's something else."

James leaned forward in his seat. "What?"

"I've been told a new story is about to run in this evening's *Times*. The papers have been investigating you. They've discovered you own a printing press. Some are saying you're a disgrace to the peerage."

James hung his head. He let out his breath. His reputation, the one he'd spent his whole life building, gone in the blink of an eye. "I see," he said calmly. "But you say I have some supporters? That's encouraging."

"Indeed you do. The lord chancellor is one of them."

James arched a brow. "The lord chancellor? Really?"

"Yes, he's firmly in your corner."

"Glad to hear it. Anyone else of note?"

"If the rumors are to be believed, the Prince Regent himself has weighed in on your behalf. He says he's anxious to hear the details straight from you and refuses to discuss the matter until he does so."

This time James whistled. "Now that is high praise indeed. Normally, his royal highness doesn't shy away from a good bit of gossip."

Abernathy nodded. "Agreed. It's a very good sign."

"And what of Kate's reputation? Everyone still believes she's guilty, don't they?"

"That's something else I wanted to mention to you, my lord. Many of the details of the case have been leaked to the papers. One wonders who knew so much. Personally, I have my suspicions that it was Lady Bettina, but the fact remains that the evidence, when presented as it has been in the papers, appears extremely damaging."

James clenched his jaw. "Are you saying there is no hope, Abernathy?"

"I'm saying I believe it's time that we explored the possibility of alternate defenses."

James narrowed his eyes on the barrister. "Alternate defenses?"

"Yes. I mentioned them to her grace when we first met. Self-preservation. Provocation."

James scrubbed his hands across his face. "Kate said no to both of those."

"Yes, but she does not know the law as I do. The way things stand, I firmly believe those are her best chances for acquittal. They might just save her life."

James nodded once. "I understand."

Abernathy's face wore a decided frown. He pulled on the lapels of his coat. "My lord, I think it's time you spoke to her grace. Explained to her that it is in her best interest to explore both options as possible defenses. You must ensure she understands."

"I believe she already knows how dire it is, Abernathy."

"But I don't think she understands how very little there is to go on without preparing a vigorous defense."

James pushed out of the chair and stood to leave. He pressed his lips together. "I'll speak with her."

"Good."

James made his way to the door and pulled on his coat. "Thank you for all of your help, Abernathy. Much obliged."

Abernathy gave him a stern stare. "Tell me, my lord. Is it worth it?"

James wrinkled his brow. "Worth what?"

"Is the pamphlet worth the loss of your town house?"

James placed his hat atop his head and tipped it forward. "I believe she's innocent, Abernathy. Now just get your runner to prove it."

CHAPTER 27

James returned to Hamphill Park the next day feeling vaguely restless. The work of repairing his town house was already under way, he'd seen to that. He'd even taken the opportunity to make some improvements to the property and was having water closets installed in all of the upstairs bedchambers. He'd also seen to it that all of the servants were installed at his other properties around town, and he had a guard standing watch over the progress at the ruined town house day and night. For the most part, everything in the house could be replaced, but Kate, if she'd been hurt . . .

Damn that mob, their small-mindedness and their assumptions. How dare they judge the woman before the court system even had a chance? He smiled wryly at his own thought. That's how everything went in London. You were guilty until proven innocent. And the court of public opinion often was more unforgiving than the most disapproving judge could be. With the way she'd already been convicted in people's minds, even if by some miracle Kate was acquitted by the House of Lords, there would still be a huge struggle to regain any semblance of innocence in the hearts and minds of the people of London. Her pamphlet might serve to alleviate a bit of that, but he made no pretensions to the fact that the pamphlet would serve more to satisfy the public's curiosity than to convince them to believe anything other than what they had already settled upon. But at least it would give Kate a chance. An attempt to sway public opinion.

Kate.

James shook his head. He couldn't stop thinking about her. Specifically, he couldn't stop thinking about their interlude in the library the other night. He'd called himself a dozen kinds of fool, cursed himself repeatedly, and vowed he would never repeat the act, but in the end, all he could do was replay it over and over in his mind. He could think of little else. Kate's velvety soft skin, her maddening sweet scent, her luscious breasts filling his hands, her red-gold hair spilling over her shoulders, her perfect full lips. He pictured her that way, over and over again. Only when he pictured it, he pictured her in his bed.

Damn it. He was getting hard again just thinking about it. And he was doing nothing more than torturing himself. No doubt if she were to clear her name—and that was a huge if—she would want nothing more to do with aristocrats and marriage and the *ton* and Society. And he bloody well couldn't blame her. But that's all James was, those things. He had nothing more to offer her. Aside from a position as the authoress of a scandalous pamphlet, of course. Better to be known as an authoress than a murderess, he supposed. But how could they ever progress into anything more when they'd met under such dire circumstances? He'd hired her essentially, and she'd used him to get out of prison. Not quite the auspicious type of courtship one dreamed of.

And what was he even thinking, calling it a "courtship"? He wasn't courting Kate. No, he was taking ungodly liberties with her whenever he had a chance because he couldn't seem to keep his hands from her. He'd suffered his own mental recriminations for it time and time again, and he'd continue to do so, but now, right now, all he wanted to do was be in her company again.

He would talk to her about her defense, just as Abernathy had requested. Perhaps claiming provocation was the best course of action. Perhaps the House of Lords would look more kindly upon her if she told them the hideous way her husband had treated her when he'd been alive. Yes, he'd speak to her about it. Later. Right now, all he could think about was seeing her face.

He quickened his step. His boots crunched over the frozen pebbled drive as he strode to the front door. Oh God, he was anxious to see her. He was nearly running. He tugged at the front door's brass handle and doffed his hat and coat. He shoved them toward the butler who looked a bit chagrined to have been thwarted in his job of opening the portal. Barely breaking his stride, James made his way to the library where Kate usually sat, writing.

He pushed open the door, a smile on his face.

His gaze darted across the room. Empty.

His smile faded. Leaving the door open, he turned on his heel and made his way back toward the front of the house to the gold salon. Was she taking tea?

He pushed open the door to the salon and strode inside. Also empty.

He frowned now. Perhaps she was napping.

He stepped back into the hall. A housemaid scurried past.

"Have you seen her grace?" James asked.

The maid cleared her throat. "No, my lord. Not today."

James frowned again. She hadn't come downstairs all day? That was unlike her. Perhaps she was feeling ill. Wanting to go up straightaway and see her, he stopped himself. It wouldn't do to indulge himself like that. No. He shook his head. He'd send up a note later and check on her. He'd ask for a meeting with her, to discuss her defense. And he would sit safely on the opposite side of the desk from her when he did so.

Hoping to distract himself from thoughts of Kate, James made his way back down the hallway, past the library, to his study.

Themis leaped up from the rug and rushed to greet him. "Good to see you, girl," he said, scratching the dog's golden head.

Themis following him, James strode over to his desk and threw himself into his chair. He scrubbed his hands across his face and expelled his breath. Something caught his attention from the corner of his eye. There was a small bundle of parchment sitting on the top center of the desk. He furrowed his brow.

He leaned closer to get a better look. His name was written on it.

In Kate's handwriting.

He grabbed up the letter, ripped open the wax seal, and unfolded the thing. His eyes quickly scanned the words.

Dearest James,

By the time you read this, I will be gone. I couldn't put you in danger any longer. I'm so sorry for the damage I've done to your life. Enclosed is the pamphlet. I hope it is all you expected it to be. I'm hiring a coach and going back to prison

where I belong. I think we both know we may never
see each other again. It's better this way. I'm pre-
pared to face my fate. Thank you for everything.
You were so good to me.
Kate

James read it again twice more, as if the words
would change if he repeated them enough times. The
sapphires, the ones he'd given her the night of their ball
lay on the desk. He clenched the necklace in his fist.

"No, Kate," he whispered, letting the note fall to the
desktop. He grabbed up the other pages and shuffled
through them. There it was, her story. The pamphlet.
What she'd wanted to say about what had happened to
her. But he didn't need to read it. He already knew.
He'd heard her story as he'd come to know her over the
last several days. She was innocent. She was innocent
and lovely, and she might die because of the callous
treatment of her husband and the failure of some snivel-
ing coward to admit to murder. It was an injustice. It
wasn't fair.

James crumpled the papers in his hands and threw
them to the floor. By God, he'd hire another runner, a
dozen runners! He wouldn't stop until they unearthed
every single fact of what had happened that night, until
they proved Kate's innocence.

He was going to save her. He had to.

CHAPTER 28

When James returned to London, he went straight to the club. He wanted nothing more than to sit there and have a drink . . . or three. He wasn't a drinker, never had been, but the pastime always seemed to help Colton and Ashbourne when they were out of sorts. Might as well take it up. And God knew now seemed as good a time as any.

James sat alone at the club. It seemed the other club members had read all about his scandal in the paper. And while the club had admitted him, he was certainly not greeted by his usual string of friends and acquaintances. In fact, the room he'd entered had managed to empty quite soon after his arrival. He took a seat near a table and rested his chin in his propped-up palm. He didn't give a bloody damn about the *ton*'s opinion of him right now. All he could think about was Kate. How was she? Sitting in the Tower? Was she cold? Scared? Lonely? Bloody hell, she must be all of those things. And he couldn't even visit her. It would be too dangerous. For her and for him and for more reasons than one.

He'd barely downed the first half of his glass of

brandy, when Colton and Ashbourne slid into empty seats next to him.

"I'm warning you both," he growled. "I'm in no mood for your antics this evening."

Ashbourne flashed a smile. "Antics?" He poked Colton in the ribs with an elbow. "Now how do you like that? Antics. And after you've been so good to him and offered to let him stay in your house, Colton."

"Thank you, but I've got plenty of houses of my own," James replied, downing the rest of his glass and calling for another.

Colton stretched out his legs and crossed them casually at the ankles. "Yes, well, I'd like to know what sort of antics you ascribe to us. We merely came here for a drink. Had very little idea you'd even be here, Medford."

James narrowed his eyes on them. "Why do I seriously doubt that? Besides, shouldn't you both be at home with your wives?"

Ashbourne snorted. "What? Don't tell me you haven't already guessed that our wives were the ones who sent us?"

"Yes," Colton replied with a nod. "They aren't welcome in the club, or I daresay they'd be here themselves."

Ashbourne glanced across the room. "Though to be honest, I wouldn't put it past Annie to climb in the window."

James growled under his breath. "Where is the footman with that bloody drink?"

Colton's eyes widened. "Well, well, well. This must be serious. You, Lord Perfect, are not one to imbibe. And two drinks in one night no less. Tsk. Tsk. Tsk."

James gritted his teeth. "Lord Perfect," he mumbled. "That damn moniker. And that's exactly what I've always been. The perfect student, the perfect peer, the perfect friend, the perfect printer." He let his voice trail off. But there were two roles he'd failed at. Two that haunted him. Not so perfect after all.

"What are you saying, Medford?" Ashbourne cupped a hand behind his ear.

James tossed a hand in the air, dismissing the question. "Let's get this over with, shall we? What exactly do you two want to know?"

"Want to know? Don't you think you owe us an explanation?" Ashbourne reached for his own brandy from the footman who had returned with three glasses.

James watched them through blurry eyes. Seemed Ashbourne and Colton had a standing drink order at the club. No surprise there.

James exchanged his empty glass for a full one. "Not particularly," he drawled.

"There's nothing you want to tell us?" Colton took a sip of his own drink.

"Like what?" James feigned ignorance.

Colton motioned to James's snifter. "Like why you're set on drinking yourself into oblivion tonight?"

Ashbourne shook his head. "Yes, Medford, I must admit I never saw *this* coming."

James growled again before taking another hefty swallow. "It's not as if I've murdered a man." He glared at Ashbourne. Ashbourne had killed a man last spring. A man who had just shot and nearly killed Colton, granted, but if he were going to judge, two could play at that game.

Colton glanced around to ensure no one else overheard them. He lowered his voice. "No, but Kate has . . . possibly."

"She has not!" James slammed his fist on the table and the glasses bounced.

Colton's brows shot up. "You sound certain of that."

"I am," James replied through clenched teeth.

"Has Horton found the proof, then?" Ashbourne replied.

"Not yet." James shook his head.

"And what of the pamphlet?" Colton asked. "Will you be printing it in time for Christmastide reading?'

James pulled the crumpled papers from his coat pocket and tossed them on the table. Colton grabbed them up, and Ashbourne leaned over and read across his shoulder. The pair was silent for several minutes while James continued to drink.

Then Ashbourne whistled. "Sounds as if the duchess had one hell of a time being married to Markingham, poor woman. This pamphlet is sure to raise a few eyebrows."

Colton tossed the wrinkled pages back onto the table. "I agree."

"I don't give a damn about the pamphlet," James ground out, tossing back a large amount of his drink.

Ashbourne whistled again. "But it's sure to be a considerable source of income for yourself, is it not?"

James's voice was savage. "I told you I don't give a bloody damn about it."

Colton rolled his eyes. "So, that's it. You just plan to restore your house, let your reputation and hers suffer, and go on about your life as if nothing ever happened?"

"No, first I intend to see Kate cleared of the charges. Then I'll go about my life." James signaled for the footman to bring him another drink.

"Please tell me you're not thinking of actually having a life with the duchess," Ashbourne said. "You do know her reputation is shredded beyond all repair. You'd have to leave London, your business, Parliament, your entire life, to be with her."

James's only reply was a narrowed-eye glare. And

then, "Haven't you seen the papers? My reputation is already in shreds. Besides, she's gone back to the Tower. I used her for what she could bring me. I wouldn't blame her if she detests me."

Colton sighed. "But yet you still want to fix it. Just like our Lord Perfect."

James half stood and leaned menacingly over the table toward the marquis, his fists braced against the wood. "I'm warning you, Colton, say another word . . ."

Colton put up his hands in a conciliatory gesture. "Good God, Medford. I wouldn't fight you in the mood you seem to be in at present. I value my life and so does my wife."

James sat back down and scrubbed a hand through his hair. He downed another gulp of his drink. "Good."

Ashbourne whistled a third time. "Drinking? Not caring about business? Mussing up your hair? Bloody hell, Medford. Look at you. You're a mess. Don't tell me you've gone and fallen in love."

CHAPTER 29

"My lord. My lord." Abernathy's voice shook as he hurried into the study James had been temporarily using at one of his other London properties. Locke hadn't even announced the man. Abernathy must have raced through the house without stopping.

James tossed his quill aside and sat up straight. "What is it?"

"I had a visit from Horton today." The older man was breathing heavily and his face was quite red.

"And?"

Abernathy paused in an attempt to catch his breath. "The Duke of Markingham's valet confessed after another one of the servants came forward and pointed the finger at him."

James's eyes went wide. He scrubbed his hand across his face and jumped up from his seat. "Say that again."

Mr. Abernathy barely paused for a quick breath. "One of the footmen at Markingham Abbey claimed the valet had confessed to him."

James sucked in his breath. No. This couldn't be happening. Could it? He braced his hands atop the desk and stared Abernathy in the eye. "Why did the servant just now come forward?"

"Perhaps his conscience was tugging at him, my lord. I don't know. But the magistrate was called in and the confession was repeated in front of him. He's on the way to report the entire affair to the lord chancellor here in London this morning."

James searched the barrister's face. "What does this mean, Abernathy . . . will Kate—"

Abernathy nodded rapidly. "She should be freed in a matter of hours, my lord."

James closed his eyes and reopened them again, slowly.

"There will be a great deal of legal work still to be done, my lord, to be sure, but once the accusation is retracted and the charges dropped, her grace shall be a free woman. And given her title, they're sure to expedite the matter with all due haste."

James slowly sat back down though he remained on the edge of the seat. "Thank you, Abernathy. Thank you very much."

"Yes, well. I wanted to let you know immediately, your lordship." Abernathy turned toward the door. "I'll just be going to see to all of it."

"Abernathy?" James's voice was steady.

"Yes, my lord?"

"Why did the valet kill Markingham?"

Abernathy shook his head. "Apparently, the duke informed his valet that morning that he intended to replace him with a different man."

James arched a brow. "Why's that?"

"It seems Lady Bettina had taken a dislike to him. She had someone in mind from her own household who aspired to the position."

James's eyebrow shot up. "Not very sporting of Mark-ingham but hardly a reason to kill a man."

"Agreed, my lord." Abernathy bowed. "From what I understand, he'd been employed by Markingham for a great many years. Had served his father, too. No doubt the man was in shock."

"And so he decided to murder him?" James asked.

"Unfortunately, the duke just so happened to have given his valet his pistol that morning. He'd asked him to see to it that it was properly cleaned. The valet was still holding it when their argument began. Seems it was a crime of passion." Abernathy shook his head. "Ill-fated timing to be sure."

James pursed his lips. "And the valet didn't seem to mind allowing the duchess to be accused of murder?"

Abernathy sighed. "Murder charges tend to bring out the coward in many a man, my lord. Apparently, the valet has been racked with guilt over having put the duchess in such a position. He said he never expected her to be charged. Said he'd hoped Lady Bettina would take the blame. But he has been too frightened to step forward and clear the duchess's name. Mr. Horton's continual presence unnerved him. He drank himself into a stupor two nights ago and revealed all to his friend the footman. That chap quickly came forward to report what he'd been told."

James just shook his head. It was amazing. Truly amazing.

"Oh, and one more thing," Abernathy added, his hand on the door handle. "Apparently the valet shot the duke in the wardrobe. The thick wooden walls of the room must have muffled the sound of the shot. He dragged his body into the main bedchamber and cleaned up the blood, it seems."

"That explains why no one heard it, I suppose," James replied.

Abernathy nodded. "It's a happy day for the duchess, my lord, to be sure. I cannot wait to go and tell her."

"By all means then, go." James gestured toward the door.

After Abernathy left, James leaned back in his chair and folded his hands behind his neck. Themis trotted up to the side of his chair, waiting to be petted. "It happened, old girl," he murmured to the dog, pulling out a hand and patting her on the head. "She's free."

Themis nuzzled his hand and let out a decidedly emphatic bark.

James pressed a fingertip to the spot between his eyes. Relief washed through him. He'd been anxious for days, hoping against hope. And now that he'd heard the news, he could scarcely believe it. He wished he could see Kate's beautiful face when she learned she was free.

James spun around in his chair. Ever since that fool Ashbourne had asked him if he was in love, it was all he could think about. Love? No. Love had always been for people who were less controlled than he, less restricted. He couldn't love Kate. Could he?

Oh, what did it matter? Even if he were madly in love with her, she wanted nothing to do with him. She'd returned to the bloody Tower after all. She'd chosen a prison instead of him and his house. And he didn't blame her. He'd inserted himself in her life during her darkest hour. Used her for her story and her circumstances. He'd placed her in an impossible position and practically forced her to write a pamphlet. Why would she ever want to see him again?

And even if she did want to see him again, what possible excuse could he conjure to imply a visit was necessary? He owed her money, but he could easily dispatch a servant with that. There was no reason for him to assume she even wanted to see him again. Hadn't she said so in her note? That they would never see each other again? No. He would not seek her out. Even if it drove him mad. Or killed him.

Or both.

When Mr. Abernathy left her cell, Kate's knees gave way. She crumpled to the cold stone floor, shudders racking her body. She was saved. Alive. She huddled in a ball, tears streaming down her face. She'd never allowed herself to hope for this. Not really. Or at least she'd told herself that lie all these weeks. But now, every bit of anxiety and emotion came pouring out. She pulled a handkerchief from her sleeve and sobbed, unabashedly sobbed, relief rolling through her in huge, crashing waves. She'd been saved. Saved. There was some justice in this world after all. Thank you, God. But it hadn't been God, had it? She had James to thank for it. The odds had been stacked firmly against her. She hadn't dared to hope. But James. James had. Despite all the evidence to the contrary, he'd hired Abernathy and Mr. Horton. He'd saved her.

She pulled herself up, her back resting against her bed frame, and hugged her knees to her chest. She wiped her eyes. She blew her nose. And she breathed. Just breathed.

What did this really mean? She was still an outcast. She'd never be able to live down the scandal. She'd still have to leave London and never come back. A little smile popped to her lips. But she was alive. Alive. And exonerated. She had another chance at life. Another chance to start over in this world. To not make the same mistake again. Despite the tears that continued to roll down her cheeks, she smiled widely this time. It wouldn't be difficult. Not making the same mistake merely involved staying as far away from Society as possible and not marrying again. Especially not a peer, and especially not one who didn't truly love her. An image of James flashed unbidden into her mind.

That was simple, wasn't it?

CHAPTER 30

"So the valet confessed. Just like that?" Lily asked, shaking her head, and taking a healthy draught from her glass of wine.

James was at dinner that evening at Ashbourne's town house with Annie, Ashbourne, Lily, and Colton. While his friends asked him a series of questions about Kate and the case, he sat staring at the wall, halfheartedly pushing his food around his plate, and being blasted awful company.

"Seems so," James replied.

"And Kate will be out of prison as early as tonight?" Annie asked.

"Yes." James nodded.

"I'm so happy for her," Lily breathed. "I just knew she was innocent. But wherever will she go? She has no family, and I cannot imagine the duke's mother will want her. Even with her dower, she would be mad to try to live there."

James grimaced. He'd been thinking many of the same thoughts all day. Where indeed would she go? He'd sent a footman to the Tower earlier with the money he owed her. He couldn't bear to think of her on the streets. At least with money, she could stay in a hotel somewhere. But the money had come back with a small note penned in Kate's own hand. "I won't take this." That's all it said. Nothing more. If he'd harbored any doubt, now he knew. She hated him. Hated him so much she wouldn't even take the money that was rightfully hers. Damn it. He'd ruined everything.

"I'm not sure what she'll do," he said quietly. "I haven't spoken to her."

"Will you see her again, Medford?" Annie asked in a too astute tone.

"No." Had his answer been too quick? Too sharp? He expelled his breath and tried again. "That is to say, I see no reason to. But I wish her well, of course."

"Well, I just cannot believe it," Lily replied. "To think, after all of these weeks poor Kate spent in the Tower and the valet was guilty the entire time. Why, he might have murdered the footman for knowing. That man was brave to come forward."

"I agree," James replied. "Kate owes that man her life."

"She owes you her life too, Medford," Annie said. "You hired the runner who eventually caused the valet to confess. Kate never would have got such a vigorous investigation and defense without you."

"She owes me nothing," James said simply. He glanced around at the other occupants of the dinner table. They each were making quite a show of being completely absorbed in their meals. Even Ashbourne didn't meet his eyes. And he better not bloody well mention love again—not tonight, not ever—or James just might jump across the table and pummel the bloke.

James turned his attention back to his own meal. He stabbed a flaky bit of cod with his fork and raised it to his lips. He took the bite, chewed and swallowed, but it tasted like sawdust in his mouth.

Minutes later, he pushed his chair back from the table and plucked his napkin from his lap. "I'm sorry, Annie. But I fear you'll have a much more pleasant evening without me."

"Nonsense, Medford," Annie said, putting down her fork, leaning over and patting his hand. "But I completely understand if you'd rather leave. You've been through quite a lot. You must be exhausted."

"Fine then, run off." Lily smiled at him from across the table. "You do still plan to join us day after next, don't you, Medford? At Colton House, for Christmas? And of course you'll be coming to Catherine Eversly's New Year's Eve masquerade ball?"

"Yes, of course." James tried to summon a smile. That's all there was to do now. To carry on with life with some semblance of normalcy. Christmastide, the masquerade. Events that came and went every year. This year was no different. Well, should be no different.

He stood, tossed his napkin to his chair, and bade everyone farewell. Then he slipped out the doors of the dining room.

That's right. He'd just have to pretend everything was normal again until it was.

As soon as Medford left the room, Lily folded her hands in front of her and leaned forward. "Poor man. But I'm a bit glad he's gone, to be honest, because there's something I wanted to speak to all of you about," she said in a loud whisper.

Devon, Annie, and Jordan all gave her their full attention.

"Lily, what are you up to?" her husband asked in a warning tone.

"Nothing," Lily replied innocently, batting her eyelashes.

"Now even I don't believe that," Annie said on a giggle.

"Neither do I," Jordan replied with a grin.

Lily winked at her sister and brother-in-law. "It's just that . . . I'm planning to invite Kate to Colton House for Christmas too."

Jordan whistled. "Do you really think that's a good idea?"

Lily pushed up her chin. "Why, the poor woman has nowhere else to go. She's still an outcast to the *ton,* and she has no family. She may be free now, but she's got no one. We cannot leave her alone on Christmas."

Devon lifted his glass. "I, for one, applaud the idea, Lily."

Lily widened her eyes. "You do?"

"Yes. You're right. Kate's got nowhere else to go. But I do think you should tell Medford."

Lily fluttered her hand in the air. "I disagree. I think it may be best for both of them if they don't know ahead of time."

"I have to agree with Lily," Annie said, reaching across the table to nab another plum tart. "Both might decline the invitation if they know the other is likely to arrive."

"And shouldn't that be *their* choice?" Jordan asked his wife.

"Ordinarily, yes," Annie agreed with a resolute nod. "But this is a special situation." She turned her attention back to her sister. "Oh, Lily, do you truly think Kate will come?"

Lily shrugged one shoulder. "I hope so. And I don't see why not. Where else will she go?"

Devon crossed his arms over his chest and regarded

his wife down the length of his nose. "Why exactly do you think Medford wouldn't want to see Kate?"

Lily gave her husband a sly smile. "Oh, I've every reason to believe Medford wants to see Kate. I just wonder if Kate wants to see Medford. And Medford's too blasted stubborn to admit he wants to see her. You heard what he said tonight."

"So you intend to trick Kate into it? Besides, how do you know she doesn't want to see him?" Devon continued.

Lily plucked a plum off the top of the tart she'd been eating and popped it into her mouth. "You heard James. She left his house voluntarily and returned to the prison without saying good-bye. She refused the money he sent her. There is obviously something amiss between the two of them."

Jordan grinned and arched a brow. "And you two intend to get to the bottom of it, don't you?" He looked back and forth between his sister-in-law and his wife.

"Precisely," Lily replied with a smile.

Annie poked at her tart with her fork. "I think it's an excellent idea. Obviously, what this delicate situation calls for is a Christmastide house party."

Jordan winked at her. "Remember, darling. House parties can get people into a great deal of trouble. We ended up married after one."

Annie gave her husband a knowing smile. "Exactly why one is necessary, my dear."

Devon leaned back in his chair. "Far be it from me to argue with the two most determined matchmakers in the country. But I would just caution you both. Be careful, ladies. Medford hasn't been in a mood lately to be trifled with."

Lily crossed her arms over her chest. "Who's trifling? We're attempting to help him."

"Help him how?" Devon arched a brow.

"Why, by placing him and Kate back together in the same house, of course. It's obvious to anyone they have feelings for each other."

Devon gave her a skeptical look. "Be careful, my love. There's more than just the murder trial separating those two."

CHAPTER 31

Kate arrived in the country at Colton House bright and early on Christmas Eve. She'd been staying at a hotel in London for the past two nights after her release from prison. The lord chancellor had seen to it that she received her dower money post haste.

Thankfully, there had been no angry mobs waiting for her when she'd left the Tower. Only Mr. Abernathy and a hired coach, waiting to take her wherever she wished to go. The city may have accepted the fact that she wasn't guilty, but she still couldn't return to her husband's property, for more reasons than one. Even given her acquittal, she wouldn't be welcomed by her mother-in-law. And Oliver, George's cousin, would have taken over the properties by now or at least would do so soon. She wasn't about to go live in the dower house with her hateful mother-in-law. And most importantly, she was free. Free not only from the Tower, but from her old life. And she refused to go back to Markingham Abbey and become a prisoner of another sort again. No, she would make her own way in the world now, somehow.

She'd readily accepted Lily's invitation to spend Christmas at Colton House, however. She needed a bit more time. Time and space to decide what she would do next, where she would go. Lily had sent Lord Colton's coach to gather her and the horses made it back to the country estate just before a light snow began to fall.

"Merry Christmas, Kate! Oh, we're so happy you've come," Lily said, hugging Kate as soon as she walked through the front doors.

Kate pulled off her bonnet and allowed the butler to take her cloak before greeting her hostess with a wide smile. "Merry Christmas to you! And thank you so much for your kind invitation, Lily."

"Come with me," Lily said, grabbing her by the arm and pulling her along. "Annie and Devon's son, Justin, and I were in the salon singing Christmas carols. Devon and Jordan are off doing something. They wouldn't tell us what. I suspect it has to do with Christmas presents."

Kate happily followed her friend, and just as they were moving through the foyer, a fox and a funny little striped gray and white animal ran past. Kate stopped and rubbed her eyes.

"Oh that." Lily fluttered a hand in the air. "That's just Dash and Bandit. Don't mind them."

Kate couldn't suppress her laugh. "James said you were a bit . . . unconventional . . . but until this moment, I wasn't entirely sure if he was jesting."

"I'm afraid he wasn't," Lily replied, shaking her head.

Another laugh from Kate. "And here I was worried I wouldn't be allowed to be a duchess with a pig."

"Nonsense," Lily replied with a laugh. "I think a duchess with a pig sounds absolutely divine."

Lily took her by the arm again and they made their way down the corridor. "In addition to a fox and a raccoon-like dog, we also have a little boy and a variety of other dogs here at Colton House. I'm sure you'll meet them all before long."

Kate squeezed her arm and Lily stopped. "Thank you again for your invitation, Lily. I don't know what I'd do without you. You and Annie are my only friends." She glanced away.

"A temporary state, I'm sure," Lily reassured her, with an encouraging smile. "I only hope you enjoy your Christmas with us."

Kate nodded. "Considering I've been convinced this would be my last Christmas and now it's not, I'm sure to enjoy it immensely," she replied with a shaky laugh.

Annie came bounding out of the door to their left. "Ah, Justin said you'd come. He was watching from the landing."

Kate glanced up to see a handsome little boy of no more than five or six with dark curly hair and equally dark watchful eyes looking at her. "Is that Justin? He looks so much like his father."

"He does, doesn't he?" Lily gestured for the boy to come downstairs. Justin made his way down the steps and bowed an adorable little bow to Kate. Kate's heart melted. Oh how she wished she had a little boy of her own. The thought hit her out of nowhere, stealing her breath.

"Justin, say 'Merry Christmas' to her grace, Duchess Kate," Lily said.

Kate shook her head frantically. "Oh no, no, no. Not Duchess Kate, just Kate." She smiled at the boy.

"Well, Kate then," Lily amended, nodding to Justin to let him know it was all right.

"Merry Christmas, Lady Kate," Justin said, with another little formal bow.

"A pleasure to meet you, Master Justin," Kate replied, laughing. She swept a grand curtsy in front of him.

The boy blushed beautifully, before turning to his stepmother. "Lily, may I have a sweet?"

Lily gave him a conspiratorial grin. "It depends. Have you been good?" She crossed her arms over her chest and stared down her nose at the boy, but the smile that lurked at the corners of her mouth belied the teasing nature of her remarks.

Justin nodded earnestly. "Quite, quite good."

This time Lily nodded. "Then yes, you may have a sweet. Tell Cook I said so."

The boy scampered off and Lily watched him go with a bright, adoring look on her face. "Ah, he's such a good boy. Such a dear. Far too intelligent for his years though, I'm afraid. Not much gets by him. The tutors tell Devon he's a genius."

"Not to mention he's adorable and extremely well behaved," Kate said with a smile, a twinge of regret in her heart for the child she would never have.

Lily and Annie each took one of Kate's arms and led her into the salon on the left. They ushered her in, and Lily gestured to a seat on the sofa. "Tea will be served momentarily."

She waited for Kate to take a seat on the sofa before she added, "Well, now, I nearly choked on my tart when Lord Medford told us the valet had killed the duke."

Annie curled up on the opposite side of the sofa and nodded emphatically to Kate. She clutched her chest. "Yes. If a man cannot trust his valet, whom can he trust?"

"I never knew him well," Kate admitted. "Tucker was always gone with George to London. It's difficult to believe George intended to let him go. They'd been together for ages. Apparently, they'd had rows before. I'd heard the other servants whispering a time or two about Tucker's awful temper but I'd never seen it myself."

Lily shook her head. "Just between us, I was always convinced Lady Bettina did it."

Annie bit her lip. "I wonder if Lady Bettina suspected the valet."

"I've thought about it all so much, and I'll never make sense of any of it," Kate replied. "I'm just glad to be free. Though I still cannot truly believe it. And please don't think less of me for not wearing mourning clothes. I fear it would be entirely disingenuous of me, and with my reputation already in tatters, I fail to see the point."

"On the contrary, we don't think less of you at all," Lily said, patting her hand.

"Absolutely not," Annie added. "You'll just have to put all that behind you now, start a new life."

Kate shook her head and glanced down at her lap. "I don't know how. I have nothing. Nothing more than my life. Though, believe me, for that I am immensely thankful."

"Let us help you, Kate," Lily said.

Kate glanced up. "No. You've both done so much for me already. I don't know how I'll ever be able to repay you. After Christmas, I'll find a way."

"You may stay as long as you like," Lily said. "I hope you know that. Either here at Colton House or at our town house in London."

Kate pulled one of the light blue embroidered pillows from the sofa up to her chest. "I couldn't take such advantage, Lily. I'm ever so thankful for the invitation to spend Christmas here, but after the new year, I think I shall go to the Continent. I'm no longer welcome in London, I realize that."

Lily squeezed her hand. "Whatever you decide,

we'll support you. And there's no need to make a decision today."

Kate smiled at that. Letting the pillow drop to her lap, she reached out and squeezed both sisters' hands simultaneously. "You're both too good to me." She bit the inside of her cheek to keep the tears from spilling from her eyes. Then she gave her head a hard shake. "So, tell me, how is Viscount Medford? I've made inquiries but . . . he hasn't published the pamphlet yet, has he?"

"No . . . he hasn't," Lily said, just before she and Annie exchanged glances. "But there is something we must tell you."

Kate's smile faded. "What? He's all right, isn't he?" She pressed her hand to her chest.

"Oh yes, he's perfectly fine," Lily hastened to say. "It's just that . . . well . . . Lord Medford will be here for Christmas too."

Kate's heart pounded. Her chest felt tight. The room tilted all of a sudden. She shouldn't be surprised. Of course James was welcome here at his friends' house. He always would be. She was the interloper. The stranger. "I should have guessed."

"You don't mind, do you?" Lily asked quietly. "Please tell me you're not upset."

Kate tried to laugh. "What sort of an ingrate would I be if I tried to tell you whom to invite to your own party?" She swallowed. "But I must say, I'm not sure he'll be pleased to see me. I would hate to ruin his holiday."

Annie patted Kate's hand. "No. No. Lord Medford has been worried about the same thing. He thinks you don't want to see him."

Kate furrowed her brow. "Why would he think that?"

Annie glanced at her. "Because you left his house

and went back to the Tower and . . . He told us you returned the money he sent you."

Kate glanced at her hands folded in her lap. "I couldn't take his money. His town house was destroyed because of me."

"Don't worry. You'll talk. I'm sure you two will sort it out." Lily clapped her hands. "In the meantime, we can all just enjoy Christmas."

Kate sighed. "It's fine, my friends. I shall not ruin your holidays with my histrionics. You've invited your friend Lord Medford to share the season with you, and I shall make no trouble for you. I should never have tried to put you in a position where you felt you had to choose."

Annie and Lily exchanged glances. "Thank you for understanding."

Kate stood up and hastily smoothed out her skirts. "Would you mind, terribly, if I go lie down for a bit, I'm just exhausted and—"

"Say no more," Lily said, ringing for a servant. "I'll have one of the maids show you to your room immediately."

After Kate left, Annie turned to Lily, her arms crossed over her chest, a catlike smile on her face. "One part down. At least, we've got her to agree to be in the same room with him."

CHAPTER 32

The snow was falling steadily by the time James arrived at Colton House. The sun had just begun to set across the Surrey countryside, and the sky was turning dark. It was speckled with the white snowflakes that wandered to the earth like fat little clouds.

James brushed through the front doors of the manor, a cold wind sweeping in with him. He shook the snow off his hat and coat and stomped his boots before turning to greet Lily with a present under his arm. Themis, whom he'd brought with him, gave a hard shake to rid her fur of the excess snow, then she quickly bounded after Bandit and Leo who had materialized from the hallway.

"Aren't they having a grand time already?" he said with a laugh, as the dogs raced away.

"Obviously they are in the Christmas spirit," Lily replied, hugging her friend. "Merry Christmas, James."

"Merry Christmas, Lily." He returned her smile as best he could, but he couldn't think of the last time he'd been so melancholy on Christmas. He'd told himself during the entire ride to Colton House that it had absolutely nothing to do with Kate. Why, he hadn't even known the woman two weeks ago, and in two more he'd have completely forgotten about her. Wouldn't he? Oh blast, even as he had the thought, he knew it wasn't true.

Where was Kate tonight? Who was she celebrating Christmas with? Surely Mr. Abernathy had seen to it that she had someplace to go. Blast it. James should have seen to it that she wasn't alone, only she'd made it quite clear that her association with him was at an end.

"Come into the library, Medford," Lily said, pulling him from his thoughts. "Devon and Jordan are there having drinks."

He arched a brow. "Of course they are."

Lily returned his look. "Don't act so smug. Devon told me he found you drinking at the club not so long ago."

Medford rolled his eyes and followed Lily down the hall, the present still tucked under his arm. "Hmm. Now that you mention it, a drink sounds perfect."

Lily led him down the marble hallway to the library. The large mahogany doors swung open to reveal Colton and Ashbourne relaxing in large leather chairs, both imbibing. Across from them, curled up on the sofa, Annie had her nose buried in a book. A fire crackled in the huge hearth across the room, and mistletoe hung above the doorway.

Colton stepped forward immediately and pulled his wife into his arms for a kiss. "Just ensuring you didn't do it, Medford," he said with a smug look in James's direction.

James shook his head. "You're funny when you're drunk, Colton." Then to the room at large he added, "Merry Christmas, everyone."

Ashbourne raised his glass. "Ah, Medford, finally here."

"Better late than never," James replied.

Ashbourne sighed. "I suppose."

Colton stepped over and shook James's hand. "Merry Christmas, Medford. Good to see you, old chap."

"I'm not sure I believe the good part, Colton. And your wife informs me that you've been telling her my secrets."

Colton shrugged. "If you're going to go drinking in public . . ."

"As if drinking at the club is such a scandal," James replied.

"Not for *me* it isn't." Colton cracked a smile. "But for you it's nearly front-page news."

James ignored that. "Where's Justin?"

"He's in his room, preparing to make way for all of his new Christmas gifts."

"Ah, perfect, this will do nicely, then." James pulled the present from under his arm and handed it to Colton. Then he turned to Annie. "What are you reading there, Countess? Hannah More again?"

Annie sprang up from the settee and came to hug him. "Oh God, no. No more Hannah More. I only read that drivel before I was married. I'm much more interested in love stories these days. I'm finding *Emma* positively delightful. Though I do so wonder which *lady* wrote it. It wasn't you, was it, Lily?"

Lily snorted. "Hardly. I retired my quill after *Secrets of a Wedding Night.*"

After kissing Medford on the cheek, Annie returned to the sofa and opened the book again.

James took a seat in a large leather chair next to the other two men.

"Drink, Medford?" Ashbourne asked.

James gave him a tight smile. "No. Thank you."

Ashbourne grinned. "Are you quite sure you don't want any blue ruin?"

James shoved his hands in his pockets. "Ah, Ashbourne. You never miss a chance to bring up our drinking contest."

Ashbourne winked at his wife who managed to give her husband a warning grunt without taking her eyes from the page. "Why would I miss an opportunity?" Ashbourne said. "I won!"

"Yes, but I tricked you. I let you win." James narrowed his eyes on Ashbourne.

Annie glanced up from her book then. "Don't make me come elbow you, Medford. We promised not to mention that, ahem, incident again." But she smiled at her friend.

James grinned back at her.

Lily shook her head. "Please don't mention it. I never found out the details of all that and I daresay I don't want to know."

James inclined his head toward Lily. "Allow me to change the subject, then. Ashbourne, where are your brothers? Why aren't you spending the evening with them at Ashbourne Manor?"

"Trying to get rid of me so soon? Why, you only just arrived." Ashbourne cracked a smile.

Annie gave her husband a warning glare. "Actually, Medford, all of Jordan's brothers are arriving in the morning. We're spending the night here, and then we'll be traveling back to Ashbourne Manor after breakfast."

James nodded. "I see. At any rate, be sure to tell the lot of them I said Merry Christmas."

"You act as if there are half a dozen, Medford. There are still only three."

Medford nodded. He was struck as usual by the fact

that Ashbourne had such a large family. While the earl's three younger brothers were not married, two of them were engaged, and all three were very close to Ashbourne. Until recently, the earl had been set on remaining a bachelor and allowing his brothers to carry on the family name. That is, until Annie had come along and swept him off his feet, as it were.

"I'm glad you've arrived before dinner, James," Lily said, scooting her chair closer to his. "There's something I wanted to tell you."

James glanced up at her. "Why don't I like the sound of that? Or the look on your face?"

Lily fluttered a hand in the air. "Oh, it's nothing dreadful. It's just that . . ." She hesitated, glancing first at Devon, then at Annie.

"Out with it," Devon prompted, while Annie gave her sister an encouraging nod.

"Yes," James agreed. "Out with it." He crossed his arms over his chest and regarded her down the length of his nose.

"It's just that . . . Well . . ." Lily bit her lip. "Kate is here."

CHAPTER 33

James slapped his open palm on the table next to him. The table bounced. Annie winced.

James's face was a blank mask. "Where is she?" he said in a flat voice.

Lily folded her hands serenely in her lap and returned his stare. "I intend to tell you, of course, but first, we must—"

"Where is she?" This time it was a thunderous command.

Colton sat forward in his chair. "Medford?" His voice held a note of warning.

"I merely want to speak with her." James's voice was tight.

Annie had snapped her book shut and slid forward on the sofa. "She took a nap earlier, but I think she went into the music room after that."

Lily gave her sister a condemning glare.

James nodded his thanks to Annie, stood, and stalked out of the library.

The music room was on the first floor at the end of a long hallway. James made his way toward it, each step making him more sure that he didn't know what he would say once he saw her. But Kate was here. Kate. Surely he'd think of something—the right thing—when he came face to face with her.

He stopped several paces from the door. The strains of "Moonlight Sonata" floated out of the room. She was playing the pianoforte again. She loved that piece.

Taking a deep breath, James opened the door without knocking. He stepped inside the darkened room. The music stopped. Only a single candelabra burned on top of the instrument.

Kate glanced up at him, her blue eyes wide.

"James."

He let out his pent-up breath. He'd thought it might be a dream, her being here, some cruel joke Lily had played on him. But there Kate was, sitting on the piano stool, across from the French doors, wearing a ruby-red gown that made him swallow. She looked like a dream come to life. He squinted. The firelight bounced off her silken hair. He longed to run his fingers through it.

"Kate," he breathed.

She shook her head a bit and the red-gold curls on the top of her head bounced. "Lily and Annie told you I was here?"

"Yes." Affecting a nonchalance he didn't feel, James pushed his hands into his pockets and made his way over to the pianoforte.

Kate stood, pushing out the stool with the backs of her knees. She wrung her hands. She stepped toward him, slowly. They were only a pace apart. He could smell her perfume. The hint of strawberries. His mouth watered.

"James, are you . . . angry?"

He furrowed his brow. "Angry? Why would I be angry?"

"That I'm here. These are your friends, and I'm intruding." She glanced away. "I don't belong here."

He had to struggle to keep his hands in his pockets. He wanted to reach out and . . . touch her, pull her into his arms.

"No, Kate. I'm not angry with you. I'm glad you're here."

She tentatively raised her gaze to his. It was pitch-black outside but the candlelight illuminated a bit of the outdoors. The snow still fell in fluffy heaps beyond the windows.

"You're glad?" she breathed.

"I wanted to visit you, Kate. I wanted to tell you how happy I was that you were freed."

She lowered her eyes. "I'm sorry I returned the money. But I just couldn't take it. Not after . . . your house."

"That money belongs to you."

"I don't care about the money." She closed her eyes briefly. "James, may I ask you a question?"

He smiled at that. "You know you can."

"Why haven't you published the pamphlet yet?"

He shook his head. "Let's not talk about the pamphlet, Kate. The pamphlet doesn't matter."

Her brow furrowed. She reached out a hand as if in supplication. "But . . . why? I'd expect it would be more popular than ever now that my name is cleared. It would sell wonderfully, pay for the repairs to your house, the money you spent for Mr. Abernathy, Mr. Horton."

"Damn it, Kate, that's not why . . . It was never about the money," James ground out.

Kate let her hand drop to her side. "I don't understand."

James paced away, toward the French doors. "Publishing for me has been a drive. A need. My father was always so blasted frightened of any hint of scandal. But now . . . I don't care about it anymore. You were right. I should use the press for good. Expose the real truth about things going on, the wrongly accused, the poor."

She closed her eyes briefly. "James, don't do that just because of me."

He opened his mouth to reply, but she put up a hand to stop him. "Wait, first, I must thank you. If it weren't for you, I wouldn't have had a defense. Wouldn't have hired Mr. Abernathy. Wouldn't have had a runner investigating my case. I wouldn't be free right now." She paused, looking down at her feet. "I owe you my life."

His voice was savage. "You owe me nothing, Kate."

She walked past him, trembling, and his fingers ached to reach out and stroke her cheek. "You didn't let me finish. I owe you my life, and I don't want you to think I'm ungrateful, but I'm leaving. I'm going to the Continent. The angry mobs may have dispersed but my reputation is still in shreds here. I will not be welcome in Society. There's nothing I can do about it. I must leave. But I'll always be thankful to you." She turned back to face him, pushing up her chin.

James scrubbed his hand through his hair. He cursed violently under his breath. "I can make this right, Kate. I can fix your reputation—"

She whipped her head around to face him, her curls falling enchantingly over one shoulder. "No you can't, James. You know that. Even you can't fix this."

He clenched his jaw and met her eyes. "How do you intend to live on the Continent?"

"I have my dower money. I can make a life."

"The money from the pamphlet is still yours, Kate. You should take it."

Her jaw tightened and anger flashed in her eyes. She turned on her heel, ran over to the double doors, and pushed them open. A blast of cold air shot through the room, and she ran out, into the black, freezing night, into the snowflakes.

James followed her, stalking out into the snow behind her. "What do you think you are doing?"

She turned on him, her eyes flashing blue fire. The snowflakes floated down her alabaster cheeks. She turned in a circle, around and around, her gown looking blood-red against the white ground. She breathed in the cold air. Her breath came in short puffs. Then she took two very deep breaths and exhaled slowly. "I'm feeling, James. Feeling. Feeling this air. Feeling the snow. I never knew if I'd feel this again."

"What does that have to do with the money, going to the Continent?"

She turned on him, eyes still flashing. "I don't want your money, James. I never wanted it."

James stopped himself from reaching for her. Instead, he clenched his fists at his sides. "What do you want, then? Say the word. I have friends. I have money. We can *make* the blasted *ton* accept you again."

She advanced on him, pointing a finger at his chest, and he retreated, slowly, shuffling backward through the snow, the cold wetness seeping through the legs of his breeches.

"You're always trying to fix everything," she said. "Always trying to make things right. That's why you hired a runner for me, and that's why you're doing this now. But my reputation is another thing altogether. Even with my name cleared I've been involved in a scandal I will never live down. Even if George hadn't been murdered, everyone knows I wanted a divorce. None of that has changed. God, James, don't you know by now that not everything can be fixed?"

James closed his eyes. He was helpless. Helpless. The one thing he wanted to fix more than all the others was standing here in the snow looking more beautiful than he'd ever seen her, and telling him he was a failure.

"I *can* fix this," he growled through clenched teeth. "I'll publish whatever you want me to, use the printing press to save your reputation. You're a duchess—"

She whirled on him, her scarlet gown flaring around her ankles, pooling against the pure snow. The flakes that still clung to her impossibly long lashes were illuminated like sparking diamonds by the candlelight that filtered from the windows of the house. "No!" she cried. "Don't you understand? I don't want to be a duchess."

James dug his fingers into his fists. "What is it you want, Kate? Tell me. I'll make it happen. I swear it."

She bowed her head. "No. No."

He took two steps forward and grabbed her shoulders. They were close enough for the little puffs of her warm breath to evaporate against his shirtfront. "Tell me," he demanded.

She looked up at him, trembling. Her eyes locked with his. "I want to spend the night with you."

CHAPTER 34

James roughly pulled her into his arms. His mouth came crushing down on hers, and Kate nearly whimpered. He pushed her head back, covered her cheeks with his strong warm hands. He invaded her mouth with his hot, bold tongue.

Kate kissed him for a moment, with all the passion and longing she felt for him. Then she pulled away. "James, I—"

"Shh," he whispered against her lips. "Just let me kiss you." He traced his mouth along her cheekbone, her temple. He kissed her forehead. Then his mouth met hers again and Kate forgot all about the cold and the snow. She was melting, on fire.

"Why didn't you tell me . . . this . . . before?" he asked in between his kisses. His hands moved up to her hair. He kept her mouth captive, shaped it, owned it. Wouldn't let her go.

Kate whispered against his lips. "I couldn't . . . couldn't keep putting you in danger."

He rested his forehead against hers and wrapped his

arms around her. "I never cared about the danger. I only cared about . . . you."

She gasped against his mouth. "That's not true, James. That can't be true."

He kissed her again, and this time she wrapped her arms around his broad shoulders. "It's true that when you first came to live with me, I wanted the pamphlet, but since then, Kate . . . all I can think about is you. I knew you didn't kill George. I knew it."

"You always believed in me."

"Not always, but after I came to know you . . . the real you . . . I knew you couldn't have done it."

He kissed her again, and she let her head tilt back, savoring the hot warmth of his mouth, the flavor of him, the smell of him, the feel of him. The last week she'd spent in the Tower before being released, those awful freezing nights in prison, she'd wondered if she'd ever see him again, and now that he was here, kissing her, she never wanted to let him go.

"I missed you, Kate," he whispered against her mouth.

She swallowed. She wanted to cry. She'd missed him too, but it didn't change the fact that she was a liability to him. They couldn't just take up where they'd left off, living together in Mayfair. Why, even if they were to lose their minds and marry, they couldn't live a normal life. The judgmental *ton* wouldn't accept them. And after James published the pamphlet, would it be better or worse? Oh, it didn't matter. The entire notion of them being together was ludicrous no matter how much she might dream of it. She couldn't love James and threaten his reputation any more than she already had.

"James," she whispered. "We . . . we can't . . ."

He kissed her again, deeply, urgently. "Can't what?"

She didn't know what she meant either. His mouth seared her ear, her throat. His lips traveled down to her décolletage, and he buried his face between her breasts. "Kate, you're so sweet. So sweet," he whispered. His thumb rubbed her nipple through her gown, and her mind went blank. His leg had pushed between the two of hers, and he was rubbing against her through the fabric of her dress. She was mindless with wanting him. Oh God, why had she run off into the snow? If they were on the sofa in one of the salons, no doubt they'd be making love to each other by now, and that's exactly what she was fantasizing about.

"James," she breathed. "Not here."

"Just let me kiss you a moment longer," he begged, pulling her closer and wrapping his arms around her waist. He kissed her as if it were the first time. He kissed her as if it were the last time, and Kate wasn't sure any more which was closer to the truth. She ran her fingers through his hair, clutched his head to hers and allowed the little cold snowflakes to infuse their hot kisses with the tiniest bit of ice. She kissed the snowflakes from his cheekbones and shuddered when his tongue roughly slid against hers. His leg was still riding between hers. She rubbed herself against him like a complete wanton, enjoying every bit of the sensation the friction their clothing created between them.

"Kate," he whispered. "I want you." He kissed her again. "I want you."

"James," she whispered back. "I want you too."

The sound of a woman clearing her throat broke them from their embrace. Kate opened her eyes slowly and focused on the candlelight behind her inside the house. James glanced behind them, a curse on his lips.

Lily stood in the open French doors, pointedly not looking at them. She appeared to be examining the weave of the carpet, actually. She'd cleared her throat, bit her lip, and was rocking back and forth on her heels, the hint of a blush on her cheeks.

James and Kate just stared at her.

"I came to tell you that dinner is ready," Lily announced in an overly loud, somewhat apologetic voice. "We'll just . . . see you in the dining room in a few moments."

She turned and hurried away then as fast as she could and the tap of her slippers down the marble hallway signaled her retreat.

James pulled Kate by the hand out of the snow and into the music room again. He shut the doors securely behind them.

They stamped the snow from their feet and Kate turned to James with wide eyes. "Oh God, what Lily must think of me . . ." She shook her head.

"She doesn't judge you, believe me," he said, pulling a throw blanket from the top of the sofa and wrapping it around Kate's shoulders. He guided her to the sofa, sat her down, and bent on one knee to pull off her wet, ruined slippers and stockings. Kate had to admit, she got a bit of a thrill from it. Then he rubbed her arms up and down to warm her. "You'll have to go up to your room, before dinner, and get new shoes."

"Yes." She nodded.

Kate accepted his ministrations with a meek smile, truly hoping they wouldn't end. "How do you know?" she asked, rubbing the warmth back into her hands and blowing into them. "That Lily doesn't judge me?"

James gave her a wry smile. "She's done worse with Colton, I'm sure."

Kate's eyes widened.

James stopped rubbing her arms and grabbed her by the shoulders gently. "Listen to me, Kate. We must talk. After dinner."

"Come to my room tonight," she blurted out. Butterflies scattered in her stomach. If he came to her room later, there was every possibility . . . Oh, but she couldn't even think about it right now. It would be too wonderful. And scandalous. But as long as they were careful, no one would ever know he'd been there.

James pulled the blanket from her shoulders and tossed it back onto the sofa. He relaxed his shoulders and offered her his hand. "Yes, Kate. I'll come to your room tonight."

CHAPTER 35

When the light knock sounded on her door sometime
well after midnight, Kate's stomach leaped. The Christmas Eve dinner with Lily, Devon, Annie, and Jordan
had been wonderful, though she'd barely been able to
meet Lily's eyes, let alone James's. They'd all talked,
laughed, and had a wonderful time, but Kate hadn't
been able to concentrate on anything other than James's
promise to visit her room later. She'd hardly eaten a thing
even though the meal had been outstanding. Seven
courses, meat, duck, jellies, puddings, breads, desserts.
All sorts of rich sauces and gravies. It had been a meal
fit for royalty and it had been spent with the very best
of company. But when James had glanced over at her
from behind his wine glass, Kate's insides trembled,
and she had no appetite. She had been forced to apologize to her hostess for not eating much of the delectable
courses that had been placed before her.

If Lily thought Kate's lack of appetite odd, she didn't
say a word. And little wonder. After witnessing Kate's
completely improper display of passion with James
earlier, Kate wouldn't have blamed Lily for tossing her

out into the snow. Apparently, she was unfazed by what she'd seen. But would Lily blame her if she knew what she was up to tonight? Kate bit her lip. What her friend didn't know wouldn't hurt her, correct?

Very well. Kate had decided weeks ago that she intended to live and living was exactly what she was up to tonight. Of course there was every possibility that James did only wish to speak to her and that he would not kiss her or touch her as he had in the snow-covered gardens earlier, but . . . she desperately hoped he would. She couldn't have a future with James. It would be putting him and keeping him in too much peril. But she could have one night with him, and it could be wonderful, magical, something for her to dream about and remember on all those long lonely nights on the Continent.

The light knock sounded again, and Kate crossed over to the door to her room, her white sheath of a night rail barely covering her. It was mostly see-through. She'd discovered that in the looking glass earlier. Halfway indecent. She smiled to herself. It was perfect. She'd let her hair down too, plucking out the pins one by one and shaking the red-gold mass until it shimmered over her shoulders and flowed down her back like fire. James would like it. He'd like it very much.

Pinching color into her cheeks, she hurried to the door, took a deep breath, and opened it with a sly smile on her face.

James stood there with his shoulder propped against the frame. He'd removed his cravat, but he still wore his black evening attire, his snowy white shirt, his black coat, his superfine trousers. One hand was shoved negligently into his pocket, and his dark hair was perfectly in place as usual.

She opened the door wider and stood aside. "Come in, James."

He straightened up and walked past her into the room. When he turned and saw what she was wearing, his eyes went wide. "Kate."

She closed the door behind him. She'd already planned exactly what she would do. She moved slowly toward the bed and slid atop it.

He swallowed audibly. "Kate?"

She nodded. "Yes."

"What are you . . . doing?"

"I thought you wanted to talk, James."

He moved toward her, stood next to the bed, and reached out and touched her face. She closed her eyes and rubbed her cheek against his hand.

"Yes, I did," he said softly. "Do you intend to talk here?" He motioned toward the bed with his chin.

"Yes." She looked up at him through her lashes. She was vulnerable. So vulnerable. And she was offering herself to him. He only had to reach out and . . . take her. "Among other things."

His eyes were smoldering green. He leaned down, his lips hovering over hers. "Are you sure?"

"Yes," she repeated.

He kissed her then. He touched his mouth to hers, so sweetly, so softly, and Kate knew in that moment that he was giving her that instant to pull away, say no. But if she didn't, if she kissed him back with all the passion she felt for him, they would do this, spend the night together and then perhaps nothing would be the same. And she was all right with that.

She'd already made her decision. She moved up to her knees and wrapped her arms around his neck. She slid her lips near his ear. "I have to tell you something."

His answer came through clenched teeth. "What?" She could tell he was fighting with himself, intent on not touching her until they established what would happen between them tonight.

"I don't feel much like talking."

His mouth hovered above hers. His sensual lips slowly formed a smile. "Neither do I."

He braced his hands on either side of her hips and leaned over, over, over, until she was lying completely back on the mattress. Then he moved up and placed his hands on either side of her head and he lowered his mouth and kissed her. He kept himself above her, hovering over her, not touching her. He stared down at her body. His eyes raking her from the tips of her toes to the crown of her head. "Kate, you look like a dream," he whispered.

She wrapped her arms around his neck and tried to pull him atop her but he wouldn't allow it. She arched a brow.

"No hurry." He gave her a mischievous smile that she felt all the way to her toes.

"Mmm," she murmured. "James?"

"Yes?" He kissed her again. His tongue met hers.

"This time will you let me take your clothes off?"

A shudder passed through him. "Absolutely."

"Oh good." She smiled against his cheek.

He pulled away from her briefly, sat on the edge of the bed, and quickly shucked his boots. Then he lay on the bed next to her, his back completely against the mattress. He crossed his arms under his head. "I'm yours to undress."

Kate smiled a catlike smile. "Excellent."

She rolled over and threw a leg across his two, then sat up, bracing her knees on either side of his hips. She watched him. His green eyes grew wide. He was obviously trying to keep his face blank. She'd just see about that. Excitement and anxiety raced through her entire body. They were really going to do this, the two of them. She'd been waiting for so long, dreaming about this moment. She didn't want it to end. She needed to remember it forever.

She reached out and ran a hand down his muscled chest. His shirt was open at the neck, revealing a bit of dark chest hair. He shuddered again, and she let her fingers trail from the patch of warm skin at the V in his neck to his waist. His muscles rippled under her fingertips, and she longed to tear the white shirt from his body and fling it to the floor.

"James?"

"Yes, love?" His voice sounded a bit strained, pained.

"How does it make you feel when I . . . touch you?"

"It's just like . . ." He closed his eyes. "Torture."

She yanked his shirt from the top of his breeches, and James sat up straight, helping her. He tugged it over his head with both hands. She took it from him and soon discarded it by tossing it to a heap on the floor. Then she sat back and reveled in the unadulterated view of him from the waist up. He was lean and muscled and perfect-looking. Lord Colton and Lord Ashbourne had spoken of their love for boxing when they'd all gone to the farm, but James hadn't mentioned his favorite sport. "How do you stay in such good . . . form?" she asked a bit hesitantly. "Surely not boxing?"

He smiled at that and shook his head. "No. I prefer fencing. I do it every day at the club. In addition to riding in the park."

She bit her lip. "I had no idea you were so . . ." Her fingers glanced off the six muscles that stood out in sharp relief on his belly. "Well made."

He closed his eyes, a grin on his lips. "By all means, look all you like."

Kate smiled at that. She intended to. Frankly, she'd never seen her husband entirely naked. Oh, he'd been nude with her, certainly, but she'd never actually . . . looked. Instead she'd been too frightened and shy, and their interactions had been over too quickly. This time, with James, she intended to look her fill and perhaps learn a thing or two, and with James she knew the view would be an absolute delight.

The firelight glanced off his velvety skin. She pushed her hands over his muscled shoulders and stroked him. Then she took a deep breath. The line of hair that trailed from his chest led down past the top of his trousers. She desperately wanted to see that part of him. She closed her eyes briefly and breathed in the intoxicating male scent of him. He was glorious, gorgeous, as if he'd been chiseled in stone. James might not be the dashing charmer that Lord Ashbourne and Lord Colton were, but he was so handsome and unassuming and funny and steadfast and true. Why any woman would look twice at a rogue when they had a man as deliciously perfect as James in their presence, she would never understand. But the other ladies' loss was her gain, and she intended to take absolute advantage . . . in every possible way.

She let her tapered nails drift down his hard abdomen and come to rest on the buttons of his breeches. James squeezed shut his eyes and moaned. "Be gentle, darling," he said with a bit of humor in his voice.

"Oh, I intend to pay you back for the exquisite torture you afforded me the last time we were alone together like this."

His teeth tugged at his bottom lip, and a surge of lust

shot through Kate and pooled in between her legs. Oh God, she wanted to rip off his breeches, pull him on top of her and beg him to take her. Instead, she braced her hand on his flat abdomen and slowly allowed her fingers to descend.

James shuddered. She slipped her fingers into the holes and, one by one, released each straining button. Through the fabric of his trousers she felt him, big, hard, wanting her, reaching for her. She traced her fingertips over him. No surprise. He was better than George in that regard too. She'd never spent much time touching George *down there,* but James's size put her former husband's to shame. She knew that much.

James groaned as she stroked him up and down through the fabric. After all the buttons were undone, she slipped her hand in his trousers and wrapped her fingers around him. His groan intensified. "Kate," he gasped.

She squeezed him. She stroked him. And then she leaned down, slowly, oh so slowly, and she kissed him. There. His hips nearly bucked off the bed. "God damn it," he cried out, his fingers tangling in her long hair.

He rolled her over then, and suddenly his breeches were completely gone. "Kate," he whispered. "I need to see you, to feel you."

"Yes," was all she said.

James pulled her flimsy night rail over her head and discarded it in a rolled-up ball that he tossed away with one hand. He leaned back and took in the unreal beauty of Kate's body. She was like a painting come to life, all alabaster skin, perfect large breasts with pink tips, a tiny waist, enticing rounded hips, and the hair and eyes of a goddess. "You're perfect, Kate. You take my breath away."

She smiled at that and met his eyes. "I was going to say the same thing about you."

His hand shook a little. The red triangle of hair between her thighs beckoned him. He leaned down and breathed in her maddening scent just before he kissed her there, just as she had done to him.

Kate gasped. Her hips twitched beneath him. She spread her legs. "James, I want you," she breathed.

"I want you too, goddess," he said just before he pulled her into his arms and kissed her. Then he moved his head to her breasts and lavished them both with his tongue. He tugged one with his mouth, while the other he tortured with his fingers, rubbing the nipple between his thumb and index finger, nipping at it, plucking at it, all the while keeping up his mouth's assault on the other breast. He kneaded it with his lips, kissed it, sucked it, and Kate arched her back off the bed and cupped his dark head to her chest.

Then James's hand traveled down her belly to the juncture between her thighs and his finger slipped into the slick folds. He rubbed her there, enough to make her mad and wet with need. He slipped a finger—a single finger—inside of her and rubbed it in and out. Kate moaned. Her head moved back and forth fitfully on the pillows. He moved his finger up to the little nub between her legs and rubbed her there too, in perfect little circles. Kate arched her hips off the bed, clutching at his hand, moaning his name, begging him not to stop.

He brought her to the pinnacle, her hips were nearly bucking off the bed, and then he moved his hand away. "No," she gasped.

He smiled against her neck. "It's better this way," he assured her, kissing her neck. "Trust me."

She wanted to sob, but she nodded. "I trust you. But I want to do it to you, too."

He opened his mouth to deny her, but she'd already rolled over and was busily moving down, down, down. Her perfect pink mouth hovered so near his hard throbbing cock he couldn't breathe. Instead, he held his breath. Time stopped. Her pink tongue flicked out to touch his tip, and his eyes rolled back in his head. "Oh God. Kate."

"Shh," she whispered, torturing him with the same words he'd used to torture her earlier. "Trust me."

He growled deep in his throat but let her do whatever she wanted with him. His hands clutched at the bed sheets on either side of his hips as Kate's hot wet mouth slid down his cock. "Jesus Christ!"

Her mouth moved in a smile just before it descended again in a maddening rhythm that made him desperate for release. She was good. Too good. Going about this too well and too fast. And it had been too damn long. He would embarrass himself and spill his seed in her mouth—oh God, dream come true—if he allowed her to continue any longer.

No, he needed to regain control of this situation and he needed to do it now. He couldn't wait a moment longer to make her his.

He pulled her up forcefully into his arms, kissed her passionately on the mouth again, and rolled over on top of her. He spread her legs with his knee wedged between hers and positioned himself in between her legs. "Kate," he whispered, nudging her forehead with his so she'd look into his eyes. "Tell me you want me one more time."

"Oh, James, I do want you. I want you. I want—"

He slid into her then, so hot and strong and hard. Kate's words ended on a long moan. She couldn't stop herself. And then he was moving inside of her, up and down. Owning her, possessing her, raining little kisses over her face, whispering words of desire and longing into her ear, making her his in every single way.

Kate had never felt such bliss. Having James inside her, filling her, kissing her, his hot chest rubbing against her breasts, the erotic friction of it making her wet all over again. She couldn't stand it. He moved his hand down between them and found the nub of pleasure between her legs again, and he rubbed it, over and over in an unending, maddening pattern. He didn't stop. Kate whimpered, her head moving from side to side on the pillow. She begged him, pleaded with him not to stop.

"I won't stop, Kate," he promised. "Come for me."

His finger moved up and down, up and down, her hips were helpless to follow his rhythm, the sensuous pace he'd set for them. She followed him, and he took her there. She raised her hips from the mattress, convulsing, just before her world shattered into a thousand tiny pieces, and she screamed his name against his strong, burning-hot shoulder.

"Oh God, Kate," he murmured, just before pumping into her again . . . again . . . and then one last time before he spilled himself inside her.

Kate surfaced slowly from the cloud of euphoria that encased her brain. James had rolled to his side to relieve his weight from her and he sat, running his fingertip along her hairline, kissing her nose, and tucking little strands of her hair behind her ear.

"You're beautiful," he whispered.

"So are you," she replied, smiling.

He rolled his eyes at that.

"What?" she asked. "You don't believe me?"

"Hardly."

She pulled the blanket underneath her arms and watched him from the corners of her eyes. "You know what I thought the first day I met you?"

The sheet was pulled up to his waist and he looked over at her, a surprised grin on his face. "In the Tower?"

She nodded and one of her red-gold curls bounced out from behind her ear, making her look absolutely adorable. "Yes."

"What?" he asked, now more than a bit curious.

"I thought you were the most handsome man I'd ever seen."

"Now I know you're just appealing to my vanity," he replied.

She propped herself up on an elbow and looked at him. "No, James, I'm entirely serious. You have no idea how guilty I felt. I knew I had absolutely no business having such indecent thoughts about you while I was in gaol for murder . . . when my husband was dead. But I couldn't help myself." She bit her lip.

He rubbed her cheek with the back of his fingers. "If you were feeling guilty, I was feeling as if I were about to be smitten with a lightning bolt given the indecent nature of the thoughts I was having about you at the time."

Her eyes widened like giant blue moons and she laughed. "James, you didn't?"

"Oh yes. I did."

She playfully slapped him on the shoulder. "You had indecent thoughts about me even though you thought I was a murderess?"

He shrugged. "I couldn't help myself. Besides, I didn't know for sure if you were guilty."

"Is that why you brought me to your house?" She grinned at him.

"I brought you to my house because you were my responsibility. I wanted to keep you safe," he replied. "I only prayed I could keep my hands off you."

"You prayed?"

"Every single day."

She giggled. "And you couldn't? Keep your hands off me?"

He looked a bit chagrined. "Guilty. As you can see."

"It's all right, James. I couldn't keep my hands off you either."

"I tried my damnedest," he said, reaching out and stroking the curl that lay on her shoulder, tempting him.

"I didn't." She laughed.

He pulled her into his arms and kissed her again. And it was several minutes later before he pulled his mouth from hers.

He tapped her nose with his fingertip. "Now that we've been so scandalous, my lady, we really do need to talk."

She curled up under his shoulder and wrapped her arm around his waist. "Oh, not now, James. We can talk tomorrow, can't we? Tonight I just want to fall asleep in your arms.

He wrapped his arms around her more tightly. "Merry Christmas, Kate," he whispered into her sweet-smelling hair.

"Merry Christmas, James."

She giggled.

"What's so funny?"

"You know what I want for a Christmas gift?" she asked with a sly smile on her face.

He leered at her. "What?"

She blushed beautifully and ducked her head under the sheet. "To do *that* again."

He pulled up the sheet and followed her underneath. "That, my lady, can be easily arranged."

When Kate awoke, the room was still dark. Thank goodness the maids weren't up yet. The curtains were still drawn. None of the bright light from outdoors filtered into the room. She sat up and eyed James. His seamless brow, his smooth forehead, the straight line of his nose. He was so handsome. Handsome and noble and . . . he probably would make the perfect husband. He was perfect in all else, why not that? But the part she liked best was how his hair was mussed. She'd never seen him with mussed hair before. The man had always looked flawless. Apparently, even James wasn't entirely perfect every minute. Though, she thought to herself with a small secret smile, last night had been. It had been exactly that. Perfect. In every way.

It wasn't possible that she would forget it any time soon . . . or . . . ever. The things he'd done to her. Oh, she shuddered just thinking about them again. Some of them were indecent. Some of them were perhaps illegal. But all of them were immensely . . . fun. She giggled to herself. Good heavens. When was the last time she'd giggled?

Oh, this man, he brought out the most unexpected emotions in her. She searched his handsome sleeping face. One of them was . . . love. She sucked in her breath. Oh God, she loved him. She did. And it was because of that that she couldn't allow him to throw away his life on her.

James stirred in his sleep. He opened one hazel eye. "Good morning." He gave her a sensuous smile and her stomach flipped.

"Good morning," she whispered back.

He sat up, pulled her into his arms, kissed her deeply, and Kate became aroused all over again by his expert touch.

He kissed her shoulder, her ear, the bend in her neck. Then he whispered into her hair. "We'll be married as soon as I can procure a license."

Kate's heart stopped. She propped herself up on one elbow, holding the sheet to her chest. "What?"

He kissed her cheek. "It shouldn't take longer than a day or two. I'll go to London tomorrow. I'll leave at first light."

She shook her head and pushed herself away a little. "No."

He looked up at her. His brow was furrowed. "No? Why? Is it because you're still supposed to be in mourning?"

She shook her head. "What? No. I've caused such a scandal already, I don't care about that. But we can't marry, James."

This time he sat up and his face wore a thunderous expression. "What do you mean? We just spent the night together, I thought that meant—"

She closed her eyes. "I want to, James. Truly, I do. But what people want and what people get are often two very different things. Don't you know that?"

He grasped her shoulders, forced her to open her eyes and look at him. "It doesn't have to be like that, Kate."

She moved away from him, to the edge of the bed, the sheet still wrapped around her. "I'm a complete outcast. The *ton* will never accept me. I can't be your wife. I'd ruin you. You must know that."

"I don't give a damn about the *ton*. We're getting married just as soon as I procure a license."

Kate didn't answer. She let her hair fall over her face, hiding her torn expression. She wanted so desperately to believe. She held the dream in her head. She cherished it. Nurtured it. Could it be real? Could she truly stay with him? Could they find love?

CHAPTER 36

James left her room. In the early morning hours, he gathered his clothes and boots, slipped into the hall, and was gone. Afterward, Kate had lain on the bed and closed her eyes, remembering all the delicious things he'd done to her body last night and allowing herself a moment . . . to dream.

The dreams she'd had while locked in the Tower were never this good. She and James, getting married. She and James, spending their lives together. She and James, with children. She sucked in her breath. She couldn't even imagine that happiness. Didn't dare to dream it. In the end, she'd told him she had to think about it, that she would give him her answer later today, but she knew he thought he'd won. He thought their marriage was a foregone conclusion. Oh, how wonderful it would be if she could believe so strongly too. James might say he didn't care about her ruined reputation and the fact that Society would cast them both out, but did he mean it?

He might mean it now while their relationship was new and they were happy. But she'd seen how quickly feelings could change. She and George had been happy once too . . . or so she'd thought. And then one day everything had changed. No, she couldn't bear it if that happened with James. Marriage was difficult enough without huge problems at the start. They wouldn't be able to survive the pressure of her blackened reputation. James would come to resent her, as George had. Just for a different reason.

A soft knock sounded at the door. Kate blinked open her eyes and quickly rolled back over and sat up. Surely it wasn't James . . . again? She pulled up the covers to her chin. "Come in."

The door cracked open and Lily's head appeared. "Good morning, Kate. May I come in?"

"Of course," Kate answered brightly. She bit her lip. Oh, what would Lily Morgan think about her antics last night? She couldn't even consider it. She looked away, a blush heating her cheeks.

"Merry Christmas," Lily said, coming to sit on the edge of the bed.

Kate smiled brightly. She couldn't remember the last time she'd had such a good Christmas morning. "Merry Christmas to you. And thank you again for inviting me here."

"I do hope I didn't wake you. I just wanted to come and check on you. The men have gone riding this morning. They took Justin with them. So it's just Annie and I downstairs for breakfast if you'd like to join us."

Kate nodded and stretched. "Yes. I'd like that very much."

"Excellent." Lily stood and walked over to the windows. She glanced outside. "My, it snowed quite a lot last night."

Kate looked toward the window, but of course she couldn't see out. "Did it?"

"Yes," Lily replied. "It's sure to be a merry Christmas."

Kate stretched and yawned this time. She wholeheartedly agreed. "I'll just see you downstairs in a few minutes."

Lily nodded. "I'll send up a maid to help you dress."

Lily made her way over to the door and opened it. She turned back momentarily. "And I just wanted to tell you again, Kate, that whatever you decide to do after the holiday, Devon and I support you completely. You can stay here, go to London, whatever you'd like."

Kate sat up straight. "Thank you, Lily. You're very kind. I haven't yet decided what I shall do, but I'm ever so grateful for your friendship."

Lily nodded. "Medford would help you too, you know?"

Kate glanced down at her hands. She traced the flowered pattern of the bedspread with her fingertip. "I know."

Shutting the door, Lily quickly moved back over and sat on the edge of the bed again. "You should consider giving James a chance. He's so noble and honorable. And I think he cares for you a great deal."

"Yes, and all I've done is ruin his reputation. I'll never forgive myself. I cannot help but think it will be better for him if I go to the Continent."

Lily frowned. "Ruined his reputation? No. Sullied perhaps. But don't worry about that. James can take care of himself. He can be very charming when he needs to be; no doubt he'll be back in the good graces of the *ton* before spring. Besides." Lily paused. "I don't think James wants you to go to the Continent."

Kate's head snapped up. "Did you speak with him . . . ? Today, I mean."

Lily shook her head. "No."

Kate expelled her breath. For a moment she'd wondered if James had told Lily he'd asked her to marry him, though he'd done it in a roundabout way. "I've no wish to see what's left of James's reputation be ruined because of me."

"Reputation is important to him," Lily amended. "But it's not the most important thing."

Kate furrowed her brow. "What's the most important?"

"I told you before, James has a deep need to fix everything." Lily squeezed her hand. She stood and walked toward the door. She fluttered her hand in the air. "Why, he even tried to marry me once because of it. Poor man. We would have made each other miserable of course. But that's the sort of man he is. He knew I had nowhere else to turn so he offered for me."

Kate went hot then cold. She clutched at the bed sheets. "Ja . . . James offered for you?"

Lily nodded. "Yes. It was months ago, and he was only doing it out of duty. He's such a dear friend."

Kate's stomach clenched. Duty. Of course. How could she have forgotten that? James might have forgotten himself and made love to her last night. But he'd only offered for her last night out of duty. Not love. Never love. Now that she considered it, he hadn't even said the words, had he? No. He was just trying to fix everything. As usual.

She pressed her hand against her belly, feeling as if she might retch. Lily didn't know it but she'd just saved her from making another terrible mistake when it came to marriage. Kate had told herself once that it didn't hurt to daydream. What a lie that had been.

She sucked in a deep breath. She had to go. Had to get out of here.

"Lily," she said, just as the other woman was about to leave.

Lily turned back around.

"Yes?"

"I believe I've made my decision."

CHAPTER 37

James came barreling into the morning room where Lily and Devon were having afternoon tea. Annie and Jordan had already left to go to Colton House and meet Ashbourne's brothers. Justin sat in the corner playing with the toys he'd received for Christmas just that morning. The three dogs sat happily watching.

"Where is she?" James tossed the note that Kate had left for him, the one that said she couldn't marry him and was leaving for the Continent as soon as possible, on the table in front of them.

Lily's biscuit dropped to her plate. She and Devon exchanged glances.

"Where is who?" Devon barely glanced up from his cup.

"Kate. She's gone," James ground out.

"Gone?" Devon's eyebrows shot up and he gave his wife a suspicious stare.

James clenched his fist. "Damn it, Colton. I'll rip this bloody house apart if you don't tell me where she is!"

Colton set down his cup and placed his hands on his

hips. He returned James's angry stare. "First of all, there is a child present." He glanced at Justin who had turned around to watch. The child's dark eyes were as wide as the dogs' collars. "And secondly, I do not know where she is, Medford. And I won't have you raising your voice to my wife who apparently does know."

Lily made a great show of smoothing her skirts. "Yes, I know. But I cannot tell you. And neither can Annie." She looked a bit guilty and a bit reluctant. "I'm sorry, Medford."

"So, there you have it," Colton replied. "Kate asked Lily and Annie to keep it secret and they are honoring her wishes."

James lunged at Colton. Lily jumped up and placed a hand on his chest. James took a step back.

The three of them stared at each other. James was breathing heavily, his eyes shooting fire at Colton. Justin raised his eyebrows and turned back around to attend to his toys.

James turned away from Colton with a jerk, straightened his jacket, and ran his fingers through his hair, disheveling it. "Fine," he ground out. "I'll find her myself." Turning on his heel, he stalked from the room.

Lily and Devon watched him go, each shaking their heads.

"Poor Medford." Lily sighed.

"What the deuce has got into that chap?" Colton asked.

"I cannot believe that was our James," Lily added.

Colton shook his head. "It seems positively impossible, I admit. But I do believe Lord Medford has fallen in love."

* * *

James spent a bloody fortune. He'd bribed the proprietors of every hotel in London and the surrounding vicinity. If Kate was staying anywhere in the lower half of the country, by God, he'd intended to find out. He nearly called Mr. Horton, to track her down.

She was not, however, staying at a hotel. And his money, in fact, was not what found her.

As he did every morning at precisely seven-thirty, Locke delivered his employer's perfectly pressed copy of the *Times*.

James accepted the paper in the midst of his stack of correspondence, his cup of black coffee, and his urgent business papers. Somewhere in between his third bite of eggs and toast, he carefully shook out the front page and casually scanned the headlines.

After dutifully reading the business news and parliamentary proceedings, James flipped the pages to the Society section. He'd had his eye on a certain story. Seemed the entire town wanted to know the answer to the same question he did. Where in the hell was the newly exonerated dowager Duchess of Markingham? And it seemed while there was quite a bit of conjecture, no one, including himself, knew. Damn it. Had she managed to leave for the Continent already? Had she slipped out of town that quickly without anyone becoming the wiser? It didn't seem possible, but as the days passed with no sighting of her, it began to seem more and more likely.

Minutes later, Locke reentered the breakfast room clearing his throat. "Lady Eversly to see you, milord."

James snapped up his head. "Lady Catherine? To see me? At this hour?"

Locke tactfully kept his eyes downcast. "She indicated it was quite urgent, my lord."

"Very well. Show her in."

Not two seconds later, Catherine Eversly swept past Locke into the room. She wore her white-blond hair in a chignon and her ice-blue silk gown clung to every curve of her perfect figure. Catherine was a beauty, and she knew it. Neither friend nor foe, she and James shared a sort of peaceable trust. She was also quite married.

"So glad you invited me in, Medford," she said with a regal shake of her head. "Or that might have been a bit awkward."

Locke gave the woman a narrow-eyed glare before retreating from the room after a nod from his master.

James stood, pulled the napkin from his lap, and bowed. "Lady Catherine. To what do I owe the pleasure?"

Catherine swept forward, her fine white-blond eyebrow arched. James always got the feeling that he was standing in the presence of royalty when Catherine entered a room. More like Marie Antoinette than Queen Caroline, however. And Catherine was always up to something.

James gestured to the rosewood chair next to him. "Please have a seat. May I offer you some breakfast?" He nodded to a waiting footman, indicating to fill a plate, but Catherine waved a well-manicured hand impatiently in the air.

"No, no, I couldn't possibly eat. I'll simply have a cup of tea."

Another nod to the footman and a china teacup appeared in front of Catherine. She slid into the chair next to James and leaned enticingly toward him. Catherine always knew how to display her—ahem—self to her best advantage even at this hour of the morning.

"You surprise me, my lady, I didn't think you rose until after noon."

Catherine smiled her infamous feline smile and

dipped a silver spoon into her teacup to stir. "My, my, we are formal this morning. You haven't called me by my title in an age. And I never rise before noon if I can help it."

James eyed her over his coffee cup. "I know you haven't come to discuss our first-name basis. So tell me, why are you here? What's got you out of your bed at such an early hour?"

Catherine picked up her cup and brought it to her lips. She took a sip and put it down with a little flourish. She nodded toward the paper James held in his hand. "See the latest?" she asked with an unmistakable sparkle in her eye.

He lifted his brows. "About?"

"Ah, don't play coy with me, James. I happen to know you have the *Times* open to page five."

James glanced briefly at the page in his lap. Page 5. He quickly folded it and tossed it onto the gleaming mahogany tabletop. "What's your point?"

"My point is, I know you are interested in the whereabouts of the dowager Duchess of Markingham."

James struggled to keep his face blank. He knew Catherine well enough to know the lady never got directly to the point. She would tell him what she had to say in due time and he would endeavor to keep from throttling her while he waited.

"Do you have news for me?" he asked in a steady voice.

She sighed and rolled her eyes. "Why else would I be here at this ungodly hour?"

His voice simmered. He spoke through clenched teeth. "Tell me, Catherine. Do you know where Kate is?"

"Of course I do, you daft man." She took another sip of her tea and regarded her fingernails leisurely. "She happens to be staying with me."

CHAPTER 38

It was exactly two hours later when James entered Catherine Eversly's town house and made his way down the hall to stand outside the rose salon where Catherine insisted Kate could be found. He'd managed to discern from Catherine, after two cups of tea and a great deal of cajoling, that Lily and Annie had been instrumental in introducing Kate to Catherine. Catherine, never one to shy away from a scandal and insert herself into the latest *on dit*, had been only too happy to play secret hostess to the most talked-about woman in London. She seemed to relish it, actually. She adored having the biggest story of the winter season living under her roof with no one the wiser.

"I thought you'd be more clever, Medford," Catherine had drawled, fluttering her long black lashes over the rim of her teacup. "I had no idea it would take you so long to figure it out."

He regarded her through half-lidded eyes. "I didn't figure it out."

"Precisely why I'm here, darling. I wanted to put you out of your misery. And get this little drama under way. It was all taking far too long, to be honest." She laughed. "Besides, I've always had a fondness for you, Medford dear. You know that. I do hate to watch you suffer."

"Thank you for that," he said in an unconvinced tone. But he'd insisted that he be allowed to visit Kate as soon as possible. And now here he was.

He took a deep breath, eyeing the door in front of him.

What would he say to her? She'd left him. Why? She'd spent the night with him, they'd discussed marriage, and then she'd vanished, leaving only an insufficient note to explain her actions. He steeled his resolve. He meant to ask her why she'd left, to tell her why she should stay, and then to leave it to her to decide once and for all. Whatever she decided, he would abide by her wishes. But she would bloody well say it to his face. No more notes. James straightened his shoulders and rapped once upon the door. This was the second time she'd left him. There would not be a third.

There was a muffled sound of movement within the room for a moment before the door swung open. Kate stood there in a pretty velvet emerald-green day dress looking radiant as ever. She also looked shocked as hell to see him.

Her hand flew to her throat. "James."

"May I come in?"

She stood staring at him for a few moments as if in a daze, then she moved aside and opened the door wider, ushering him in.

He brushed past her into the salon.

"How did you find me?" she asked, closing the door behind him.

He turned to face her. "Don't worry, Lily and Annie

kept your secret well. I spent the last several days bribing every employee of every hotel across the city."

She arched a brow. "Breaking rules? That doesn't sound like you."

"I assure you. Nothing I've done in the past few days sounds like me."

She pushed her hands down her skirts. "But how did you find—"

"Catherine paid me a visit."

She looked down and nodded. "I see."

"Don't blame her. She was doing me a favor."

Kate twisted her fingers. "I'd never blame her. She's been so kind to take me in." Her gaze searched his face. "Are you all right, James?"

He smiled a humorless smile. "How can you ask me that?"

She moved over to the window and looked out, wrapping her arms around her middle. "Why did you come?"

His voice was tight. "Funny. I thought I'd asked you to marry me, and you never gave me your answer. Or did you forget?"

She traced her finger along the windowsill. "I thought my answer was clear when I told you I was leaving."

He narrowed his eyes on her. "You left me a note. A note I ripped into a hundred pieces."

Her voice cracked. "I'm sorry, James."

"Tell me to my face that the answer is no," he demanded. A muscle ticked in his jaw.

She swung around to face him, tears welling in her eyes. "I'm leaving for the Continent in two days, James."

* * *

Kate eyed James. His hair was disheveled, his cravat askew. He looked completely mussed and endearingly handsome. And she'd done this to him. His house was destroyed, his reputation in danger, and now he was apparently willing to completely obliterate it for her. She couldn't allow it.

When he'd asked her if the answer to his proposal was no, she couldn't say it, couldn't drag that one word past her dry lips. She wanted so badly to say yes, but she couldn't say that either.

He didn't love her. Had never said as much. He'd offered for her out of a sense of duty. A misguided sense of duty. Just like he had with Lily. He was trying to fix it all.

There were some things you just couldn't fix. But that wasn't the worst part. The hardest part. The fact was, Kate loved him. She'd fallen in love with him, truly, deeply. And she couldn't allow him to sacrifice himself for her. She was a social outcast, a pariah. She had nothing to offer him but ruin. If he had truly loved her, truly wanted her, she might be tempted to accept his offer. They might be able to make it work. But she couldn't let him ruin himself over someone he didn't even love. No, she'd spent years in a loveless marriage before and she refused to repeat that mistake ever again.

"James," she whispered, turning to him. "I cannot allow you to ruin yourself over me."

"That is my decision to make."

She dug her fingernails into her palm. "No it's not, actually. It's mine too."

He cursed under his breath. "I didn't mean—"

She closed her eyes and put up a hand. "I know. You're just trying to do the right thing. But I cannot allow you to."

"Damn it, Kate. You're not allowing me—"

Her eyes snapped open again. "James, I know you. You're so noble, so full of honor. You want to do right by everyone." She couldn't say Lily's name. Not now. And what did any of it matter? Even if he'd never offered for Lily, the situation was untenable because of her own blackened reputation.

"Kate, don't do this." He moved toward her, reached for her, and she had to close her eyes, hoping he wouldn't see the unshed tears. He wasn't making this easy for her. She'd just have to play her very last card. She whirled around, turning her back on him, staring unseeingly out the frozen panes of glass in the window. "Marriage is hardly a panacea, James. The first time I married, everyone acted as if I'd been given a gift from the heavens. I quickly realized that was far from true. You'll forgive me if I don't think marrying another nobleman is the answer to my prayers."

There was a long, painful pause before he answered in a tight, clipped voice. "Is that how you truly feel? You equate me with George?"

Again, she couldn't drag the word past her lips. Instead, she merely nodded. She shut her eyes. "Goodbye, James," she whispered.

Seconds later, she heard the door close behind him and the click of his boots on the marble in the hallway. She rested her forehead against the freezing windowpane and let the tears she'd been holding back flow freely down her cheeks. Sobs racked her body. Oh God, she'd just performed the most selfless act of her life, letting the man she loved walk away.

CHAPTER 39

James tossed the small glass of gin into the back of his throat. He gritted his teeth. It tasted like hell. But the Curious Goat Inn was as fine a place as any to drink his troubles away. They'd given him a table in the back, a full bottle of liquor, and a questionably clean glass. Perfect.

He tipped the bottle to the mouth of the glass again, clicking the two together. Damn it all to hell. He'd done the one thing he swore he would never do. He'd actually gone and fallen in love. Of all blasted things. It's true that he hadn't completely ruled out marriage. Hell, he'd proposed to Lily a matter of months ago. She'd turned him down of course, but love had never been a factor. And it wouldn't be. Or so he'd vowed years ago. Years and years ago. Marriage and children were one thing. Love was another thing altogether.

He'd only ever loved, truly loved, one other woman in the world, and he'd both never met her and been responsible for her death. Love meant a great deal of pain and a great deal of risk, two things he wanted no part of. His tightly controlled life had been a study in perfection, yes. And perfection involved making the right decisions too. Love made nothing but messes. Big, odious messes. Ones that needed to be cleaned up posthaste.

Right. Love had no place in his world. But he'd bloody well gone and fallen in it regardless. Despite his vows and best intentions, he'd fallen in love with Kate. And she'd rejected him. And it hurt, damn it. Her standing there telling him she couldn't allow him to ruin himself over her. That had been nothing more than an excuse. If she loved him, truly loved him, she wouldn't let anything stand in the way. Just like he wouldn't. What did a reputation matter when compared to true love? Bah. He couldn't even listen to his own thoughts anymore. He was turning into a blasted bad poet. Bloody hell. He'd thought he'd found the one woman he could finally love, and instead, he'd found the second woman who could mortally wound him. And that sort of loss of control he could not allow. He curled his hand around the bottle of gin and squeezed.

Sloshing the contents of the bottle into his glass, he tossed back a second drink and then a third. It all began to make a bit more sense. Very well. He'd lost his head for a time. But just like anything else, reason and logic could easily overcome it. And that's exactly what he intended to do. Reason through it. And reason told him that not only was he to stop loving Kate immediately, he would never open himself up to that sort of pain again. His drunken brain finally allowed him to admit the truth. It began and ended with his mother. Deep down, he'd always known that. He'd lived his entire life with the pain of losing the only woman he ever loved. And now he'd lost the second one. It was over. Kate couldn't hurt him any more than she already had. He'd already lost her.

And now he would steel his heart against the smallest bit of weakness, the tiniest inclination to fall in love again. Done. Over with. Finished.

And he'd ensure all of it. Tomorrow.

Tonight? Tonight, he was going to drink.

The door to the tavern opened. The patrons' heads swiveled to stare at the two fine gentlemen who'd just entered. The tall men strolled leisurely through the gin-drinking set until they happened upon James at the back of the room.

Ah, right on time. His companions had made it. Who better to drink with?

Jordan Holloway whistled. "Now this I truly had to see to believe. Tying one on, Medford? What has the world come to?"

"Shut up and have a drink," James replied, scraping the bottle across the wooden table toward his friends.

"And in a seedy tavern of all places." Colton glanced around the public house. "Why aren't you at the club drinking properly?" He gestured toward James. "Instead of sitting here, at a dirty table, with your cravat half untied, your hair a complete mess, a smudge of dirt on your shirt, and . . . is that a blackened eye? What the hell happened to you?"

James growled. "I don't want the patrons of Brooks's to see me like this. Bloody snobs, the lot of them. And as for the eye, some bloke said something I didn't particularly agree with earlier."

"Fighting in a public tavern, Medford? Really?" Ashbourne shook his head while obviously trying to hold back his laughter.

James narrowed his eyes on the earl. "Don't give me another reason for a fight."

Ashbourne held up both hands in a conciliatory

manner. "Don't think I—" He looked twice. "Holy God, man. Are you drinking gin?"

"Yes," James replied, slurring the word a bit. "And I intend to drink more gin and more after that. Now sit down. I summoned you to drink with me, not to judge me."

Colton and Ashbourne exchanged knowing looks, pulled out two dirty stools, and took their seats.

Ashbourne's grin spread across his entire face. "You've summoned the right chaps. Far be it from me to argue with you when you're in one of your moods, Medford. Tell us, did you find the duchess?"

"Don't call her that," James snapped, frowning at them.

Ashbourne shook his head. "Oh no, Medford, please don't tell me you're an angry drunk. And here all this time I'd pegged you for a jolly one. It's ever so much more endearing to be jolly . . . like me."

James grunted. "Yes, I saw her."

"And?" Colton arched a brow.

"And she refused me." James tossed back another shot of gin.

Another whistle from Ashbourne. "Did she now?"

"Do you think I would make that up?" James spat.

"Look on the bright side, man," Ashbourne replied. "You won't have to be leg-shackled. Besides, not quite the best form to ask a new widow to marry you. If you two weren't already courting scandal, God knows you'd be run out of town after a fast marriage. She's supposed to still be in mourning."

James lunged out of his seat at Ashbourne. Colton stood up quickly and held him back. "Now, now, now. No need to take a swing at the bloke," Colton said, ensuring that James grudgingly sat back down.

Ashbourne snorted. "Right. You don't want your other eye blackened."

James merely growled at him.

"You can hardly be angry, Medford," Colton continued. "It's not even as if she's the first lady you asked to marry you."

James propped his elbow on the table, letting his fingers weave through his hair. "This is completely different."

Ashbourne and Colton exchanged glances again.

"Hand me the bottle." James reached across the table for the gin.

"Hold on," Ashbourne said. James watched while he and Colton both received their own dirty glasses from one of the barmaids and tipped the bottle into their own cups.

Ashbourne raised his glass. "If you're going to do this, you might as well do it properly," he said, tipping back his drink. "Let's go."

Hours later, with James passed out on the table, Colton and Ashbourne stood up, tossed an indecent number of coins on the table, and each took one of Medford's arms. They pulled their friend's limp body and hefted him up to rest on their shoulders.

Ashbourne shook his head. "And to think of all the years we've tried to get the good viscount to relax and have a good time."

Colton nodded over Medford's head. "Seems he learned a bit too well."

Ashbourne flashed a grin. "He always was a perfect student."

"Too good," Colton agreed, also grinning. "But of course, tonight he learned from the very best tutors." He hefted Medford up again. "Let's get him home."

Sticking his hat on his head and wrapping his cloak loosely around his shoulders, they pulled him out into the street where they maneuvered him into Colton's waiting coach. "I'll take him to my house. Keep an eye on him. God knows the man's probably never suffered the aftereffects of a night of drinking. Things may not be good in the morning."

"You know what we must do, don't you?" Ashbourne said, climbing into the coach with his friend.

"What's that?" Colton replied.

They propped Medford in the corner where his chin rested on his chest. Ashbourne leaned against the opposite seat. "This bloke here has done us both a good turn when we were in similar pitiful circumstances."

Colton arched a brow. "You mean being in love?"

"Quite right," Ashbourne replied, leaning back against the seat, stretching out his legs and crossing them at the ankles.

Colton shrugged. "So?"

"So, it's our turn, Colton. We owe him one. It's our duty to assist the poor sop."

CHAPTER 40

When James awoke the next morning, the bed was turning in sickening circles. He cracked open one eye and surveyed his surroundings. His stomach lurched. He swallowed. Correction. It wasn't the bed. The *room* was turning in sickening circles. He glanced around. A room he didn't recognize. He struggled to sit up and groaned, pushing a hand to his pounding forehead. He pulled himself upright against the pillows and grasped his pulsing head in his hands.

Where the hell was he? What had he done last night? His mind traced back. Bloody hell. That's right. Blue ruin. The tavern. Colton and Ashbourne. He must have passed out. He couldn't remember anything after perhaps the fifth—the sixth, was it?—glass of the stuff. He groaned. Colton or Ashbourne must have taken him home and tossed him into a spare room. Wonderful.

A knock sounded at the door and James winced. "Come in," he croaked.

The door cracked open and Lily stepped into the room, a bright smile on her face.

Hmm. Apparently, he was at Colton's house. James

glanced down to ensure he was decent. Oh bloody hell. He was still wearing his clothing from last night. Even better.

"Good morning, Medford," Lily said. "I've been waiting to hear you stir." She held a glass in her hand filled with a yellowish-green substance.

James leaned back against the pillows and pushed a palm to his forehead. "Please lower your voice. What are you doing here?"

Lily laughed and then stopped short to whisper. "What are *you* doing here is the better question. You're in our house. Devon tells me he and Jordan had to carry you up here last night." She clucked her tongue and shook her head at James. "What happened to your eye?"

"Long story."

Lily shook her head again. "I must say I'm a bit shocked actually, Medford. I've never seen you so . . ." She eyed him up and down and gestured to him with her free hand. "Disheveled."

Without opening his eyes, he groaned. "I've never felt like this."

"Like what?"

"As if an entire orchestra were playing in my head, and I'm about to toss the contents of my—"

"Oh yes, well, as to that." Lily held out the glass to him. "Devon says to drink this."

James lifted his head and popped open one eye. He arched a brow and gave the glass a suspicious look. "What is it?"

Lily shrugged. "I have no idea. To be honest, I'm not sure I want to know. But Devon went into the kitchens and mixed it himself. It looks absolutely dreadful and smells worse, I'm afraid, but Devon swears it'll fix your head."

"Colton made this? What is he, a bloody apothecary now?"

Lily gave him a stern stare. "Be nice."

James reluctantly lifted his hand and took the glass. He stared at it. He sniffed it. "It smells worse than I feel."

Lily cracked a smile and plunked her hands on her hips. "That may be true, but do you doubt for a moment that *Devon* knows how to relieve a sick head?"

James growled. "Unfortunately, for me and my palate, I don't doubt it at all."

He slowly moved the noxious substance to his lips, took a sip, and shuddered. "Good God. I refuse to drink that."

"Oh, I nearly forgot," Lily said, pointing one finger in the air and wagging it. "Devon said to pinch your nose and down it quickly all at once. Don't taste it. Much easier, according to him."

James narrowed his eyes on her. "Thank you for telling me that *after* I've tasted it."

She affected a curtsy. "My pleasure."

James shuddered. Might as well get this unpleasant task over with. Colton of all people had probably invented this stuff. The man was a drunkard. Pinching his nose, James tossed the entire contents of the glass into the back of his throat. He swallowed, then coughed, and gagged. "Jesus. That was disgusting."

Lily winced. "Yes. Devon said you'd say that too."

James shook his head, doing his level best not to gag. He pounded his chest with the side of his fist. "I think I'd rather be sick."

Lily patted him on the foot through the covers. "It shouldn't take long to feel better, according to Devon. We'll have the coach brought round to take you home when you're ready." She moved back toward the door. "Just say the word. By the way, it's nearly noon. Don't forget that you must get ready for this evening."

James let his head fall back against the pillows again and shut his eyes. He scowled. "It's nearly noon? No wonder I never took to drinking. Half the day is gone." He paused and opened one eye. "Wait. This evening? What's this evening?"

"Why, Catherine Eversly's New Year's masquerade, of course. You cannot miss it. She'll be devastated if you do."

James groaned. "I'm not about to go to any—" His voice rose, and he winced. Blast. He'd been too loud. That hurt.

"Oh, you're coming all right," Lily replied in her most matter-of-fact voice. "Even if we must march over to your house and drag you there."

The knock on her bed chamber door made Kate's stomach clench. She couldn't open it. What if it was James again? Seeing him yesterday, sending him away, had nearly killed her. She couldn't do it again. If he were back with a pocketful of outrage, demanding that she marry him, she just might give in and forget her plans to go off alone to the Continent. But she had to be strong, for her sake . . . and for his.

"Who is it?" she called tentatively.

"It's Lily and Annie," came Lily's voice through the wooden door. "We hope you don't mind. Lady Catherine let us in."

Kate closed her eyes briefly and said a prayer of thanks. She hurried to the door and swung it open. She smiled at her friends. Lily and Annie hugged her one after another.

"I was afraid you were . . ." Kate glanced away. "It doesn't matter. Come in. Come in."

Kate stepped back and Annie and Lily moved into the room. "Please, sit, sit." She gestured to the little seating area in the corner of her room.

"Lord Medford came, didn't he?" Annie asked, plucking off her gloves and taking a seat in a chair by the window.

Kate nodded. "Yesterday."

Lily shook her head. She'd remained standing and had moved over to the window, looking out to the street below. "We didn't tell him you were here, Kate. We promise. I have no idea how he found out."

Kate nodded. "I know. He told me. Seems he bribed his way through all the hotels in London. And then Lady Catherine paid him a visit."

"Medford giving bribes?" Annie's brow was furrowed. "That doesn't sound like him."

Lily turned to face Kate. "He was so upset when he found out you were gone, Kate. Truly. You should have seen him. He raised his voice at me."

Kate bit her lip. She didn't want to hear this. She was barely hanging on to her resolve as it was. "I can't . . . that is to say, I'd rather not talk about James if that's all right with you."

Lily walked over and looped her arm through Kate's. "Absolutely, we completely understand."

"Yes, we just came to see how you are doing," Annie added.

"And to ensure that you're coming to the masquerade ball tonight." Lily winked.

"The masq—" Kate's mouth dropped open. "Masquerade?"

Lily squeezed Kate's arm. "Yes, it's here, tonight. Didn't Lady Catherine tell you? She holds one every year at this time. It is the most fun. You simply must attend."

Kate pulled away from Lily and shook her head. "Lady Catherine mentioned it to me but I thought she was just being polite. She must know . . . You must know . . . I cannot come to a *ton* event. It's impossible. I won't be welcome."

"Ah, but that is the beauty of the masquerade," Lily replied with a wink. "We've already spoken to Catherine, and we all agree. No one will know who you are. Annie and I can introduce you as our cousin on a visit from the country. Everyone will be drinking and toasting the new year. It will be perfectly safe."

Kate bit her lip. She adored parties and would love the opportunity to dance again. Once she went to the Continent, she wouldn't have the chance, perhaps ever. If she made friends there at all, the odds of her being accepted into social events were fairly slim. No, masquerades were not in her future.

"Besides," Annie added with a wide smile. "Lady Catherine is our friend, and she insists you be there. She says she's looking forward to it. And she'll keep entirely quiet about your identity."

Kate threaded her fingers together. "I just don't know if it's safe."

"It's perfectly safe," Lily replied. "Devon and Jordan will be there, and Catherine and her servants will be on the lookout. You needn't worry about a thing."

"But I'm leaving for Dover in the morning and—"

"All the more reason why you should spend your very last night in London at a masquerade."

Kate squared her shoulders. Lily was right. All the more reason. "Very well." She nodded and smiled at the sisters. "I'll come." She wanted so badly to ask if James would be there. Perhaps he would forgo the party.

Perhaps he would assume she would be there and stay away. No, why would he assume the biggest outcast in the *ton* would be attending the grandest ball of the new year? Even if she was Lady Catherine's houseguest. But he was friendly with Lady Catherine too, so it stood to reason that he would be invited. Wouldn't he? Oh, Kate mustn't think such thoughts. She would be in disguise regardless, and so would James, if he came. The ball was sure to be crowded. They probably wouldn't even see each other. Though it would be nice to see him . . . one more time.

"Oh, I'm so glad you've said yes," Annie replied, jumping up from her seat and giving Kate a quick hug. "We'll just go back to the coach and get your costume then."

Kate blinked. "My costume?"

"Yes." Lily winked at her. "We brought it with us as we were so hoping you'd say yes."

Kate couldn't help her laugh. "By all means, then, go and get it. I cannot wait to see my costume."

CHAPTER 41

Kate felt like a fairy princess. Perhaps because she was dressed like one. Her gown was a midnight-blue concoction with wide skirts and two tiers of underskirts, a fitted, nearly indecent bodice and long sleeves. Her mask was just as daring, a demimask also made of midnight-blue satin with two wide feathers, one blue and one black, sweeping above her right eye. Annie and Lily had assured her that she would be unrecognizable in the mask and they'd been right. Except for her hair and eyes of course. She sighed. She supposed she had the element of surprise on her side. Who in the *ton* would expect the scandalous dowager Duchess of Markingham to be attempting to sneak into a masquerade ball?

Lily was dressed in dashing jade green with an equally impressive matching demimask and Annie wore her favorite pink accented by a pink and white mask.

Lord Ashbourne and Lord Colton were dressed entirely in black. The blackness of Lord Ashbourne's mask set off the man's intriguing silver eyes, making him look quite the rogue. Colton wore a silver mask that slightly relieved the darkness of his hair and eyes. Both men and their lovely wives looked positively splendid, Kate thought as their coach pulled to a stop in front of Lady Catherine Eversly's town house. Lily and Annie had decided their ruse of introducing Kate as their cousin would be more plausible were she to arrive with them, so the two sisters had brought Kate to Annie's house earlier to prepare for the ball. Now they were returning, all dressed up.

They waited in the seemingly endless line to enter the ball and Kate couldn't help but rise on tiptoes to see if she recognized James. Lily and Annie hadn't said a word about James all afternoon. She'd asked them not to speak of him earlier so she could hardly make a show of asking about him now, could she? If he were here, he hadn't come with his friends. Perhaps he wasn't invited after all. Oh, she desperately wanted to ask Lily if that were true. But she held her tongue.

If asked, Kate was pretending to be Lily's cousin Althea. She could only hope that no one looked too closely. Apparently, Lily's cousin lived in Northumberland and hadn't been to town in years. Thankfully, she too had red hair. She pinched the inside of her arm. "Courage, courage, courage," Kate whispered to herself.

Catherine Eversly was dressed entirely in sparkling silver. The beautiful blond woman swept over to their little group soon after their arrival and hugged each of them individually.

"Who have we here?" she whispered conspiratorially, in her lovely, sultry voice. "My, but you all look like a merry band of misfits."

She turned her crystal-blue gaze toward Kate and winked and Kate was suddenly quite glad to have come after all.

"Thank you very much for the invitation, Lady Catherine," Kate replied. "I am very honored to have been invited." And then lower, "And I cannot thank you enough for all you've done for me."

"Yes, well, welcome one and all," Catherine said. "But beware." From behind her mask, she arched a brow at Kate. "We have a tradition here. We count down the seconds to the new year and when the clock strikes twelve and the church bells ring, we all remove our masks."

Kate bit her lip. She'd have to be gone by midnight.

Catherine turned back to Lily and the others. "By the by, your friend Medford is already here. I must say, the man's drinking more than I've ever known him to." She looked off into the crowd. "He was over by the French doors the last time I looked. If I see him, I'll send him over. I daresay he'd love to meet your cousin." She gave Kate a little smile.

Kate's stomach lurched. James was here? Lily and Annie rocked on their toes and exchanged glances. Kate narrowed her eyes. Why did she have the feeling she was in the middle of a very large and carefully orchestrated conspiracy?

She turned to ask Lily a question and something caught her eye. A flash of red, a laugh, a set of deep-set dark eyes on a woman across from them.

Lady Bettina.

Lily saw her too at nearly the same moment. She squeezed Kate's hand. "Let's go," she said. "I'm sure we can find a more inviting place to stand."

"No," Kate insisted, pulling away from Lily's grasp. "I have something to say to her."

Lily shook her head. "Kate, you can't. If she learns who you are, that you're here—"

"Don't worry," Kate added. But she wasn't even listening to Lily any more. Instead, she found herself moving toward Lady Bettina as if her feet were not under her own control any longer. She walked straight up to the woman but didn't remove her mask.

"Lady Bettina?"

The dark-haired beauty stopped laughing at whatever the man next to her had said and turned to look at her. "Yes?"

It was clear she didn't recognize whom she was speaking to. Thank God.

"I wanted to tell you how sorry I am about the Duke of Markingham's death."

Lady Bettina narrowed her eyes. "Who are you?"

"It doesn't matter. I'm merely an old friend of the duke's."

The gentleman next to her laughed. "Yes, well, it's too bad that Markingham got shot by his own valet, no less, but his loss is my gain."

Lady Bettina smiled at that and the man, whom Kate didn't recognize, leaned down and kissed her on the neck. Kate sucked in her breath. Not only were the man's words cruel but Lady Bettina had clearly already taken up with a new lover. Here she'd been feeling a bit sorry for her, thinking that she'd truly been in love with George, and all the while she'd been out finding a new protector.

"Oh, you're bad, Kingston, very bad," Lady Bettina purred. Turning her attention back to Kate, she said, "Yes, well, dear, I've never been much for mourning, as you can see." And she laughed, took a long sip from her champagne flute, and rubbed her hand possessively over Kingston's chest.

Kate felt ill. There was no reason to confront this woman, reveal her identity. She felt sorry too, actually, sorry for George. He'd believed the woman loved him and obviously she'd only been using him for his title and money.

Without saying another word, Kate turned away from the sickening pair. She was through with them, through with her old life and everyone in it. Tonight she intended to have fun. She made her way back to Lily's side. "I want to dance," she whispered to the marchioness. "I want to dance and dance."

"Then dance you shall," Lily said with a smile. She tapped Devon on the shoulder and soon Kate was whirling around the room with the handsome marquis, a glass of champagne in one hand and a smile on her lips. And suddenly it didn't matter why she was there. It didn't matter that she didn't know where James was and that Lady Bettina was detestable. Kate was having fun again. And she intended to have a great deal more of it.

After dancing with three more debonair gentlemen in a row, Kate made her way over to the refreshment table to retrieve another glass of champagne. The crowd had long ago separated her from Lily and Annie and their husbands. And with so many people wearing such elaborate costumes, it was difficult to know just who was who.

She pressed her palm against her stomach. James was here. He was here in the crowd somewhere. But she'd never know him. Never find him. She had no clue how he was dressed. What color was his mask? Oh, it was better this way, not to know. If she knew what to look for, no doubt she'd be constantly scanning the ballroom, looking for him, searching him out, hoping to get a chance to see him, talk to him, hear his voice.

Oh, who was she fooling? She was already looking for him. With every male voice that drifted to her ears, she strained to hear a familiar tone. With every male costume that crossed her path, she scanned the gentleman's eyes, hoping to see the hazel she knew so well. She tossed back her second glass of champagne. That was it. She had to stop thinking about James. A London New Year's masquerade ball was something she'd never been to before, and would never attend again. And she intended to enjoy herself.

She turned to leave the refreshment table, to go in search of Lily and Annie, when a snippet of conversation to her right caught her attention.

"I heard the duchess is leaving for the Continent as soon as possible," said a shrill female voice.

Kate glanced over her shoulder. She didn't recognize the hefty woman dressed in a horrendous puce color or her older male counterpart dressed in bright peach, but Kate was rooted to the spot.

"Yes, well, it cannot happen quickly enough if you ask me. She should leave this town as soon as possible," the man answered.

"I've heard she's staying in a hotel," the woman said in a disgusted tone.

"Wouldn't surprise me," replied the man. "Some establishments will take in any riffraff."

The woman took a sip of champagne. "I, for one, shall never believe she didn't kill him. The valet may have confessed, but I don't believe it for one moment."

The man nodded and his jowls shook. "Neither do I."

Tears of anger stung the backs of Kate's eyes. She turned to move away from the conversation, not wanting to hear a bit more of it. This was why she couldn't come into London Society. Ever. Even if she were wearing a disguise. She wasn't welcome here and she never would be. She would find Lily and Annie and give her regrets, and quietly slip upstairs to her guest chamber. She never should have come.

She took her first step, just as a tall man wearing all black with a dark green mask pushed past her. He addressed his comments to the couple who'd just been speaking.

"Please tell me, Lady Cranberry, that you were not just speaking of Kate, the dowager Duchess of Markingham," the tall man said in a clipped voice.

Kate's breath caught in her throat. She couldn't move. She knew that voice. Familiar and deep and wonderful. *James.* She hadn't recognized him when he'd brushed past her, but now there was no mistaking it. He was here and he appeared to be coming to her defense. She moved to the side of the table again and picked up another glass of champagne, trying to look as inconspicuous as possible, but a small crowd had already begun to form around the threesome since James had raised his voice.

"Lord Medford, is that you?" Lady Cranberry straightened to her full height, which wasn't very high at all.

"It is," he replied through clenched teeth.

Kate moved into the corner behind a potted palm and clutched her champagne flute, her gaze darting back and forth. The group around the other three was growing and no one was paying a bit of attention to her, thank heavens.

"What if we were speaking of the duchess?" Lord Cranberry cleared his throat. "Do you dare to defend that trollop?"

James took two steps toward the shorter man and towered over him. "Yes. I. Do." There was no mistaking the tightly controlled anger in his voice.

The crowd was growing larger and larger.

Lord Cranberry straightened his shoulders too. He hefted his girth as if he were trying to suck it in. "Seems you would have learned your lesson, Medford. Harboring her. I'm surprised Lady Catherine let you in the door tonight. She's clearly not attending to her guest list properly."

James's voice was a low growl. "What in the hell is that supposed to mean?"

"Only that you keep company like that and you get what you deserve," Lady Cranberry retorted, her nose in the air. "Everyone knows your town house was destroyed because you were harboring that rubbish."

James's voice thundered loudly enough for the entire assembled crowd to hear. His feet were braced apart and he shook with unleashed fury. "Know this. The dowager Duchess of Markingham is better than either one of you will ever be. She's a kind, generous, loving person who was falsely accused and who has since been exonerated."

Lord Cranberry's face turned cranberry, and it did not go well with peach. He tugged at his lapels. "She may have been exonerated but that doesn't prove—"

"Yes. It. Does. You small-minded twit," James replied. "And if I ever hear you breathe another unkind word about her, you'll have *me* to answer to. Do you understand?"

Lord and Lady Cranberry huffed and puffed. They searched around as if looking for friendly faces in the crowd to agree with them. Everyone else seemed suddenly preoccupied with their conversations, as if they hadn't all just been staring aghast at Medford's confrontation with the couple.

James turned to the assembled group, his glass of brandy sloshing over his hand. "Does everyone hear that? The same goes for all of you. Anyone who utters a word against the duchess will answer to me."

Complete silence.

James stalked off then. Pushing through the crowd,

he made his way out of the ballroom. The mass of people erupted in a sea of whispers and speculation. The entire ballroom, it seemed, was talking about him. And her. Oh, he'd really gone and done it now. But he'd defended her. Gloriously, wonderfully, heroically defended her.

Kate watched him go, with tears welling in her eyes.

CHAPTER 42

Kate downed the rest of her champagne for courage and hurriedly set the empty flute on a side table. Tears blinding her, she pushed her way through the crowd. She elbowed and shoved. The partygoers were wall-to-wall, all whispering, giggling, and conjecturing. She couldn't get past them. They all seemed to be headed in the opposite direction, trying to get to the back of the ballroom to see what all the fuss was about. But Kate, Kate was trying to get to the front of the ball-room, to follow James out the door.

She finally made it, pushing past scores of people, her wide blue skirts not helping at all. She threw open the double doors to the ballroom and rushed into the cold corridor, looking both ways. In the shadowy dark-ness, she glimpsed the black of James's evening attire slipping through a set of French doors onto a balcony at the end of the hallway. She picked up her skirts and ran, her blue slippers slapping against the marble floors.

By the time she made it to the end of the hallway,

she was breathing heavily, her chest aching. She dropped her skirts and grasped the handles to the French doors, pushed them open and stepped out onto the balcony. The freezing wind whipped across her face, but she could barely feel it.

James was there, alone, his arms braced on the balustrade, his drink still in his hand. He stared off across the rooftops, his breath making streams in the night sky.

He was so noble and handsome and . . . perfect. Her heart wrenched. She wouldn't have believed it before. If she hadn't heard his speech to the Cranberrys. But those hadn't been the words of a man who was just trying to do the right thing. Those had been the words of a man who cared. Truly cared. Loved her, perhaps? Every word he'd said had seared her heart and she couldn't leave without giving them one more chance.

"James," she breathed.

He turned around at the sound of her voice. He paused. He set his jaw. "I didn't know you were here."

"I came with Lily and Annie, and I am, here that is, and I . . . I heard what you said . . . to the Cranberrys."

He spat his words through a clenched jaw. "The Cranberrys don't know what the hell they're talking about."

"James." She moved over to him and touched his sleeve. "Thank you."

He stood up straight and took a drink. "You're always thanking me, Kate. And you have nothing to thank me for."

"I have everything to thank you for."

He eyed her up and down. "I assume you are still leaving for the Continent tomorrow."

She struggled to breathe evenly. Oh God, she knew

it. The next few moments would decide their entire future. "It . . . depends," she murmured.

He narrowed his eyes on her. "Upon what?"

"On whether you still want to marry me." Her voice broke on the last two words.

James lifted his free hand and let it fall back to his side. Then his face went hard, like stone, and Kate's stomach dropped.

"What do you mean, Kate?" His voice was too hard.

She searched his face. His hazel eyes looked positively green from behind his emerald mask. "Do you want to marry me, James?"

He turned. Setting his glass aside, he braced his hands on the balustrade. "Damn it, Kate. I did. God knows I did."

"And you don't anymore?" She held her breath, cold tears trembling on her lashes. He couldn't mean it. Things couldn't have changed so much in merely a day. Not to mention, he'd just given the most chivalrous speech back there on her behalf. He had to love her. Didn't he?

He expelled his breath hard, another white puff in the freezing night sky. "I asked you to marry me, Kate, and you left."

She reached for him, grabbed his sleeve. "James, I love you. I just couldn't tell you before. I didn't want you to give up your life for me. Give up your reputation for me. But back there . . ." She gestured to the ballroom. "I realized. You already have."

"I told you that already, Kate. What makes tonight any different than Christmas? Didn't you love me then?"

"Yes. Yes, of course, but I didn't want to hurt you."

He looked down and shook his head. "You wouldn't have hurt me, Kate."

She dug her nails into the palm of her opposite hand. He was talking about it all in the past tense. As if there were no hope. She couldn't stand it. What was it her mother had always said? There was nothing two deep breaths won't cure. Kate took two very deep breaths and exhaled. "I didn't understand that then. I thought . . . Lily told me you'd offered for her last spring and I was convinced you were just trying to fix things again. I didn't think you loved me. Do you, James? Do you love me?" He'd turned to face her, and her eyes frantically searched his face.

His jaw was tight. "Don't make me answer that, Kate. It doesn't matter now."

Tears streaked down her cheeks. They nearly froze in the cold wind. "Why? Why not?"

"I've never felt the way I do about you for any woman before. I've never— Damn it. I didn't want to lose you. Lose the only other woman I ever gave a damn about losing. But I already did. I lost you." He glanced away and there was a distant, dark look in his eyes. One that made Kate's heart plummet. "I cannot do it again."

"No, James. Listen to me." She stepped forward and grabbed his shoulders. "Can't we start over? Ask me to marry you again, James. Ask me—"

From inside the ballroom, the crowd grew louder. It had to be nearly midnight. Kate held her breath, watching James's stony face. He remained completely silent.

From inside the ballroom, the crowd began to chant. *Ten. Nine. Eight. Seven. Six. Five. Four. Three. Two. One.*

The crowd erupted into a mass of cheers as the church bells all over the city rang.

Kate ripped the mask from her head and searched

James's face. "Ask me, James," she whispered brokenly. "Ask me."

He pulled her hand away from his shoulder and placed it back at her side. He shook his head. "It's too late."

CHAPTER 43

Somehow James had ended up back at Colton's town house. After his discussion on the balcony with Kate last night, he'd gone back into the party, ignored the stares and whispers, and danced, and drank and drank and danced some more. He was vaguely aware of the fact that Lily and Annie had left. They'd probably taken Kate up to her room, but Colton and Ashbourne dogged his steps the rest of the night, and now he was staring down another glass of that foul-smelling concoction that Colton had forced on him the day before. How in the hell had Colton and Ashbourne handled all of this in their younger days? James had been doing it for only two nights and already felt half dead. Though he had to reluctantly admit, whatever was in that awful concoction, it had worked. After drinking it the day before, he'd felt better almost immediately.

Lily brought the stuff again. She carried it on a silver tray along with a note from Colton asking James to meet him in his study in half an hour.

"How are you today, Medford?" Lily asked, watching him carefully.

"Not good," he answered.

"You know, Kate—"

"No!" He held up a hand. "I do not want to talk about Kate."

Lily slid the silver tray onto the bed next to James and then she plunked her hands on her hips. "I have something to say, my lord, and I'm going to say it even if you don't want to hear it."

James rubbed his temples. "Fine." He groaned. "Get it over with."

"I spoke to Kate last night and . . ." Lily bit her lip. "It seems I'd accidentally told her at Colton House that you'd offered for me and . . . well, she didn't quite understand. I'm sorry, Medford. I didn't mean to complicate matters, I apologized to Kate. I explained our friendship and why you'd offered for me."

James's face was blank. "I fail to see why that matters."

Lily sighed. "You obviously don't know women like you think you do."

He arched a brow and gave her a wry smile.

"Look. We both know you only offered for me because your heart wasn't involved. If it had been, if I could have truly hurt you, you wouldn't have offered."

He glanced away and cursed under his breath. "I hope you're about to get to your point."

"You're angry with Kate," she said. "I understand. But you know what I think?"

His voice was clipped. "Something tells me you're about to say it even if I don't want to hear it."

Lily cracked a smile. "You're right." She folded her arms over her chest. "I think you are pushing Kate away now because she *does* have the power to hurt you. She has the power to hurt you very much and you cannot allow it."

James expelled his breath and closed his eyes. "Are you quite through?"

Lily let out a frustrated breath and pushed the silver tray closer to him. "Yes, I'm through. But I wish you'd at least consider what I have to say." She pointed at the green drink on the tray. "Drink this. Feel better. Then meet Devon downstairs. Perhaps *he* can talk some sense into you."

"Don't count on it," James bit out.

He watched Lily stomp off, slamming the door behind her without a care for his pounding head. He winced. He supposed he deserved that. He'd been a complete ass since the moment she'd walked in the room. But he refused to listen. He knew exactly what he was doing. Using reason. Using logic. Since when had those two things ever let him down?

And now Colton wanted to speak to him. Perfect. He'd entertain a conversation with the marquis for exactly five minutes, thank him for his glass of green whatever-it-was, and be on his way. Lily and Devon may have found true love and a happily ever after, but both of them would do well to realize that they were fortunate. Happy endings didn't happen for everyone.

Pinching his nose, James downed the vile liquid in one horrible gulp, washed up as best he could using the basin in his room, and made his way down to the study a bit early.

Firming his resolve, James pushed open the doors to the room and walked inside. Colton was nowhere to be seen, but Justin was there, sitting on the sofa in the middle of the study with a book open on his lap. The two dogs, Leo and Bandit, were perched on either side of him.

"Good morning, Uncle James," Justin said in a bright, happy voice. James smiled at that. "Lily told me you were here," Justin added.

James strolled in and sat down in the chair across from the five-year-old, regarding him. "Good morning, Justin," he replied. "Lily was right. I'm here again. What are you reading?"

"A book about Egypt," Justin said. "I intend to go there someday. I'm going to travel all around the world."

"Ah, you have lofty aspirations. That's good."

Justin nodded matter-of-factly. "Have you traveled around the world, Uncle James?"

James cracked another smile. "Not around it, entirely, lad, but some of it, to be sure."

"I intend to travel around all of it. I want to go to India, Constantinople, the Americas. Everywhere!"

"What about the Continent? Do you intend to travel through Europe?"

"Oh yes, of course." Justin nodded again. The child tilted his head and regarded James through dark, assessing eyes. "Why are you here, Uncle James? I've never known you to stay at our town house before."

James cleared his throat. Justin was too astute by half. Always had been. "I had a bit of an . . . overzealous evening last night, I'm afraid."

Justin righted his head. "Lily says you're sad."

James frowned. "She did, did she?"

"Yes. Why are you sad, Uncle James? Is it because your house burned down?"

James nearly had a coughing fit. "Who told you my house burned down?"

Justin shrugged. "Lily and Aunt Annie."

"Of course." James shook his head. "No. I'm not sad because my house burned down. It was only a house."

Justin appeared to consider that for a moment before closing the book and setting it aside. Bandit moved out of the way to allow for it. "Then why *are* you sad, Uncle James?"

"I'm not—" James sighed. He scrubbed his hand across his face. No use pretending with Justin. Children had a knack for getting to the heart of things, particularly this very intelligent child. "I'm just . . . a bit . . . unhappy."

"Why?"

There was that question again. James regarded the boy. Astute, this one. He shrugged. "It's complicated."

Justin folded his little hands in his lap. "When people tell me it's complicated they usually mean they don't want to explain it to me because they don't think I'll understand."

James struggled to hide his smile. "Is that right?"

Justin nodded. "Lily told me that you and I have something in common. I think it's what makes you sad."

James looked twice. "Something in common? What's that?"

"My mother died when I was born. Lily told me yours did too."

James expelled his breath as if a punch had just landed in his gut. He'd never even thought about it before, but it was true. Justin's mother was Colton's former mistress. Colton hadn't known she was with child. Alone and penniless, she'd given birth to the boy in a poorhouse and died the same day. The other women who lived there took pity on the baby and cared for him. If it hadn't been for Colton's father attempting to use the boy as a pawn for his own reasons and retrieving the lad, Justin might have grown up without a father too, without any family. Justin would have had a very different life. But the boy was right. The two of them did have that in common. Their births had caused their mothers' deaths.

"I'm sorry your mother died," James said solemnly.

"I'm sorry yours did," Justin replied just as solemnly.

He petted Bandit who hopped up to try to lick his face. "You know what Mrs. Appleby told me about my mother?"

James braced himself, something about angels and being watched over, no doubt. He was glad that sort of thing could comfort the boy, but it was hardly something that could help him. "What's that?"

"Life is for the living."

James snapped up his head. His brow furrowed. "What?"

"Life is for the living," Justin repeated. "I used to be sad because my mother was dead and because I'd never know her or see her. But Mrs. Appleby said that my mother wouldn't want that for me. She said my mother would hate to know I'm spending my time being sad for her."

James narrowed his eyes on the boy. He'd always known Justin was uncommonly clever for his age, Lily had told him so on more than one occasion, but the lad had surprised him. No doubt about it.

"I'm sure she would," James replied.

"You know what I think, Uncle James?" Justin asked.

"What's that, lad?"

The boy stood, picked up his book, and made his way to the door. The two dogs hopped from the sofa and followed close on his heels. "I think your mother wouldn't want you to be sad about her either. She would want you to live." Justin slipped through the door and James watched him go with what he was sure was a look of complete amazement on his face.

He scratched his head. Had he just received a life lesson from a five-year-old? He considered the boy's words. Life was indeed for the living. James had spent his whole life in pursuit of perfection, in an effort to make up for the loss of his mother. He couldn't see it in his own life, but when he considered Justin's situation, it seemed so clear. Of course Justin's mother didn't blame him. He'd been an infant, an innocent. There was nothing the boy could have done to prevent her death. And a normal father like Colton never would have blamed him, even if he'd been madly in love with the boy's mother. A sane person doesn't blame an infant for a mother's death. James had known his father was mad, but it hadn't hit him so squarely in the chest as it did after his discussion with Justin. By God, the child was right. Life was for the living and it had taken a little boy to teach him that.

James sprang up from his chair. Kate had hurt him, it was true. She'd hurt him by leaving and he'd been reluctant to make his heart vulnerable again. But the reason he'd been so scared of being hurt had always been about his mother. That truth he'd been able to admit to himself that night at the gin house. And Kate had tried to make things right. She'd followed him onto the balcony last night and begged him to give her another chance. He'd refused her. He'd hurt her. God. They were even.

He hurried out of the room and down the hall, calling for the butler, Nicholls, to bring him his coat and hat. He had to go, immediately. He had living to do, by God. Living without the constant guilt of losing his mother. Living without the censure of his father. Living the life he wanted, the life his mother would have wanted for him.

And he knew just what he must do first.

CHAPTER 44

When Lily brought Kate the pamphlet, she set it face-down on the side table next to her bed and refused to look at it. She'd spent the past few days writing in her journal . . . that, and trying to decide what exactly she would do next. The Continent was probably still the best choice, but she hadn't been able to bring herself to leave. Not after seeing James at the masquerade, so disheveled, drinking . . . imperfect. What had she done to him? And would he realize that they were meant for each other? He'd been speaking of his mother when he'd told her he wouldn't allow the only other woman in his life to go. She knew that much. He might not have mentioned her by name, but Kate knew. He blamed himself for so many things. And that's why the man had the constant need to be perfect. Everything in this life rested on his strong, square shoulders. He took all responsibility upon himself. Just knowing it made her heart ache.

Thankfully, Lady Catherine had been kind enough to assure Kate that she could stay at her house as long as she wished. And of course, both Lily and Annie had

offered their homes to her as well. But Kate preferred
to stay with Catherine. Much less of a chance of seeing
James. Much safer . . . for her heart.

She glanced warily at the pamphlet. It sat there like
a little papery recrimination. Mocking her. She was
glad James had decided to finally publish it. It made
sense that he should recoup his losses on his house
with the profits from the thing. And she'd already read
the words before, knew every one of them by heart.
She'd spent such agonizing hours writing them. But she
just couldn't bring herself to pick it up, open it, and read
it again. It was out there now, for all of London to see.
They would judge her one way or the other. At least
now her side of the story would be told. Would Lord
and Lady Cranberry read it? Would it change their
opinion one bit? Probably not. But she hadn't written it
for relentless gossips like the Cranberrys. She'd written
it for . . . James.

She knew that now. She could admit it to herself.
She'd been so concerned about whether he believed
her. And he had. In the end, he had. He'd seen to it that
her defense was the best it could be, he'd saved her
from the mob, taken her to his country house, offered
for her . . . And she'd rejected him.

No, she would not read that pamphlet. She couldn't.
Not now. Perhaps not ever.

Two days later, Lily arrived at Lady Catherine's town
house and rapped on Kate's door. Kate let her in, regarding her friend with a weary sigh.

"You must come riding in the park with me today,"
Lily announced.

Kate sighed again. "I'm just not up to it. Not to mention it's freezing."

Lily rested one hand on her hip. "I refuse to take no

for an answer. You've been shut up in this room for days, seeing no one, doing nothing. The brisk air will be good for you."

Kate pushed up her chin. "I've been doing something. I've been writing in my journal."

"Not good enough. I insist you get out. You'll go mad in here."

"What if someone sees me?" Kate replied.

"The devil take them." Lily tossed her hand in the air. "If they say a word against you, they'll have to answer to me . . . and my riding crop."

Kate couldn't help but smile at that, though she shook her head.

Lily tapped her foot on the rug. "I'll wait while you put on your pelisse."

"Lily, truly, I don't want—"

Lily arched a brow. "You're coming and that's it. I'll brook no further discussion on the subject."

Kate made her way toward the wardrobe, grumbling. "Obviously, you're the one who's gone mad, but very well."

Lily's voice contained a smile. "Don't worry. There are few people in the park this time of year at any rate, far too cold."

Kate grudgingly pulled on her wrap. She had to admit, it would be nice to get out of the room. "Very well, let's go."

Lily looped her arm through Kate's and led her toward the door. "Excellent. Now that that's settled, I've been on tenterhooks. What did you think of Medford's pamphlet?"

Kate stopped short. "I haven't read it. I couldn't."

Lily turned to Kate, her eyes wide. "You *must* be jesting."

Kate returned her stare. "No. I'm not. Besides, I already know what it says."

Letting go of Kate's arm, Lily marched over to the side table and swiped up the pamphlet. "Let's go." She motioned toward the door, shooing Kate out.

Kate rolled her eyes. "What are you planning to do . . . force me to read it?"

Lily pulled the door shut behind them. "If I must."

As it turned out, Lily had been right. *Very* few people were in the park at this time of year. And for good reason. The cold was biting. But the brisk air felt good on Kate's face for a change, and the bashful January sun had decided to make an appearance today. Kate raised her cheeks to the light and closed her eyes, breathing in the crisp afternoon air, while Lily maneuvered the curricle with a sure hand.

"Have you seen him?" Kate finally asked, breaking the silence between them. Then she cursed herself. Apparently, she couldn't go fifteen minutes without mentioning James.

Lily gave her a sly smile. "Medford?"

Kate nodded. "Yes. How is he?" She twisted her skirts with her gloved hands.

Lily let out a long sigh. "The truth is, I've never seen him look so poorly and I told him as much."

Kate's hand flew to her throat and she clutched at the fastening to her pelisse. "Really?"

"Yes, really." Lily nodded.

Kate bit her lip. "I know I should go to the Continent, but I just can't seem to make myself leave."

"May I give you a bit of advice?" Lily watched her from the corner of her eye.

"Yes, of course."

"You might begin by reading the pamphlet." Lily inclined her head toward where the folded paper lay on the seat next to them, exactly where Lily had placed it when they'd climbed aboard the vehicle.

Kate turned her face away. "I told you. I can't."

"Do you intend to take my advice or don't you?" Lily asked in a singsong voice.

"Lily." Kate couldn't keep the exasperation from her voice. She rolled her eyes. "I know what it says."

"Read it," Lily prompted, pointing at the pamphlet with her riding crop. She gave a stern shake of her head.

"Lily, I don't—"

This time Lily rolled her eyes. "Will you stop being so stubborn and read it?"

Kate set her jaw. She didn't want to relive those feelings, that pain, the moment when she'd found George's body. They were all there in stark detail. And she didn't want to revisit that dark place. Not today, perhaps not ever. Why was Lily so intent upon forcing her to?

Kate plucked the pamphlet off the seat, glanced down at it, and steeled herself.

"SECRETS OF A SCANDALOUS GENTLEMAN."

She blinked and looked twice. That wasn't supposed to be the title. Not at all. Her eyes scanned the first several words.

"The truth is that this pamphlet was supposed to be the confessions of Kate Townsende, the dowager Duchess of Markingham."

Kate's heart beat faster.

"But it is not that. It is a confession still, but not the duchess's confession. In fact, it is mine."

Kate swallowed hard. "James, no," she whispered.

"I am James Bancroft, Viscount Medford, and I am the owner and publisher of the press that published

this pamphlet. My work includes Secrets of a Wedding Night *and* Secrets of a Runaway Bride. *I've delighted in bringing you, the good people of London, scandal in the form of salacious pamphlets. I had intended to bring you the duchess's story. But someone very young yet very wise taught me something recently, and now I understand that publishing scandal is not my true purpose."*

Kate's eyes filled with tears.

"By now, you have learned that the duchess has been exonerated on all charges of murder. I personally reviewed every bit of the evidence and know that she is innocent, but then I've known that for quite some time."

Kate pressed her hand to her chest. Lily gave her a sideways smile.

"The duchess was wrongly accused of murder and wrongly accused of a great many things in the minds and hearts of all of us. Only such ignorant hatred could cause an angry mob to destroy my town house. Only ignorance and judgment could incite such violence."

Kate swallowed the lump that had formed in her throat. She couldn't read fast enough.

"I write this not to convince you of her innocence, because I know you will each make your own decisions on that score. I write this instead to inform you with no uncertainty that I stand with her."

Kate gasped. Tears dropped from her eyes, landing in fat little splashes on the page and smearing the ink. She frantically brushed them away and continued to read.

"You see? The secret I am revealing here is not that I am the publisher of scandal, though no doubt that will come as a surprise to many of you. The secret, in fact, is that I am in love with Kate Townsende, madly in love, and my only hope is that she will become my wife."

Kate glanced up at Lily. She could barely speak. The lump was permanently lodged in her throat. "Where is he?" she sobbed.

Lily gave her an empathetic smile. "I believe he's at his town house. The one on Regent Street where he's been staying while the other is repaired."

"We must go." Kate choked on the words.

"Say no more." Lily had already deftly turned the conveyance around. They trotted out of the park at a brisk clip.

CHAPTER 45

Kate hiked up her skirts and rushed up the steps to James's town house as fast as she could. Her slippers slap-slap-slapped against the stone stairs. She pounded on the door and then stood back, wringing her gloved hands and staring at the portal intently as if she could force it open with her sheer will. Moments later, the heavy door swung wide, and Locke's large form filled the frame.

As soon as the butler recognized Kate, a wide smile spread across his face. "Your grace?"

Her breath came in short pants. "Tell me, Locke, is James here?" She bobbed her head, trying to catch a glimpse around the butler, into the house.

Locke's face transformed into a frown. "I'm sorry to say he is not, your grace."

Kate's heart sank. She frantically searched the butler's face. "Where is he?"

"His lordship has gone to Parliament this afternoon. The new session has just begun."

Kate leaned up on her tiptoes and deposited a kiss

on the older man's leathery cheek. He blushed and stammered. "Your grace, why, I—"

"Thank you very much, Locke." She whirled around and rushed back down the stairs and out into the muddy street where Lily sat impatiently on the seat of the curricle.

"Well?" Lily asked, her eyes as wide as the curricle wheels. "Where is he?"

"He's in session at the House of Lords."

Lily sighed and shook her head. "How do you like that? Most inconvenient. Don't worry. I'll take you back to Lady Catherine's and we'll return later when he—"

"Like hell you will."

Lily's head snapped around. Her expression could not have been more shocked had Kate just slapped her. "Pardon?"

"I said like hell you will!"

Lily's mouth dropped open. "Why, Kate. What exactly do you plan to do?" she asked breathlessly, her hand fanning out across her breastbone.

With a sly smile on her face, Kate gathered her skirts, climbed back up onto the conveyance, and took a seat next to Lily. She nodded toward the matched pair of horses. "You're taking me to Parliament. Now."

Lily gaped. "P-P-Parliament?" she stuttered, her mouth opening and closing.

"Yes. Now. Please," Kate added for good measure.

Lily shook her head. "Kate, we can't."

Kate arched a brow. "Can't or shouldn't?"

"Both!"

Kate turned to Lily and met her gaze. "With all due respect, Lady Colton, I determined several weeks ago that I intended to live. And if this isn't a moment for living, I don't know what is," she finished with a resolute nod.

Lily eyed her carefully. "But Kate, have you any idea the kind of scandal it will cause if you interrupt Parliament?"

Kate threw back her head and laughed. Now that she'd made the decision, a curious calm had come over her, a curious calm paired with a giddy happiness. "I am the original scandalous bride. I'm already an outcast. Are you seriously telling me you think I'm worried about causing another scandal? Truly?"

Lily opened her mouth to retort but quickly snapped it shut again. "When you put it like that . . ." Lily clucked to the horses and shook out the reins. The team took off at a fast pace. Kate pressed her bonnet against her head and swayed with the jolt of the carriage's movement.

What was she thinking? She moved to pinch the inside of her arm. Could she do it? Could she truly march into the Houses of Parliament and retrieve James? A thrill raced down her spine. She pulled her hand away and settled it in her lap instead. Yes, by God. She could do it and she would. *Courage. Courage. Courage. Live. Live. Live.*

Minutes later, the curricle pulled to a stop in front of Westminster. Kate stared up at the grand Gothic buildings and gulped.

"Are you quite sure about this?" Lily asked.

"Quite."

Kate squared her shoulders. She'd come within weeks, perhaps days, of a death sentence. She'd caused a spectacular scandal. Telling the man she loved that she couldn't live without him one moment longer wasn't about to stop her from rushing into the House of Lords. Hell, she'd rush into the Prince Regent's bathing parlor if she had to. Though no doubt she wouldn't like what she saw.

Kate pulled her skirts to the side and jumped from the vehicle. She turned and winked at Lily. "If I'm arrested, I expect you to call upon Mr. Abernathy."

"I shall do so with all haste," Lily replied, pressing her lips together as if to keep from laughing. "Rest assured. And good luck. Now, go." She motioned with her chin toward the buildings. "Oh, and one more thing."

"Yes?" Kate replied.

"If you see Devon, don't tell him I'm out here," she said with a wink.

Shaking her head at her friend's irreverence, Kate turned on her heel and faced the imposing Houses of Parliament. She took a deep breath, sucking cold air into her lungs. Steeling her resolve, she made her way to the south side of the Commons where the House of Lords sat. She marched up to the tall green wooden front doors. The gatekeeper, an enormous man, stood at attention. "What business do you have?" he asked in an imperious tone.

What business indeed? Hmm. She hadn't quite thought this far.

"I am the dowager Duchess of Markingham, and I have urgent information for Viscount Medford," she said in the most commanding voice she could muster. She raised her chin and stared the man straight in the eye. Unless the bloke had been unconscious for the past two months, he must have heard her name before. But would he believe she had urgent business?

His eyes flared. Ah, so he did know her name. He looked her over, up and down. She narrowed his eyes on him. *What's the matter? Never seen the subject of a scandal before?*

Finally, he stood aside. He bowed to her, then straightened and nodded. "Down the corridor, your grace. Just through those doors."

Kate expelled the breath she'd been holding since she approached the cavernous building. Good God. She'd never been so thankful to have the detested duchess title to bandy about in all her days. She had to admit, it opened doors, that title. It opened very large, grand doors.

"Thank you very much." She nodded regally to the guard and made her way past him along the corridor, exercising a degree of patience she didn't know she possessed. She longed to hike up her skirts and run, but she imagined the beefy guard tackling her and carting her off to the Tower if she attempted such a thing. No, better to remain calm and carry on as if she were just going to slip James a quiet, orderly little note.

She walked up to the side of the gallery and took two deep breaths. She stood outside the door, trying to quell the sick scared feeling in her belly. Then she pressed open the stately carved doors with shaking hands and stepped inside the large hall.

"Will the honorable gentlemen—" The loud voice that had been speaking immediately stopped and all heads swiveled to look at her.

Kate gulped but managed to raise her trembling chin. She felt like a tiny pebble lost in a sea. There were dozens of men in the room, possibly hundreds. And they were the bishops and the peers of the land. The illustrious House of Lords. The men who would have sat in judgment on her had she gone to trial. She tightened her fist. *Courage. Courage. Courage.* She'd decided to do this, and do this, she would.

"Your grace?" a man's voice commanded, and Kate turned to see the lord chancellor himself staring straight at her.

She nodded. "Lord Chancellor." Apparently, her reputation preceded her. She should have expected as much.

He arched a brow. "May we help you with something?" His voice echoed off the wood-paneled walls.

She cleared her throat. "As I believe you already know . . . I am the dowager Duchess of Markingham. And I'm here to see Viscount Medford."

Muffled gasps rippled through the gallery. If every eye hadn't indeed been trained on her before, they certainly were now. She pushed up her chin another bit. Where was James?

A great deal of coughing and mumbling ensued. Her gaze scanned both sides of the gallery. As soon as he stood, she saw him. James raised himself from a bench in the center of a large group of men on the right. "I'm here, Kate." He stared at her with reverence in his eyes. Her breathing hitched. Her chest hurt. She broke into a run.

"Your grace, what's the meaning of this?" The gavel cracked, and the lord chancellor's voice thundered across the gallery, filled with outrage and indignation.

Kate didn't care. She ran, her slippers slapping against the marble floors. She ran straight into James's arms. He'd climbed over the side of the wooden box in which he was sitting and grabbed her and hugged her. He spun her around.

"I thought you'd never come," he whispered in her ear as tears ran down her face.

"I only read the pamphlet today," she said against his rough, wonderfully familiar cheek.

"Your grace." The gavel cracked again and the lord chancellor's angry voice rang out. "It's completely improper—"

Keeping her eyes fastened on James, without turning to the lord chancellor, Kate summoned the loudest voice she could muster. "Oh, we're far past improper, my lord." She smiled to herself as she imagined the scandalized look that surely rested on the dignitary's face. Poor man.

James ran his hands along her cheeks and kissed her then, and her knees almost gave way. "Kate," he murmured. She felt so much in that one word.

"James," she murmured. "I'm waiting for you to tell me you love me."

He crumbled then. Pulling her into his arms, he kissed her fiercely then moved his mouth to her ear. "I love you, Kate. I love you. I love you."

"And I love you, James," she said between kisses and tears.

"You know your reputation will be completely gone if you marry me," she said, with a bit of a laugh.

He kissed her cheeks, her temple. "It's already gone. I don't miss it."

"You know you won't be able to fix it?"

He glanced around at the crowd staring at them with a mixture of shock and anger. James smiled a wry smile. "After this little scene, I doubt we could fix anything. Besides, I'm through trying to fix the wrong things." He stepped back and smiled at her.

She kissed him again. "Does that mean you plan to stop publishing?"

"No. I intend to use my press to help people from now on. It's as you told me, Kate. I never wanted to publish anything for the sake of scandal. I've always been trying to use my press to fix things. First the plight of the frightened bride, then to satisfy the curiosity of the young women who'd considered running off to Gretna Green. But now, now, Kate, I intend to use it for an even greater purpose, to fix things . . . the *right* things. To change the lives of those who are wrongfully accused."

A younger man leaped from his seat. "Hear, hear."

James and Kate swiveled their heads toward him. "Who is that?" Kate asked.

"That is Oliver Townsende," James replied, the hint of a smile on his face. "The new Markingham. Good chap."

Ah yes. Now she recognized him.

She didn't have long to contemplate the new duke. The lord chancellor cracked his gavel against his podium so hard, Kate was sure it must have split in two. Oliver Townsende sat down. "Lord Medford," the chancellor thundered. "What in the devil's name are you talking about?"

"My pamphlets, gentlemen. And my press," James called out. "That's right. I'm sure you've all read it in the latest edition. And I have absolutely no intention of resigning my seat in Parliament. You'll just have to get used to the idea of having a scandalous viscount among your ranks. Now, if you'll excuse us. My future wife and I are leaving." He bowed to the gallery and led Kate by the hand down the aisle and straight out the doors.

EPILOGUE

London, late March 1817

Kate sat next to her husband on the front seat of their curricle as they prepared to ride through the park. They'd been holed up all winter. Today was the first good day for riding.

"Are you sure you want to do this?" James asked, regarding her from the corner of his eye.

"Yes." She nodded. "I don't care if we get the cut direct from every single person in the park. We have just as much right to be here as anyone. And I am feeling beautiful in my sapphires today." She touched the jewels on her neck.

"Your wish is my command, Viscountess Medford." He winked at her. "Let's go." He clucked to the horses and they took off down Rotten Row.

Kate laughed. "I thought I couldn't be any happier after you got me Margaret the Second from the farm as a wedding present," she said. "But I do love my sapphires." She touched them again and smiled.

He grinned at her. "The sapphires don't do you justice. You far outshine their beauty. And as for Margaret the Second, I daresay you'll be the only viscountess with a pig in her town house."

"Yes. But I'm in excellent company, with a marchioness who owns a raccoon and a countess with a fox."

"Very true." James nodded.

They pulled to a stop in a little grassy nook off to the side of the dirt road. Lily and Annie and Devon and Jordan were already there. They waved to their friends.

"Ah, the viscount and viscountess, welcome," Lily called.

James helped his wife down from the vehicle and escorted her over to the gathering. Kate had their picnic basket tucked under her arm.

"If it isn't Lord and Lady Scandal," Ashbourne called to them, a wide grin on his face.

Annie slapped at her husband's sleeve. "Oh, don't listen to him," she said to James and Kate. "Your wedding was just beautiful. Even if it was just the six of us and Justin. Who cares if you didn't wait the requisite year of mourning?"

Kate nearly choked on her laugh. "Who cares? Why, I believe that would be the entire town."

Lily shrugged. "Not us."

"The entire town but for the four of you, and Lady Catherine," Kate amended with a wink. "But we decided we were already such a scandal we might as well just get it over with."

Lily sighed. "What is it that Lady Catherine always says?"

"If you're going to be a scandal, darling, be a *complete* scandal," Annie said in a voice that sounded exactly like the low, sultry tones of Lady Catherine.

They all laughed.

Lily shook her head. "I, for one, cannot tell you how happy I am that everything has worked out. Now, if only the rest of the *ton* would stop being so self-righteous."

Kate lowered herself to the quilt that lay atop the grass. "I still cannot believe it. I can't believe I was accused of murder. I cannot believe I was acquitted. I cannot believe I was ever married, actually. The first time, that is." She smiled at James. "The entire last ten years seem like an awful dream from which I have finally awoken."

"I admit, I'll never understand why the valet suddenly confessed," James replied.

Lily elbowed her husband and Devon coughed. "Tell him," she prompted. "It's time."

"Time to tell me what?" James's brow was furrowed.

Devon frowned at his wife.

"Yes, tell us what, Lord Colton?" Kate asked, narrowing her eyes on Colton.

Devon cleared his throat. "Oh, very well. The fact is, I may have put up a bit of money . . . for the truth to come out."

"An insane amount of money," Jordan added on a fake cough.

James frowned. "What do you mean?"

Colton shrugged. "I offered anyone with knowledge of the murder a purse for their story. Their *true* story, that is. I arranged the whole thing with Mr. Horton."

Kate gasped.

James's eyes were wide. "And that's why the footman told on the valet?"

"Never underestimate the knowledge of servants," Colton replied. "In my house they know absolutely everything. I was convinced . . . if someone else did it, a servant knew. I merely enticed the right chap to come forward with the knowledge."

"I cannot thank you enough, my lord," Kate said.

"I am forever in your debt, Colton," James said, his jaw tight.

"No, now we're even. I'd been in your debt for your help securing my wife." Colton smiled at Lily who winked back at him.

"Yes, well, I just cannot believe that despite our very best efforts—and believe me, Medford, we tried—we've actually grown to like you, Lord Perfect," Ashbourne added with a bark of laughter.

Annie elbowed her husband again and James narrowed his eyes on his friend.

"I notice you're not wearing your cravat as—ahem—straight these days, Medford," Lily said, pouring him a glass of wine.

James jerked at the cloth around his neck. "That's right. It's decidedly askew, and I couldn't care less."

"Yes," Kate replied. "You wouldn't believe it. He allows messes to sit around the house for hours at a time now, and even the papers on his desk aren't always straight."

James beamed at his wife. "And I love every moment of it, my darling." He kissed her cheek. Then he leaned back on his elbows and stared into the blue spring sky. "It's true. In fact, every so often, I misalign a stack just for good measure."

Lily, Kate, and Annie were busily pulling out the items from the picnic baskets and arranging them on the quilts the men had spread along the grass. They had all settled down to enjoy their meal when they noticed a crowd gathering along the row behind them.

"What do they want?" Jordan said, glancing over his shoulder.

James narrowed his eyes. He put an arm around Kate's shoulder, guarding his wife. "If there's any trouble . . ."

Devon and Jordan exchanged knowing, alert glances, their bodies tensed to fight, if necessary.

One man stood forward. "When will your next pamphlet be published, Lord Medford?"

"Hear, hear," came the shouts from the growing crowd.

"Yes, when is it?" someone else called.

James furrowed his brow. They were referring to his new venture, the pamphlets he'd been printing in an effort to tell the true stories about certain Newgate prisoners. He and Kate had scoured the dungeons of the prison, meeting with the dirty, downtrodden patrons, listening to their tales. They'd just published one such story about a widow who had been falsely accused of stealing. She'd been sentenced to hang. Had the sentence been carried out, she'd have left four small children at home. Orphans.

James and Kate had hired Abernathy and Mr. Horton to examine the facts and the truth had been revealed. The widow hadn't even been in the town where the theft had taken place. She'd been released from prison shortly after. London had been mesmerized by the story and the pamphlets had sold nearly as well as the scandalous ones had done, amazing as it was to both James and Kate. They'd expected their pamphlets to be completely snubbed by all of London. Though they weren't about to let that stop them.

Lily's eyes were wide. "Did they just ask when the next pamphlet will be published?"

"Imagine that," Annie breathed.

"It shall be published in a fortnight," James called back. "My lovely wife wrote it." He leaned over and kissed Kate. Wild applause erupted from the crowd.

Kate smiled. "I cannot believe it. You never could have convinced me that being scandalous would be so popular."

"Apparently, scandalous is all the crack this Season," Lily said with a laugh.

James snorted. "And here I was just beginning to relish the challenge our tarnished reputations hold."

Lily's jaw dropped. "I cannot believe it. I swear I just heard someone say they always knew Kate was innocent. She couldn't possibly have committed such a vile act."

"Ah, the fickle, fickle *ton*," Devon said.

"They'll get their pamphlets," James said with a nod.

"What are you working on next, Medford?" Annie asked, laying the plates out on the blanket.

Kate answered. "The next one is about a woman named Flora who was accused of killing her husband. There is almost no proof and very little evidence at all."

"Of course, we're very careful about whose stories we take on," James assured them. "After all, there are many criminals who are just that, guilty."

Annie passed the plates of food and Kate rested her head on her husband's shoulder. "Yes. But there are many who are not," Kate whispered. "I was very lucky."

"Not as lucky as I am, my love." James raised her hand to his lips and kissed her knuckles.

Kate leaned back and whispered in his ear. "Remember that night when you took me from the Tower and carried me to your town house on horseback?"

"Yes." He nodded.

"I said a prayer that night. I prayed to believe in love again. To find it again. And I have. Oh, James, you did that for me. I love you so much."

The crowd cheered once more when James kissed his wife again.

"You're right, Lily," he said, glancing back at the bystanders. "Scandal seems to be all the crack this Season."

Kate sighed and leaned against him. "I'm very glad to hear that because I'm very, very scandalous."

James pulled her into his arms. "I wouldn't have you any other way, my dear. Not any other way."

Look for the first two novels in this sensational series by

VALERIE BOWMAN

"This fast-paced, charming [series], sparkling with witty dialogue and engaging characters, marks Bowman for stardom."
—*Romantic Times Book Reviews*

SECRETS OF A WEDDING NIGHT
SECRETS OF A RUNAWAY BRIDE

Available from St. Martin's Paperbacks